BURN

THE SAINTS OF SERENITY FALLS

LILY WILDHART

Burn
The Saints of Serenity Falls #1
Copyright © 2022 Lily Wildhart

Cover Designer: The Pretty Little Design Co.
Editors: Encompass Editing & ACourtOfSpicyEdits
Proof Readers: Sassi's Edits & Puddleduck Proofing
Interior Formatting & Design: Wild Elegance Formatting

Burn/Lily Wildhart – 1st ed.
ISBN-13 - 978-1-915473-05-9

*To everyone who has braved the dark and faced their demons
and to those still fighting.
There is always a way out, a light at the end of the tunnel.
No matter how dark it seems in that moment.
You are not alone.*

CONTENT WARNING

This book is a dark, college, why choose romance with some aspects of bullying.

It contains scenes and references of drug use (off page), abuse/ sexual assault to a minor and sexual assault that some readers may find triggering, along with graphic sex scenes, cursing and violence.

LILY WILDHART

ONE

There is nothing quite like coming home to discover your entire world has changed. I was only gone for one summer. One fucking summer.

A few months of bliss away from my mom's neurotic ways and zero contact with her because I needed the break. Not that she wanted to hear about my time with my dad and his new family anyway.

But getting off of the plane to find a message from her saying that she's away on her fucking honeymoon, with a new address for me to go to when I land... I didn't even know she was dating someone, let alone getting married.

Freaking married!

I pinch the bridge of my nose while I wait at the baggage claim, wondering how the hell this is my life.

My phone buzzes again and I almost don't want to look, but the type-A part of my brain will not let me ignore it.

Mom:

Oh, and sweetheart, Chase has had you enrolled at Saints U for college rather than the community college we had you planned for! It's closer to the new house and will be much better for you. Wasn't that nice of him? Can't wait to see you! We should be home in two weeks. Sorry I won't be there for your first day.

I take a deep breath and hold it, trying to find some of the zen I thought I'd built up while being away. Times like this, I really, really wish I could just live with my dad on the West Coast, but his new wife just had twins, and she already has three young boys from her previous marriage. That is not the sort of chaos I can cope with.

Then again, maybe without the havoc my mom causes in my life on a regular basis it would even out.

Not that they have space for me with the twins around now. Spending the end of summer sleeping on the couch wasn't exactly the highlight of my trip.

When Dad left, he didn't take me with him because he didn't have a house or a job, or at least thats what he said. Personally, I think he's a little too much like mom, and is more than a little selfish. I had to beg him to let me stay with them this summer because I needed to get away from mom.

I'm sure he only agreed because his new wife made him.

I shake my head, trying to get out of my funk. I've got this. I can totally handle this.

Please, God, let me be able to handle whatever the fuck this new situation my mom has gotten us into.

Grabbing my luggage, I head toward the exit, juggling my suitcases as I go down the escalator. As I step off the moving staircase, I spot a guy in a suit and hat holding a sign with my name printed across it.

If this doesn't scream *Taken,* I don't know what does.

I might have watched one-too-many movies with my dad over the summer, and his obsession with that movie is real.

I shuffle toward the driver, hoping to fuck this isn't me being the stupid white girl in a horror movie heading to her death.

"Uhm, hi? I'm Briar Moore."

Wow, I don't even sound awkward or anything.

S. O. S., save my goddamn soul from my internal sarcasm.

"Good afternoon, Miss Moore. I'm Tobias Adams. Your mother asked me to collect you since they were away. I understand she told you about the new residence?"

This guy is eloquent, I'll give him that. He doesn't even double take at my ripped jeans, fading band tee or my beloved but worn thrift store boots. Obviously a professional. He leans forward to take my bags after I answer his question with a simple nod, and my eyes go wide when I see the gun on his hip.

Who the fuck did my mom marry?

Before this we lived in a shitty two-bedroom apartment in the city, and even with my part-time job on top of school, we barely managed to make ends meet. Which I'm all too aware of because I was the one who handled our rent and bills. My mom isn't great with numbers... or much of anything, to be fair. The divorce definitely ended better for my dad than it did my mom. Not that I blame him for leaving. My mom is... well, she's fucking batshit crazy most of the time.

I follow behind Tobias as he leads me out of the terminal to the waiting town car, and once again I wonder who the hell my mom has married. Not that I'm about to ask the *armed* driver. It's more than a little weird for me not to know, but again, my mom isn't the sort to quibble about such *trivial* details.

Tobias opens the car door for me and I slide inside along with my backpack, feeling weird as fuck about letting him put my luggage in the trunk. I watch through the heavily tinted glass as people pass, the car getting more than a few stares from tourists entering the city.

A few moments later, Tobias climbs into the driver's seat. The privacy glass is up, so I guess even if I did want to ask questions, he isn't the guy to be asking. Instead, I sit back and buckle up as he starts the engine.

I check my mom's messages again for the address she gave me earlier. I didn't really pay much attention to it, considering the whole marriage bomb.

My eyes go wide when I notice where I'm going to be living for the foreseeable future. I say *foreseeable* because, well, anyone putting up with my mom for long doesn't seem like much of a probability.

At least I can technically move out now if she gets to be too much once this one dumps her. Because he will.

Serenity Falls.

Fucking *Serenity Falls*.

Where the assholes who are too rich for the city go…

Gross.

I should've known when she mentioned Saints U, but still…

I take in the cuffs of my faded hoodie that has holes where my thumbs are looped through and think about everything packed in my luggage, including my ratty converse that are my second favorite shoes and the array of thrift store gems I've acquired over the years.

Oh yeah, I'm totally going to fit in in fucking Serenity Falls.

Thanks, Mom.

Groaning, I lean back against the seat and watch the city pass us by. I love the hustle and bustle; the fact that no one knows your name, and no one gives a fuck. Everyone's too busy going about their lives, dealing with their own shit, to try and stick their nose in yours. The anonymity of living in the city is one of my favorite things about it.

That and being in the heart of somewhere with so much culture.

Serenity Falls is going to fucking suck. It might be less than an hour from downtown, but fuck my life. That means the few friends I had are all going to be an hour away. All of my favorite bookstores, coffeehouses, everything.

I repeat. Serenity Falls is going to fucking suck.

I don't even have a car. I've never needed one before. The joys of the subway.

The city gives way to greenery and my heart sinks a little. But I can survive this. If I can survive my dad leaving, and having to—at fifteen—pick my mom back up after he left, then I can survive dealing with the snobby assholes in Serenity Falls.

I hope.

I spend most of the drive reading on my phone. It's a shitty one, but it still runs my reading app, so I'm not complaining. It's a way to escape reality, and I am all about it. I look up and see a 'Welcome to Serenity Falls' sign. Jesus fucking Christ, even the sign looks pretentious.

The mechanical whir of the privacy screen grabs my attention as Tobias clears his throat. "We're nearly at the house, Miss Moore. Do you need anything picked up before we arrive?"

Pulling at the loose thread on the cuff of my hoodie, I shake my head. "No, I don't think so. Thank you."

"Okay, well I know the kitchen is fully stocked, so if you want to eat, there should be something for you. If not, then one of the staff can always run out and get what you need. Or you can take one of the cars in the garage if you'd rather. I know that

Mr. Kensington has added you to his insurance plan, and Master Kensington isn't at the residence until tomorrow, so you won't be able to take his car mistakenly."

"Master Kensington?" I ask, more than a little confused.

I catch the surprise on his face in the rearview mirror and heat splashes across my cheeks as he gets a little insight into just how much my mom doesn't think of me. "Yes, Miss Moore. Mr. Kensington's son from his previous marriage. I believe he's a year older than you. He's been on vacation with his friends for most of the summer, but I'm sure you'll see him before you start school next week."

So I have a new brother too. This day just keeps getting better and better.

"Okay, thank you, Tobias."

"Not a problem, Miss Moore."

I groan a little. "Please just call me Briar."

"As you wish, Miss... sorry, Briar." He smiles warmly at me and I return it.

"Thank you."

"Not a problem. We're here."

I look out of the window, my eyebrows practically in my hairline, and take in the giant wrought-iron gates with a K in the center.

I ask myself, yet again, who the fuck did my mom marry?

The gates open and we drive onto the property. The driveway is a giant U shape, with gates at each side and a chunk of lawn in the middle with a giant oak tree in the center. *Fancy.* Not as fancy as the giant house in front of me though.

It's like something out of a movie or a TV show.

Red brick surrounds the ground floor, lined with white columns to match the white doors and window frames. The top floor has light wood siding decorating it, with red brick chimneys coming from the gray-tiled roof.

There are so many fucking windows, and I'm pretty sure the place has fucking *wings.* It's a huge L shape, and I just can't...

"If you give me a moment, I'll grab your luggage and I can take you on a tour of the property," Tobias says, chuckling softly at my slack jaw.

"Yeah okay," I manage to get out as I just blink at the place. I wrack my brain, trying to work out if I know who the fuck the Kensingtons could be... but I come up blank. It's not that I stick my head in the sand, but rubbing elbows with this part of society isn't exactly something I've ever done.

Or wanted to do.

Climbing from the car, I spin in a slow circle, trying to acclimate my brain to the sheer size of this place. I follow Tobias through the double doors and into a giant foyer.

"The stairs to your left will take you up to the second floor where your bedroom is. On the left you have the theater room, the library, and Mr. Kensington's office. To the right is the formal dining room, the kitchen, the morning room, and the staff quarters, but if you follow the hall down past the morning room, you'll find your mother's day room and a tennis court. As well as a mud room that leads out to the garage."

"I'm going to get lost," I mutter. This one floor has more rooms than our old apartment had. What the actual fuck?

"The other staircase to the left goes down to the basement, but I can show you that later if you like. There is a second media room down there, along with a climbing wall, full gym, spa area, a reading nook, and access to the basement level of the garage."

"How many cars do you need to have to warrant a double-level garage?" I ask, not really expecting an answer as we climb the stairs.

"This side of the second floor is the master suite. Your mother has put you in the east wing. So if you'll follow me," he says as he heads down the long hall. "This room here is the laundry. If you ever need something and you can't find anyone, this is where you'll find extra towels and the like. Though, the rooms here are serviced daily unless you specify otherwise. This is Master Kensington's room." He tilts his head toward one of many doors and I nod, following him as we round the hall to the other side of the house.

"This wing is mostly empty unless Mr. Kensington has guests, but you were given the biggest suite available. It's been left as a blank canvas for you as per your mother's instructions. If you would like to decorate, please, just let me know. As the estate manager, I can help with anything you need." I smile as he glances back at me, still more than a little flustered by all of this. "And this is your suite."

He opens the door at the end of the hall and my eyes go wide. This room alone is bigger than our old apartment. It's so bright from all the windows, and decorated in neutral colors, which just adds to the clean, giant look of the place—even if it does look pretty stark. "This is your sitting area, at the far right is your bath, you have your own small kitchenette in here since your mother said you like to have your independence. It's not currently stocked, but if you let me know what you'd like in there, I'll arrange for it."

I blink in shock as he explains everything to me.

"And through this door is your bedroom. There's also a second bedroom in here should you wish to have anyone stay. Do you have any questions?"

"An absolute fuck ton," I blurt, then blush. "Sorry, this is all…"

"A little overwhelming?" he says kindly, and I nod. "I understand. I'll let you get settled in. Your mother has arranged for your closets to be stocked, and Mr. Kensington arranged for your own bank account, so the card for that is on the kitchen counter. You have also been given access to the gold card account. If you need anything that goes over the expense limit on that card, just let me know and we'll arrange for it. Hopefully this will all be suitable until you move into your dorm, and will be here for you whenever you want it."

I gulp, what the fuck could I possibly want that goes over a limit on a gold card? Also, dorm? I'm moving into the dorms?

Just awesome. One more thing to worry about.

I realize he's waiting for me to respond while I stand here like a mindless moron. "Thank you?"

He laughs softly. "Well, I'll leave you to get acquainted. I'll be in the staff quarters if you need me."

He lines my luggage up against the wall and leaves me in the giant, bright space.

What sort of twilight zone have I just stepped into?

Still reeling from everything that's happened today, I drop a text to Emerson. My phone rings instantly. I groan because I like talking on the phone about as much as I like pins in my eyes.

"Hello?"

"Don't you *hello* me, sweet cheeks. I'm at your apartment and it wasn't you that answered the door. What the fuck?" she screeches down the line, and I smile. I might not have many friends, but Emerson is the closest thing to a friend I've ever had.

"Pretty much what I said when I landed to find out my mom got married over the summer and moved us out to Serenity Falls." I sigh as I roll over on the giant cloud of a bed that's in my room.

"Serenity Falls?" she squeals. "Holy shit, that's…"

"It's gross," I tell her.

"Gross? Bitch, that's where those houses I dream about are. And you're living out there. Who did your mom marry?"

"No idea. Chase Kensington is the name I have but that's literally it."

She cackles down the line. "Typical Sofie move. I don't recognize the name either, so I'm about as much use to you as taste buds in an asshole. Does this mean you're not coming to college with me?"

I shake my head, then roll my eyes because I remember she can't see me. "Nope. Apparently Chase has had me enrolled in Saints U out here."

"Oh, shit!" she exclaims, and I can see the look on her face in my head. Her big brown eyes open wide with her statement red painted lips in an 'O'. "Well, that sucks. This was supposed to be our fresh start, taking on the world with a big bang."

"Don't I know it. I think I'd rather pull my nails off with pliers than go to a preppy college full of snooty assholes."

I hear the telltale sounds of her hitting the street, the crash of a door in the background. I miss the city already. "Well, since it's Friday, and officially our last weekend before college starts, you want to hit a party with me tonight?"

A deep sigh escapes me. Parties are so not my thing.

"Come on, B. It's one party and I haven't seen you all summer. You should let loose just once. What's the worst that could happen?" she whines down the line, and I roll my eyes, already knowing I'm going to give in. I don't normally drink, so parties are pretty much a bust for me. Being the sober chick around a ton of drunk idiots isn't exactly my idea of a good time. But really, what else do I have to do except walk around this empty monstrosity I'm now forced to call home?

"Why don't you come here? We could do a movie night, you can check out the new house? Then you still get to see me and I don't have to go to a party."

I cross my fingers knowing it's useless. Emerson is a friend, probably in the loosest form of the word, but she's also the only one I have. She's also not the 'stay at home' type, so I know I've basically wasted my breath before she even responds.

"Don't be such a loser, Briar. Who wants to stay in on a Friday night when there's a party with booze and hot guys? I thought you'd have loosened up with your summer away."

Yep, called it.

Rolling onto my front, propped up on my elbows, I cave. "Fine, fine. Gives me an excuse to spend some time in the city anyway."

"I mean, you could, except the party is out in Oakwood." I can hear her grin down the line as I drop my head onto my arms.

Of course it is.

Why would it not be in the next town over? Oakwood isn't as pretentious as Serenity Falls, but it's still not great.

"Fine, fine. Way to not lead with that little snippet though."

"You know I love you, really."

"Uh-huh. Course you do." I roll my eyes while flipping over onto my back, staring up at the ceiling. "Drop me the address and I'll meet you there?"

"Sounds good to me! Can't wait to see you."

"Yeah, yeah. See you later." I sigh and she ends the call.

Apparently I'm going to a party.

Yay me.

Instead of focusing on the party, since I have a few hours before I need to get ready, I set an alarm on my phone and lose myself in my book and the academy of underworld types. It's not your typical assassin book, but I am so here for it. This girl is living the dream: shoots like a badass, multiple guys falling at her feet. What's not to love about it? My fantasy life inside these pages is far better than real life.

My alarm pulls me from the assassin world and I contemplate telling Emerson I'm sick. I'd much rather spend my night reading than going out, but I don't know when I'm going to get a chance to see her again since we're not going to college together anymore.

I run through the contents of my suitcases in my head and realize I have absolutely nothing to wear to a party. Especially not one in Oakwood.

I'm going to have to bite the bullet and look in the closets at the clothes Tobias mentioned earlier. Fun.

Groaning, I climb off of the heavenly bed—which might just be my favorite thing about this new situation of mine—

and head over to the closet. Opening the door, I roll my eyes. This isn't just a closet, it's a fucking closet slash dressing room combo that's probably the size of my old bedroom.

Rails line three of the walls; more clothes than you'll find in a normal fucking store hang on them. That's before I even get to the drawers that run along the bottom half of the closet.

Or the wall of cubed shelving that holds shoes.

Who the fuck needs a shoe wall?

This is not my life and I feel so fucking out of place. I never thought I'd miss our shitty two-bedroom apartment, but I do. It might not have been much, but it was home. Yes, the hot water left a lot to be desired and the water pressure was basically non-existent, but it was still home.

I brush my hand across the ridiculous amount of clothing, taking in the different textures. I feel like I'm living in one of my romance novels. This shit just isn't real life.

With the choices I have in front of me, I should be able to find something to wear.

The problem with that is, none of these clothes are me. I really am the torn jeans and ratty hoodie or oversized cardigan kind of girl. Skirts, heels, crop tops... yeah, not exactly what I'd usually wear.

Except for the row of brand new Converse, each pair a different color.

Apparently, my mom did at least try to consider my clumsiness when she put this part of my new wardrobe together.

Heels and my coordination do not work.

After spending too much time rummaging through my new gigantic closet, I find a pair of jeans and a black crop top. The jeans are, thankfully, a little like the ones I'd usually wear.

And then I can at least put my black cardigan with it and hide myself a little better. It's not that I'm ashamed of my body, but my curves aren't exactly comparable to the runway models that flit around the city. Pretty sure Serenity Falls is going to be full of the same sort. Not that there's anything wrong with them, I'm all for body positivity, I'm just not tall, leggy, and stick thin like Emerson. I have tits and a dump truck for an ass.

Outfit chosen, I jump in the shower to wash away my day of traveling, doing a little happy dance, not just at the size of the shower stall, but at the delicious, powerful spray of hot water too. This bathroom is like something from the movies and as much as my new situation is a little upside down...

Maybe there are some perks to this new life of mine.

BURN

LILY WILDHART

TWO

I jump out of my cab, wrapping my cardigan around me, feeling more than a little self-conscious as my long red locks blow around in the breeze. I'm not self-conscious about my body—I adore my curves. I wouldn't call myself plus size necessarily but I definitely have some extra ass and boob that I'm not sad about. No, what I'm self-conscious about is what I've put on it. This outfit is so not me. Not even a little.

The music from the house across the street from me is crazy loud, but no one else on the street seems to mind. Whoever this is must have really friendly neighbors. Not that the next houses are all that close. This house isn't quite the monstrosity that I get to call home now, but it's still insanely big, and people are somehow spilled all over the front lawn.

"Hey, bitch!" I turn, hearing Emerson's voice as she struts

toward me, all legs and long, straight hair. Of course, she's in booty shorts and a tight tee. Paired with skyscraper heels, she looks fucking fabulous, as always.

"Hey!" I smile as she reaches me and wraps her arms around me.

"You look fucking awesome, your hair is *hot!*" she says, lifting some of the long bright red strands. "And you added bangs. I love that for you!"

"I wanted a change over summer," I say with a shrug, and my cardigan falls open.

Her eyes go wide as she takes in the crop top. "Briar, you look hot as hell. You *have* to ditch that hideous cardigan before we go inside."

"One, no. Two, where the hell would I put it? In a fucking bush?"

She laughs at me like *I'm* the one saying wildly outrageous shit. "Come on, let's head inside before my pre-buzz wears off."

I choke out a laugh. Of course she's already buzzed. She wrestles my cardigan from me, cackling once she has it in her clutches, and drags me across the street toward the masses of people before I can cover my stomach with my arms.

Someone save me. From her or myself.

We work our way inside and the heat slaps me in the face. Okay, so maybe losing the cardigan was a good idea, but walking around with my arms wrapped around my stomach isn't exactly a great look either. My jeans are high waisted but I still have skin on show with the crop top, and my girls are on display to an almost obscene degree. I take a deep breath and lift my head. I can do this.

"Come on!" she shouts over the music, and I follow her to where a keg is lined up with a ton of liquor. She pours two shots of tequila and hands one to me. "What's the worst that could happen? Loosen up, live a little! You're starting a whole new life at Saints U, might as well send the old one out with a bang."

She gives me her puppy dog eyes and I take the glass, throwing the fiery liquid down my throat. Fuck me, that burns.

I take the next one she hands me and do the same thing.

Maybe just a little buzz will make this night bearable. The last thing I want to do is leave her out here alone, where we don't really know anyone.

"Let's dance!" she squeals before slamming back another shot. Throwing her hands in the air, she lets out a scream as she heads toward the throng of people bumping and grinding in the middle of the room.

This is so not me.

But who said I have to be me tonight? Maybe one night of mindless fun is exactly what I need. I spent the entire summer being me, and that was about as much fun as holding hot coals.

So fuck it.

I throw my hands in the air and squeal right along with her, the shots giving me just enough courage to get on board and dance with her.

The music is absolute fire. There's a live band and I lose myself in what they're playing. Emerson feeds me shots like I need them to survive, but it keeps me dancing, and for the first time in a long time, I'm actually enjoying myself.

I don't even notice when she basically abandons me to dance with some guy. Instead, I just keep dancing and enjoy the hell out of the guy who's singing. It's like he's singing just for me as I watch him, almost hypnotized. His dark hair is messy, falling into his eyes as he croons into the microphone. He looks completely at ease up there as his steel blue eyes lock with mine, promising mischief. But there's something about him that screams money.

Though considering where we are, I'm pretty sure that ninety percent of the people here scream money.

The band finish their song and put down their instruments, someone putting on the sound system to take over as the groans go up in the silence. I leave Emerson to it as she tries to touch the guy's tonsils, and stumble back to where the alcohol is to pour myself another shot. Might not be the brightest idea, but also, I'm chasing this buzz because I'm having too much fun.

"I didn't figure you for a tequila girl." I turn around and lock eyes with the guy who was just singing as he grins down at me.

"Woah, you're super tall." I cover my mouth after the words spill from it and he laughs softly, the edges of his eyes crinkling as he does.

"I don't think I've met you before," he says, taking a sip

from his red Solo cup.

"Unlikely that you have. I'm not usually in these parts." I shrug before taking the shot I poured.

"Well, you and your friend seem to be having fun." His scent wafts toward me and he even smells like heaven. Like wood and outdoors, but clean.

I lean back against the wall, becoming increasingly aware of the slight sway of the room. "I am. She's usually the party girl, but tonight, I want to be a party girl too."

His two friends join us, and holy fuck. I wasn't paying all that much attention when they were playing, but shit. Just looking at them makes my brain go haywire.

"What's your name?" the singer asks, watching me as one of his friends says something that I miss.

"Does it matter?" I ask with a shrug.

"I guess not. Want to come party with us?" I look between the three of them, wondering if this is possibly the stupidest idea I've ever had, but then glance behind them to see Emerson has disappeared.

"Sure, why not?" I mean, hanging out with three beautiful musicians is hardly a bad night, right? Might be stupid, but it's not like I'm ever going to see them again.

"Cool," the singer says, grabbing an unopened bottle of tequila and another of whiskey. "Let's go downstairs."

I nod and follow behind him, his friends behind me. When he opens a door on the opposite side of the room and descends the staircase, I question if I should do this but shake it off. Tonight, we're not being bookish Briar. Tonight, we're nameless party girl, and nameless party girl wouldn't question hanging out with three hot-as-fuck guys.

I hear the turn of a lock and look back to see the blond one checking it's engaged and he winks at me when he turns back.

Oh yeah, he's going to be trouble. I can already tell.

I reach the bottom of the staircase and find it opens out into a smallish room with couches and a table in the middle. While the thump of the music reaches us down here, it's significantly dulled, so the singer's friend—the dark-haired one—heads to the phone dock in the corner of the room and a few seconds later, music starts playing.

Dropping into one of the chairs, I fold my legs and get comfortable. I hadn't realized how hot I was before and fight the urge to fan myself. At least the room isn't swaying anymore.

"Drink?" the singer asks, and I'm captured once more by the blue of his eyes.

"Sure," I nod, brushing my red bangs out of my face. "Why not?"

"She's my kind of girl," the blond rock god says as he drops onto the couch beside me. "Tequila or whiskey?"

"Tequila." I grin. Might as well stick to one, I guess. Plus, it doesn't seem to be hitting me all that hard now that I've sat down, so tequila feels like a good decision.

He passes me the bottle, letting me open it, which seems

nice. At least I know he's not trying to drug me. I break the seal and take a swig while they pass around the bottle of whiskey between them.

The guy who put on music sits opposite me. His dark brown eyes, like melted chocolate, stare over at me. "Want to play a game?"

Feeling bold as his eyes skim down my body, growing heated, I nod and bite my lip before answering him. "Sure."

"Truth or Dare?" the blond guy says as the singer laughs.

"Sounds fun. Who goes first?"

"You do, party girl," the dark-eyed stranger says. "Truth or dare?"

I bite the inside of my lip before taking another swig of tequila. "Dare."

"Ohhh, she's feisty. I like her," the blond guy says. "Come dance for me, pretty girl."

A blush spills across my chest, but I take another swig and stand up. The room spins a little again, but I move toward him, trying to channel Emerson, and sway my hips to the music. He stands, placing his hands on my hips and dances with me. I get lost in the warmth of him and the beat of the music.

"Your turn, pretty boy," the singer quips, and I realize I've been dancing longer than I probably should've. I try to scurry back to my chair, but the blond pulls me down onto the couch, sitting between him and the singer. "Truth or dare?"

"Dare." The blond god with mesmerizing green eyes grins,

and I giggle at the smile on his face. He seems almost fearless. "Okay, dare. Let's let our beautiful guest decide, shall we?" He raises an eyebrow, like he's challenging me, and my mind goes blank.

"Uhm... Lose your t-shirt?" I say, feeling awkward as hell, but I'm not exactly a Truth or Dare pro.

"Going easy on me, I knew I liked you," Green Eyes says with a wink, pulling off his black t-shirt, and I think I drool at the number of abs he has hidden under there. Six? Eight? Fuck, might as well call it a dozen.

"Your turn, Travis," he says to the singer. Huh, I probably should've got names already. "Truth or dare?"

"Truth," Travis responds, and the blond laughs behind me.

"Okay, truth. How much would you like to fuck our pretty guest?"

What the fuck did he just say? I mean, I'm not a prude, and I'm not a virgin, but still... they don't even know my name.

Travis looks at me, his heated gaze running over my body. "I'd definitely enjoy showing her a good time."

"Would you like that, pretty girl?" Brown Eyes asks, and I'm not sure if it's the tequila making me feel bold or what, but I find myself nodding. I mean, he's hot as fuck and his voice was like a balm to my soul when he sang.

I try to buy myself some time out of this conversation by looking across at the dark-eyed bronze god and ask, "Truth or dare?"

He just grins, almost feral. Like he knows exactly what I'm doing but loves the fact that my attention is now solely on him, despite the fact that Green Eyes beside me just put his arm around my shoulders, pulling me into his chest. Oof. He smells like a sea breeze, but also, like home and it's freaking heady. I swear I could get lost in that smell and never be sad that I didn't come back.

"Dare." I have no idea what to do with that. Of the three, he seems the least interested—a bit aloof—except now he's staring at me like he wants to devour me.

My gaze bounces between the two guys on either side of me as I try to figure out what dare I should offer up, but I come up blank.

"Take out your cock." The blond one grins; his teeth are straight and almost blindingly white. Smiles like that don't exist in real life, do they? Just how much tequila did I drink?

His words finally register and I gasp. Not that the bronze god seems to have a problem. The two of them stare at each other, as if they're having a silent conversation.

"Fucking hell, Sawyer," Travis groans. I guess that's blondie's name, but I'm not paying much attention because in front of me, Bronze God gets to his feet.

His eyes burn into mine as he slowly unbuttons his jeans, and my mouth literally waters at the sight of his thick fingers pulling down his zipper. Shock flits through me as I take in his bare cock. Hard and thick. I gulp, wondering if I'm going to be up to this.

"I think our boy likes you, too, Red." I frown at Sawyer's new and unoriginal nickname for me thanks to my hair, but for the first time in my life, I don't mind it. It might be because it's him, but it's also very possible that it's the tequila.

Travis leans into my ear and asks, "Do you want to suck his dick, pretty girl?"

Absent-mindedly, I lick my lips, and all three of them groan like I'm torturing them or something.

"Fuck, my dick is so hard right now," Sawyer groans. I turn to him, but instead of looking at his face, my eyes go directly to his crotch. The bulge is unmistakable. Out of curiosity, I look at Travis's crotch and yep, he's sporting a major hard-on too.

For me? All three of them are turned on by me?

The thought is empowering as fuck and makes me so wet I wonder if I'm losing my mind.

It has to be the tequila.

At least that's what I'm telling myself.

We've got this. Nameless party girl is totally game for this.

"Truth or Dare?" Sawyer whispers in my ear as I watch Bronze God languidly jacking himself off.

I answer immediately.

"Truth."

"Interesting. How about this, Red? You wanna have some fun with us? No holds barred?"

I should say no, right?

I mean, sure, tonight is about being the nameless party girl and letting loose, but maybe I should have some limits? Maybe a foursome isn't quite the way to go? I toss it about in my head back and forth for a minute and land on, 'What the hell?'

Thanks, tequila.

How many times in my life is this opportunity going to present itself to me with complete and total strangers? It's not like I'll ever see them again. They don't even know my name, so finding the details of tonight splashed all over social media isn't something I have to worry about.

Before I can chicken out, I blurt out a yes and bite my bottom lip, waiting to see what they do next.

Sawyer lets out a whoop beside me. "Hot damn! This night just became my favorite ever."

But I don't look at him. I'm still watching those deep, dark eyes that devour me as the bronze god's hand strokes his cock in front of me.

"Take your clothes off, pretty girl. I want to taste you," Travis says as he brings his mouth to my neck and licks a slow, wet line all the way up to my lips where he parts the seam and introduces me to his talented tongue.

We kiss, softly at first, but then his hand goes to the back of my head and he deepens the kiss, adding a bit more force to it as he tangles his hand in my hair. He tugs on it a little and I let out a moan.

That shouldn't feel so good.

When he pulls back, he removes his hand and grips my chin. "Undress."

Lifting my ass up, I shimmy out of my jeans, Sawyer helping me pull them off completely before helping me out of the crop top.

"Beautiful," Travis mutters, kissing me and gripping my chin once again.

I turn my head to the other side where Sawyer is waiting, a devious grin making him even more gorgeous than he already is.

He takes my face from Travis's grip, his hands on my cheeks, his thumbs at the corners of my mouth, before he leans forward and kisses me softly. I whimper as Travis reaches around my chest and pinches my nipples. "Isn't she fucking delicious?"

Sawyer pulls back from our kiss, his tongue licking a path across my bottom lip. He glances over my shoulder to Travis and nods once; the agreement sending a shiver down my spine. Sawyer turns my head to the front and I'm met with a very hard, very big cock pointing at my lips. My heart pounds in my chest as I realize I'm definitely doing this, and I'm not even a little sorry about it.

"Suck his dick, pretty girl."

Licking my lips, I look up at Bronze God and smile. Sawyer's instruction makes me feel bold. I open my mouth wide and let my tongue out just a little, my eyes flashing up at him.

"Fucking hell," Travis mutters, and my bronze god grins in

response. He steps forward, putting the head of his dick on my tongue, so I lick it like a goddamn lollipop and he groans at my touch.

It's fucking hot as hell and I almost wish I could watch from a distance.

On either side of me, the other two lean in and kiss my neck.

"Fuck her mouth, Cole," Travis commands. "I want to see how far she can take you."

That must be the bronze god's name. It suits him.

Travis pulls my head back by my hair and caresses my neck with one hand as Cole slowly pushes his dick to the back of my throat. It hurts a little at first, the sheer size of him is impressive and uncomfortable. Travis strokes my neck gently as Cole slowly fucks my face. I'm held in place as Sawyer slides his hand beneath my panties, making me cry out with pleasure as he dips a finger inside of me.

"Fuck me, she's so fucking wet," he groans as I reach out and grip Cole's dick, trying to ease up his thrusts down my throat. I look up at him and he holds my gaze as Sawyer works my clit.

"Make her come," Travis instructs Sawyer, who slides his fingers back inside of me. I feel like it's Travis who gives all the orders around here. Also, I don't think this is their first rodeo, but what the fuck do I know?

"Breathe through your nose, Red," Sawyer says by my ear as I almost gag on Cole's dick.

When the head of his cock bumps against the back of my throat, I almost gag again but do as Sawyer said, and suddenly it's a little easier.

Blind, but feeling bolder, I reach out my free hand for Sawyer's cock and squeeze, earning me a grunt by my ear. All the while, my mouth is getting thoroughly fucked.

I buck against Sawyer's hand as Travis' grip tightens on my throat, whimpering as I feel my orgasm coming.

"That's it, pretty girl. Come for me," Sawyer whispers as I soar over the edge, seeing stars as my orgasm rips through my body. Cole slows his fucking of my throat, pulling out, and I go almost boneless.

Travis and Sawyer move around me. When I reopen my eyes, I realize all three of them are fully naked.

Hot fucking damn.

I think I might've died during my orgasm, because how is this reality right now?

"Pretty girl, I really want to fuck you. You down with that?" Travis's voice is like honey, just like when he was singing. But that's not what spurs me on.

I want to live this.

I want to be able to say I had the courage to spend this night with them.

"Do you have a condom?" I might be a little reckless tonight, but I'm not completely stupid.

"Fuck yeah, we do." Sawyer dips down to his jeans and

grabs a condom, holding it out to him. I can't help but watch as Travis slides the condom over his cock. His huge fucking cock.

Holy shit, is that even going to fit?

I look at him, wide-eyed, and he grins. He sits beside me and taps his thigh with one hand while the other holds the base of his cock.

"Fuck me, you're all way too fucking hot," I blurt out and they laugh.

"You too, Red," Sawyer responds, and I feel a little better.

I stand and turn toward Travis, but he shakes his head with both of his hands on my hips. He turns me to face a still-very-hard, very big Cole in front of me.

Sitting back with Travis's guidance, I hold on to Sawyer's arm so as not to fall on my face, or worse, hurt Travis, as I slowly sink onto his huge dick.

We both gasp, then sigh as I take him all in.

For a minute, neither of us moves as I try to adjust to his sheer size.

"She looks so fucking good on your dick, man. I'm a little jealous." Sawyer laughs as I look straight at Cole.

"She feels like a fucking glove, man. I need to fuck her so badly right now," Travis mutters behind me, but then I hear Sawyer groan.

"What?" Travis asks.

"Her mouth is open like a good little slut and I'm so fucking turned on right now." Naturally, I reach out to Cole and he pushes his massive dick into my mouth. At the same time, I wrap my fingers around Sawyer's dick and squeeze while letting Travis guide my hips.

I groan as he moves me, because holy fuck, he feels so goddamn good.

This is definitely going to be a night to remember.

Travis holds my hips hard enough to bruise, but it feels too good to complain as he slides in and out of my pussy, hitting a spot deep inside me that I thought was a myth.

"Cole, grab her hair and fuck her mouth just the way you like it," Travis commands, and Cole does as he's told. It's all I can do to not lose my mind.

If it weren't for Travis holding me upright, I'd be a complete mess.

Travis snakes one hand around to my pussy, his fingers flicking over my clit, and I think I see fucking stars.

Fucking hell.

Who knew being wild for one night could feel so fucking good?

Tequila, that's who.

Sawyer moves closer, tracing his fingertips up my ribs before moving to my tits. He caresses them, adding to the overwhelming sensations assaulting my senses. Leaning forward, he takes one of my nipples into his mouth, and when he bites down, my entire body goes taut with bone-jarring pleasure.

Holy shit, I think I might come undone again.

I groan around Cole's dick and he drives harder into my mouth as Travis pounds into my pussy.

"You look so good on those cocks, Red," Sawyer groans as Cole comes down my throat. I swallow it down after he pulls out.

Travis slows and Sawyer takes the spot where Cole had been standing, grinning down at me. "Open up, Red."

Travis fucks me harder and I cry out. Sawyer seizes the opportunity to fill my now-open mouth and grips a fistful of my hair as Travis wraps his hand around my throat once more.

"Fuck, pretty girl," Travis growls in my ear. My pussy tightens as a shiver runs down my spine and he bites down on my shoulder as he comes inside of me then stills as Sawyer continues to fuck my face. I wrap my hand around his dick and he groans, releasing his grip a little, letting me take some control.

It's not long before he comes down my throat too. I swallow him before crawling off of Travis' lap and collapsing on the couch in a boneless mess.

"Holy shit, Red... that was incredible," Sawyer says as I manage to sit back up, feeling a little bashful.

I can't believe I just did that.

I wake up the next morning, cold, alone, and my head pounding.

That'll teach me to slam back so much tequila, I guess.

The soreness between my legs reminds me of everything that happened last night as I sit up. Who was I last night? Because I sure as hell wasn't myself. Fucking around with three guys after I just met them? Yeah, that's not a Briar thing to do. It might be an Emerson thing, but it's definitely not a me thing.

I realize my cardigan is in my lap, so Emerson obviously found me at some point and just left me here. Well, isn't she awesome?

I slide my jeans back on, pulling my cardigan tight around myself. Leaning down to put my Converse on makes the world tilt, so it takes me a few tries, but once I'm dressed, I feel a little better.

Standing slowly to try and get out of here, I suck in a breath and pat myself down, relieved to find my phone still in my jeans pocket.

I need to get home, shower, and just… contemplate if last night is something I should regret.

After ordering myself an Uber, I tiptoe my way upstairs and through the masses of sleeping bodies. Apparently, I'm not the only one who passed out here last night, and something about that makes me feel better.

I get outside just as my car pulls up, and I try to ignore the look on the driver's face as I creep into the back of the car. He can fuck off. This is my first, and only, walk of shame.

I'm never drinking that much tequila ever again. Scratch

that… I'm never drinking *anything* again. Last night it seemed like a good idea, but in the bright, harsh light of day? Well, it seems like a fucking awful idea.

We pull up to the front of the house and I crawl out of the car. Thankfully, the gates are open, so no need to call on anyone and let them see that I spent the entire night out.

Way to spend your first night here, Briar.

I tiptoe into the house and hear music coming from the kitchen. All I want to do is go upstairs, but my mouth is as dry as the fucking Sahara, so I suck up the embarrassment and head toward the kitchen. I can get a bottle of water and scurry away.

Totally fine.

Simple even.

Pushing open the door to the kitchen, I freeze.

The door swings closed behind me as I look at the three guys from last night. They all stare at me in silence, while I just blink at them, slack-jawed.

Why are they here?

"Oh, Miss… Briar. Sorry!" Tobias calls out as he enters the room from the other door. "Good morning. I'm just making breakfast for Master Kensington and his friends. Would you like to join them?"

Holy fuck.

No. No. No.

This isn't happening. This cannot be happening. I have to be asleep and this is some fucked-up nightmare.

Travis glares at me from where they're sitting.

Please let the ground open up and swallow me whole. If there is a god out there, I will disappear right the fuck now.

"Briar?" Tobias says again, and I swing my gaze to him.

"Sorry, no. I just wanted some water," I squeak out, feeling like I'm going to pass out. "Kensington?"

"Yes, Briar," Travis growls. "Travis Kensington."

Fuck my life, I fucked my new stepbrother.

BURN

THREE

Here I was, thinking the highlight of shittiness in my new life was my mom abandoning me with her new family. Oh, how fucking wrong I was…

I want to run from the room screaming, but I get the feeling Tobias will follow me and ask me what's wrong, so instead I'm rooted to the spot while he pours me a glass of water.

"Are you sure you wouldn't like some breakfast, Briar?" Tobias asks, but I can't rip my eyes away from Travis. The unfiltered hate pouring from him is enough to make me feel like I'm burning from the inside out.

I blink, breaking the connection between us, and look back to Tobias. "I'm sure, thank you." Taking the glass from him, I take a sip while I glance at the other two.

First and last time I have a one-night-stand anything.

Holy shit, could this really be any worse?

The door swings open behind me and a double of the blond at the table walks in with four Rottweilers on his heels. Two fully grown, and two puppies.

My heart goes squishy at the puppies when the guy pauses to look at me. "Who are you?"

I look at him properly and realize I was wrong. He is *almost* the double of the blond, but there are definitely differences between the two. The one at the table, Sawyer I think, has this golden retriever energy. He looks a bit like the quarterback in every film you watch about high school football.

This version of him, who I should probably think of as his twin, has thick black-rimmed glasses, his hair is a shade darker, his lip is pierced, and there's ink covering one of his arms. The tank he has on with his jeans does nothing to hide it. He has a whole geeky emo thing going on and it's hot as hell.

Jesus, I need to dial back thinking with my vagina.

"I'm Briar," I finally answer with an awkward as fuck wave. I crouch down as the dogs approach. One of the adults stays with the geeky god, but the puppies rush at me while the other adult watches with caution.

"I'm Asher," the geeky god says. "Seems Shadow likes you." He nods to the puppy jumping all over me.

I pet the dogs, trying to drag my focus from the daggers I can feel being stared into my back.

Tobias serves up breakfast and leaves the kitchen as Asher

sits with the other three. "Any reason you're looking at the new girl like she pissed in your cornflakes?"

I turn to face them, wincing when Sawyer laughs. "Bro, that's the chick from last night."

Asher's eyes go wide when he glances at me. "Oh shit. Well, that's fucked up."

"And on that note, I'm going to go."

"Good idea," Travis sneers. I look at the others and no one else seems to be hating on me too much. In fact, Sawyer keeps looking at me like he wouldn't mind a repeat of last night but Cole hasn't said much at all. Still, no one contradicts Travis, which isn't surprising considering the dynamic I picked up on last night.

"Hold up," Asher says, patting the chair next to him. "Maybe I want to get to know the new girl. Sorry, Briar." He winks at me and my stomach rolls.

"Sorry, I'm really not feeling great and I need to think about getting ready to sign up for classes on Monday." I fake an apologetic smile, pet the dogs one last time, and haul ass from the kitchen. I hear a yip behind me and realize one of the puppies has followed me out.

I wait a second but no one comes to get him, so I scoop him up and run up the stairs. I check the tag on his collar and realize this is Shadow. "At least you don't hate me, huh?"

I kiss his squishy little face and he licks my cheek back. I always wanted a dog, but living in a tiny apartment, I never got to have one. I'm taking this as one upside from this morning. I get puppy cuddles.

I don't even know who he belongs to, but for now at least, he's mine, and I'm going to steal him for as long as I can get away with.

I curl up on my bed, wondering how, in all of fucking Oakwood, I managed to sleep with my new stepbrother. Shadow curls up in a ball in front of me like he's the little spoon in this equation.

Grabbing my phone to see if there's anything from Emerson, I'm not all that surprised to see there isn't, so I drop her a message instead.

Me:

Please tell me you're alive.

I drop my phone onto the bed, not expecting to hear from her any time soon, only a little pissed that she straight up abandoned me last night. I should've known better. She's always been like that. Some would probably call her a frenemy rather than a friend, but she's always just kind of been there. Which makes me sound like a shitty friend too, I guess.

I close my eyes as the room starts to spin. Here was me hoping that the shock of finding all three boys from last night in my kitchen would be enough to counter the aftereffects of the tequila, but of course I'm not that lucky.

Not today.

My phone buzzes and I groan as I open my eyes. Shadow grumbles quietly, like he begrudges the movement too.

Emerson:

I'm alive. You have fun last night?

I contemplate telling her what happened and decide against it. This isn't something I intend to publicize. Like, ever.

Emerson might not be going to Saints U, but she also has a big fucking mouth.

Me:

Yeah it was okay, couldn't find you when I left.

Emerson:

Yeah sorry, I left with that guy. Glad you had fun.
Let me know when the frat parties start, I think I'm going to enjoy the preppy frat boys.

I groan, rolling my eyes.

Me:

Will do.

There is no way in hell I'm inviting Emerson to Saints U.

I'm going to stand out like a sore, poor thumb all on my own. Having Emerson around isn't going to help me blend in, which I've decided is all I want to do.

I never really thought about college properly, knowing I'd probably never be able to afford it. And, while I'm smart, my last priority the last few years were my grades—I was more worried about keeping a roof over our heads, so how Chase managed to get me a place at Saints is beyond me.

Except now I have to think about a major and classes, and I have absolutely zero idea what I want to do. I always saw my future as working some dead-end job just to keep me and Mom afloat.

My head pounds and I close my eyes again. Now is not the time for thinking. First, I need sleep. Then I can think about my future. At least I have a few days to work it out.

For now, I'm going to snuggle my stolen puppy and sleep off the rest of this tequila and hope that this entire morning was just a bad dream.

Yep, that sounds like the best idea I've had since I landed.

"Briar." The soft voice pulls me from my deep sleep and my eyes flutter open. I squint against the bright light and see the geeky god that is Asher standing above me. "Briar, wake up."

I groan and cover my eyes with my arm. "Why? Sleeping is

so much better."

"Well one, because you're holding my dog hostage, and two, I wanted to talk to you." The bed dips and I turn my head to find him lying beside me.

Way to be familiar there, guy.

"Talk?" I ask, wishing he wasn't so close. Damn I forgot to brush my teeth this morning. And since I can smell his minty breath mingled with whatever heavenly cologne he has on that smells like a bonfire on a fall night, I know he can smell my gross morning breath.

He flips to his side, watching me with those green eyes of his, his hair falling into his eyes as he stares down at me. "Yes, talk. You know, that thing people usually do."

I roll my eyes at him, but his smile is so freaking disarming that I find myself giving in. "So… talk?"

His smile widens and I fight the urge to roll my eyes again. I haven't had enough sleep to deal with that smile. "So, you're Travis's new stepsister."

"It would appear so, though I really wish someone would have pointed that out *before* this morning." I grimace, thinking about my new reality again.

He chuckles, stroking the sleeping puppy between us. "Pretty sure that's one of the few things you and Travis feel the same about right now."

I run a hand down my face and groan. "I get him not exactly being chill about it, but there was some serious icy rage rolling from him earlier."

"Yeah, Travis… well, he has issues. Lies are a big no for him, and it's not that you knew who he was, obviously, but he feels deceived. It's triggered him. I'm not making excuses for him, just explaining."

Well slap me upside down if that little nugget doesn't just make me want to ask why, exactly, it's a problem, but even if I did, I'm fairly certain Asher isn't going to say any more than that.

"My brother and Cole, however, clearly aren't even a little sorry. And me, well, I missed out on all the fun, so we're obviously good." He winks at me and I face-plant my pillow.

"This was not how I expected my freshman year to start. Any of it. I didn't even know my mom got married until I landed yesterday."

"Seriously?" Asher asks, his shock obvious.

I flop onto my back and shrug. "Me and my mom aren't exactly close. I don't know how much time you've spent with her or if you've even met her, but she's… flaky."

He stays quiet, like he's waiting for me to expand, but I don't exactly want to trash talk my mom either. Especially when this conversation is likely going to be rehashed with Travis and co. later.

"So, what did you really want to talk about? Other than giving me the spiel about Travis?" I ask, peeking over at him.

He watches me closely and then shrugs. "Nothing really.

I was just intrigued by the girl who got my brother and two closest friends to let down their guard for a change. Last night isn't exactly a norm for them."

"It wasn't for me either," I grumble.

He nods before sitting up and scooping Shadow into his arms. "I could see that much earlier, but I do think you just made this year a hell of a lot more interesting. I'll see you on campus, Briar."

He stands and leaves, and I pull the duvet back up over my head.

Yeah, because interesting is exactly what I was going for.

Fuck my life.

I pull the car into the lot for Saints U and stare up at the building. Oh yeah, I'm never going to fit in here. I felt awkward as fuck asking Tobias to use the car this morning after my conversation with Asher, and when he gave me a choice of options, I went for the most low-key one I could find, which still ended up being a fucking Porsche Panamera.

Because of course.

The building before me is a huge brownstone building with ivy climbing the walls, surrounded by the biggest lawn I've seen in my life.

I'm definitely not in the city anymore, but there's something about this place that makes me wish I had my sketch pad with me.

There's a metal-railed wall that's broken up by brick pillars lining the grounds, which leads to giant iron gates at what looks to be the main entrance.

I'm going to get so fucking lost, I can tell that already and I'm only looking at a fraction of the campus. I'm already late for orientation. Most people will have gotten the drop on it weeks ago, so I'm dreading finding out which classes are going to have space left.

Especially when I still have no idea what I want to do. I used to want to work with children, but I've been so focused on surviving rather than living up to this point that I never thought it would be an actual decision I'd have to make.

Taking a deep breath, I climb from the metal monstrosity these people call a car, pull my bag onto my shoulder, and make my way toward campus.

First task: get through orientation. Then, find my freaking dorm.

Why I need a dorm when I can drive here in under an hour is beyond me, but at least I'll be able to sleep more. Unless the person I share my dorm with is an absolute asshole, but here's hoping the fates aren't that cruel.

Though, looking at the last few days, they might just be.

There are people milling around the main pathway through the quad toward a huge building, which I'm really hoping is where I need to go. Being absolutely clueless about all things college really isn't helping me, but I'm also too stubborn to ask for help.

Especially when the only people I could maybe ask are Travis or Asher, and there is no way in hell I'm asking either of them, even if Asher was nice to me.

I haven't seen any of them since this morning, but Tobias told me they have a house together close to campus, so I guess that's where they'll be. Mostly, I'll miss the puppy cuddles, but it will be nice not having to dodge and avoid the boys who come *with* the puppies all the time.

I'm just hoping this campus is big enough that I don't run into them too much either.

I head into the main building, following the signs on the walls for the office, trying to ignore the looks I'm given. I get it. I definitely don't look like I belong here, probably because I don't. Everyone I've seen on this campus is polished and refined and looks like they're about to walk a fucking runway in New York Fashion Week.

In my torn jeans, band tee, and Converse, I definitely do not fit that description. My outfit is topped off with a messy bun, chipped nail polish, and my band-patch-covered backpack. Though I'm sure that my bright red hair doesn't help how obvious it is that I don't belong here. If I still had the vibrant red… well, the stares I've gotten here have been bad enough already.

LILY WILDHART

I knock on the door labeled 'office', trying to push down the urge to run away and hide from this place. I've never felt more like a fish on land than I do right now.

The door opens and a woman who looks like the main character from *Stepford Wives* smiles tightly at me. "Yes, dear? Are you lost?"

She runs her judgmental gaze up and down, her disdain obvious in her eyes, even if the rest of her face doesn't move even a millimeter. She kind of reminds me of Fiona, Sam's mom in *A Cinderella Story*. Her voice is even nasally enough to make me want to wince.

"I'm not sure," I start, wanting this over as soon as possible. "My stepdad enrolled me here late, Chase Kensington. I need to pick my classes and find out my dorm assignment."

Her entire demeanor changes at the name Kensington. "Oh, yes of course. You must be Briar, we've been expecting you."

What I'm sure passes as a smile for her graces her face before she steps back and waves me into the office space. It's all very... fancy? Wood paneling, thick carpets, earthy tones, and it screams old money.

Not that I'd expect anything else from the school for the elites of the East Coast.

"Please, sit. I'll get you a list of classes that still have space. While you're looking through that, I'll find the paperwork on your dorm. I believe Mr. Kensington requested a single."

I smile for the first time all day as I sit on the plush leather sofa she motioned to. At least I won't have to share a room with someone, because I can't imagine having anything in common with anyone here.

Like, ever.

She heads over to what I assume is her desk, tapping away at a few keys before the printer whirrs to life. It's a bit old school, but I like a bit of old school sometimes. There's nothing quite like the feel of a real book in my hands, or an actual paper sketch book. Don't get me wrong, I love digital drawing—not that I've done it much, because well, money—but the feel of charcoal on my fingertips is almost therapeutic.

She hands me the paper and I stare at it like it's written in Japanese. "Don't worry, I've just emailed the academic advisor, she has a slot in about an hour to talk through your options with you. That should give you plenty of time to check out your dorm room beforehand. Unfortunately, it doesn't seem like you have a single."

I take another stack of paper from her, including dorm information, a campus map, and God only knows what else.

"I've circled the dorm building you're in. Make sure to introduce yourself to your RA when you get there. That will be your base for the year, unless, of course, you intend to rush for a sorority." She smiles at me and I have to swallow my laughter.

"Nope, not for me," I say with as little sarcasm as I can manage. "Thank you for all of this. I'll head to the dorm now, the Marshall building?"

"That's the one. The academic advisor's office is three doors down from this one, so just head back within the hour." She hands me a key for the dorm room before she ushers me from the office, and I thank her as she closes the door in my face.

I guess the Kensington name only grants so much fake kindness.

Checking out the map, I muddle my way across the campus, thankful for my years waitressing so walking around this much isn't too much effort, but jeez, did they have to make this place so freaking enormous?

After ambling around lost, I finally find the Marshall building, catching the door as some girls leave. They glare at me when they see me entering, but I ignore it. It's obviously going to be a thing here, so I might as well get used to it.

I try to ask someone where to find the RA, but after being ignored three times, I just head to the room number on the slip of paper the woman gave me. She also happened to write down the name of my roommate—Penelope Reed. Finding myself at the end of the corridor on the top floor, I knock tentatively on the door.

When no one answers, I use the key to unlock the door, opening it slowly. The screeching starts the moment I step into the room.

"Who the hell are you and why the fuck are you in my room?" The redhead looks like she's about to take my head off. Even at five-foot nothing in her crop top and cutoffs, she looks fucking terrifying.

"I'm Briar, and I guess I'm your roommate," I say before moving to the bare side of the room with the stripped double bed.

Fancy.

"So you're the bitch who took my solo room joy from me. Awesome. I'd say nice to meet you, but it's not. Stay on your side of the room, keep your hands off my shit, and we'll manage to coexist."

Awesome, so everyone here is hostile. Just great.

Maybe it's not that different from the city after all.

"Sure thing," is all I respond, and she rolls her eyes, flicking her hair over her shoulder. She slides her dainty feet into a pair of flip-flops and storms from the room.

Well, that was a fun start to Saints U.

Things can only get better from here…

Right?

LILY WILDHART

FOUR

Staring up at the ceiling, ignoring the fact that the clock beside my bed says it's nearly two in the afternoon. At least it's a Sunday and no one is waiting on me. I pick up my phone and scroll through the mindless stream of social media, paying absolutely no attention as I try to not go over the horrific day I had yesterday, but I'm failing.

Between my so-not-happy-to-see-me new roomie and the longest meeting ever with the academic advisor, my brain was officially cheese.

Holey, gooey cheese.

After pushing me to pick a major, I landed on Psychology with a minor in Art, because I have to find some joy somewhere right? Plus, the human mind has always fascinated me. Yes, I'm one of those basic bitches that loves serial killer books and documentaries. Anyone that wants to come for me should know that, at this point, I basically know how to get away with murder.

Well, in theory anyway.

Just thinking about my course load this semester has me looking forward to the New Year already, especially when I couldn't get any art credits in this semester and still make my schedule work. Seven classes will be easy, right?

At least this way I can get through my associates degree in just five semesters and spend as little time at Saints U as possible. The thought of being indebted to Chase Kensington makes my teeth ache. Even if he is my stepdad now, it still feels like I'll owe him, and that thought makes my skin crawl. Just having the credit card in my wallet feels like a lead weight.

I groan as I cover my face with my hands. Really, I should be packing, ready to move into the dorms later today, ready for classes to start tomorrow, and getting used to being there with Penelope, but all I want to do is curl up and hide in my closet. Maybe sleep for a few days.

Part of my reluctance could, just maybe, be the fact that Travis will be on campus. I can't deal with his brand of hatred right now. I only had a small taste of it on Saturday, and I can't cope with that on top of all the change right now.

Usually, I'm the steady ship in stormy waters. I can adapt to almost any change, but something about the icy hate he shot at me has me off-kilter.

Stop, Briar. Enough. Focus on school.

Maybe I should get a job. Then I wouldn't need to use the stupid credit card, at least. But juggling a job plus seven classes in my first semester doesn't exactly feel like a good idea.

I shake my head, hating myself for being such a whiny bitch. Sad little poor girl is thrust into the rich world and complains about having money. Makes zero sense, but I'm also just not that girl. I like to make my own way. Some might call it stubborn or strong-minded and, personally, I don't usually give a fuck, but I also don't want to offend Chase.

Goddamn, I wish my mom would have talked to me about all of this rather than dumping it in my lap upon landing back on this side of the country. But no, that isn't how my mom operates.

To be fair, I should consider myself lucky she warned me at all. It's more than I've ever had before.

No more whiny shit. Suck it up and get on with your crap.

I take in a deep breath and let it out slowly before sitting up, popping a cherry Lifesaver in my mouth and staring at the closet. I really don't need much, and it's not like the house is far from campus. I spent most of Sunday unpacking my suitcases, so I grab the biggest one and start repacking for my dorm while trying to go through my schedule for the week in my head.

I'm probably most excited about Abnormal Psych from my first semester course load. Peering into the human mind is fascinating, and maybe, just maybe, I'll get an insight into my own damage. Pretty sure my trauma would take a trained professional years to unpack, but a little self-help never hurt anyone.

Probably not something I should be worried about. I'm only eighteen, nearly nineteen, but I've been an adult for a really long time. Pretty much since my dad skipped out and my mom stopped showing up as a parent.

I say this, knowing that sometimes I make really stupid decisions that I don't consider consequences for.

Case in point—fucking three guys I didn't know the other night and now being in this insane situation.

Epic plan, Briar. Don't be your normal awkward self for a night, Briar. What's the worst that could happen, Briar? Fucking genius.

I finish packing up my suitcase and stare at the room that's mine, but absolutely isn't. I doubt this will ever feel like home. Then again, nowhere has ever really felt like home, so I can't even be sad about it.

Deep breath, Briar. We might hate the how of what's in front of us, but this is an opportunity to be the version of ourself we never thought we'd have the chance to be.

Picking up my suitcase, I make my way back down through the Kensington mansion and head outside.

This is a new start, and even if I hate how I got it, I don't intend to waste one fucking moment of it. I have the chance of a future beyond a dead-end job for the rest of my life, and I'll be damned if I'm going to let it slip away.

I pull my t-shirt down, trying to keep my hands busy as I make my way across campus. My first night in the dorm was hellish. Penelope definitely isn't happy that I'm there, but I woke up with my hair still on my head, my eyebrows on my face, and my stuff not torn to shreds.

I'm taking the win, because, from our brief encounter, she definitely seems like the spiteful, petty bitch type.

But I'm still positive living in the dorm will be better for me than living with Mom and her new husband. Because *ick* doesn't quite cover how I feel about my mom in the honeymoon stage. You'd think after the men she's carouseled in and out of my life I'd be used to it, but it's not something I'll ever get used to.

Just like I never got used to watching them hit her. To trying to stop it. Getting hit myself for trying to save her when she never once attempted to save herself.

But that was my job.

To save us. To protect us. To keep us safe.

I'd love to say I didn't resent her for all the bullshit I lived through, but I'm not that much of a well-rounded human. God only knows how that shit will trip me up later in life, but that totally isn't the point.

At least I know I can both take and throw a punch. Which might just help me with a crazy roommate like Penelope.

Running through a mental checklist of what I need to do today, including grocery shopping for my essentials, I try not to focus on the sheer amount of people milling around on campus.

How does this feel busier than being in the freaking city?

I take a deep breath as I head to the coffee cart, telling myself that Psych as a Profession isn't the worst subject to have as my first class of the day. It could totally be worse. Human Origins: Evolution and Diversity—better believe I did *not* choose to take *that* class this semester. I can't think of anything more brain melting considering my workload, but I know it's one of my requirements to get my degree.

It could definitely be a worse start.

I fumble with putting my headphones on, pressing play and letting the soothing—to me at least—sounds of The Maine's *Black Butterflies and Deja Vu* fill my ears while I wait in line for what smells like some amazing coffee.

I keep my head down, staring at my phone, putting out my best *please don't talk to me* vibe, until I reach the front of the line. "Oat milk mocha, with an extra double shot, peppermint syrup, and extra whip, please." I smile at the guy serving, because I'm not a total asshole. Plus, he's making me coffee. I'm aware that ordering oat milk with cream is a little odd, but just because I'm lactose intolerant doesn't mean I'm giving up one of the few things in life that brings me joy, and dairy is one hundred percent a joy factor. My smile must not come off right because he looks a little shocked and turns to make the coffee without saying a word.

I drop my smile, refusing to look back up until I see the cup on the counter.

"Four fifty."

I drop a ten onto the counter, grab my coffee and haul ass away from the counter. Did I want change? Yes. Will I be going back to that cart ever again? Absolutely not.

In my hurry to get the hell away, I don't pay enough attention to where I'm going, and the next thing I know, I'm on my ass, staring up at a now coffee and cream-covered Cole who is glaring down at me like I'm the anti-Christ sent to Earth to ruin his existence.

He rips off his t-shirt, grumbling about third-degree burns, using his top to mop up the rest of the coffee staining his very lickable, very defined abs and chest.

Reminding myself not to drool, I open my mouth to speak, then close it again when I notice him watching me just stare at him.

Please let a hole open up beneath me so I can disappear. Any time now would be good.

Dramatic? Maybe. But it's not even eight in the morning and this day already sucks ass.

"I am so sorry," I start, but he just shakes his head and walks away. I'm not about to complain about him not bitching me out, because he looked like he might murder me, and with the sheer size of him, I'm convinced he could.

I'm also not about to complain that I somehow have zero coffee on me.

It's only when I notice people staring at me while I'm a crumpled mess on the ground that I jump to my feet and hightail it in, what I hope is, the direction of my class.

I really need coffee, but there's no way I'm getting back in that line, and after my literal run in with Cole, I don't trust myself not to trip over thin air and scald someone else with my freshly-brewed, life-giving heaven in a cup. Apparently I really am living out my nightmare of being an awkward potato with a good seasoning of klutz.

Just awesome.

So much for a fresh start. Apparently, some things you just can't outrun.

After spending twenty minutes wandering around aimlessly, hoping I'm going in the right direction, I put my stubborn streak in my back pocket, finally caving and looking at my map of the campus.

Am I on the total wrong side of campus? Abso-freaking-lutely.

Fuck my actual life.

Now there *really* isn't time for a coffee break. Sometimes I wish I wouldn't be such a stubborn asshole. It only ever shoots me in the foot.

I scramble across campus, sliding into one of only two spare seats left in the lecture hall, paying exactly zero attention to my surroundings, just glad I made it before the professor.

Catching my breath, I grab a pen and notebook from my

satchel, pulling up the syllabus for this class on my phone, but before it loads, a woman in a pantsuit and heels struts into the hall, followed by a student who dives into the chair beside me.

"I thought you might want this." I look up and see the guy from the coffee cart holding out a takeout cup that smells like my mocha.

I open my mouth to say thank you and to ask how the hell he knew I would be in this class, but the professor starts speaking and I nearly drop the cup again.

"I don't know what unfortunate thing you did in a past life to end yourself up in my class, but know that this will not be fun. It will not be easy, and if you miss more than two lessons, I will cut you from the class and it will be an instant fail. Half-hearted input is not welcome in my classroom. I will expect you to work, and you will hate me for it. So before we get started, does anyone want to leave?" I stare at the dark-haired woman, her deep eyes boring into the souls of each of us momentarily as she scans the room.

I swear her intense stare turns my blood to ice, and as much as I want to run from this class right now, I'm too freaking scared to move a muscle.

When no one leaves, she smiles at the room, and it's fucking terrifying. This woman should not smile. "Good. Welcome to Psychology as a Profession. I'm Professor Rainwater and you just passed your first test."

With my brain feeling like cheese after a morning of Psych as a Profession and Intro to Statistics—which is an awesome start to the week… *not*—I'm ready to go back to my dorm and curl up in a ball. But I really need food. I'm severely lacking in sustenance today, and if I actually want to survive college, I can't afford to forget to eat, despite the fact I've been living that way for years.

I pull my satchel strap over my head so it's crossbody and bring up my maps on my phone to work out where the nearest grocery store is.

Feeling more than a little exhausted after my day's classes, I try to pay attention to my surroundings this time rather than run into someone else. Which is exactly how I spot Travis, Asher, Sawyer, and Cole on the quad with what looks like a bunch of frat guys who would happily suck their dicks, and sorority girls hanging from them, who look at them like they are the reason the Earth spins.

At least Cole has a top on now, even if it is a white t-shirt that clings to every ripped freaking inch of his dark skin.

Deciding today is not the day, and now is most definitely not the time, I attempt to keep my head down and rush past the group, but unsurprisingly, with how this day is going, I am not that lucky.

"Is this your new gold-digging whore of a leech?" one of

the girls asks Travis, who looks at me with more hatred than I care to examine.

The girl steps into my path and I let out a deep sigh. "Excuse me," I say, trying not to get sucked into their stupid little rich kid games.

She ends up being flanked by two of what I'm assuming are her sycophants and I look up to the sky, wishing for strength to deal with more petty rich bitches today. Because dealing with Penelope apparently isn't enough.

"You don't belong here, skank. You should leave now, before we make you," the brunette to the right says, and I can't help but bark out a laugh.

"I'm not sure you'd be able to fight dirty enough to make me do anything," I say, rolling my eyes, wishing I could stop my mouth from moving. No such luck.

"What did you say, bitch?" the original girl says, raising her hand to slap me. Someone grabs her wrist before she gets the chance.

"She's not worth it, Melody. She's just a slut. She'll be gone right along with her whore mother when my dad gets bored of her open legs. That's all trash like her is good for. Don't waste your energy." Travis's icy words are like daggers in the back of my brain, triggering a memory I forgot I even had.

"That's it, you piece of trash. Open your legs for me, just like your mama does. You two bit whores aren't worth any more

than that." I scream as I try to fight off the drunken letch my mom brought home. I locked my door, but the flimsy frame snapped when he kicked at it.

I scream and call out for my mom, knowing it's useless because she's never saved me a day in my life.

The alcohol-smelling, stain-covered t-shirt-wearing, pot-bellied guy with his yellowing teeth laughs before he hits my face so hard I think I might pass out. "You can scream all you like, sweetheart. Your mama said you would pay for the goods I gave her. She's enjoying them, while I get to enjoy you."

He presses his body onto mine, despite me trying to punch and kick at him, but he just laughs as my body pushes against the mattress underneath his weight.

"Oh, I do like 'em feisty." His grin widens and I think I'm going to be sick. Of all the things my mom has done to me, this has to be the worst. "Even if you are just trash. This is all you're good for. Now open your legs for me, sweetheart."

I scream as he paws at me, but it's only when the whoop of sirens on the street outside sound that he scrambles from the bed, zipping up his fly. "Good for nothing whore. Just like your mama. I'll be back to collect the rest of my payment."

He scrambles from the room and I curl up in a ball, hating him, my mom, and myself for not being stronger. For not fighting harder.

If it hadn't been for that siren and the flash of lights, he would have raped me and there would have been nothing I *could've done about it.*

I shake my head, pulling myself from the darkness inside my own mind, and find everyone staring at me like I have three heads. The concern on Asher's face makes me pause and that's when I feel the wetness on my cheeks.

"Fuck all of you," I hiss before turning on my heel and storming off in the opposite direction. Fuck them. Fuck him. Fuck all of this.

They have no idea what I survived to get here, and I might have stumbled here by accident, but I'll be damned if they're going to get rid of me that easily. Not when the possibility of a real future is in my grasp if I can just work hard enough to leave here with my degree. I stand up taller and turn back around to head to the grocery store, smashing into the first girl with my shoulder as I pass by, being just as much of a petty bitch as she is.

I've fought worse monsters than them and won, I'm not about to give up now.

FIVE

I only got lost three times, which I'm taking as a win. Who would've thought Serenity Falls would be big enough to get lost in? Sure as hell not me. After grabbing ramen, coffee, hot chocolate and granola bars, I found some cherry Lifesavers, which are my absolute weakness and the absolute holy grail, so I grabbed a few packs of those too along with my Pepsi Max. I'm not thrilled to spend any Kensington money, but after today, I deserve a little bit of happy and if it pisses Travis off in the process, well, extra awesome sprinkles on top for me.

I make my way back to campus listening to Halsey's *The Tradition* on repeat, full blast, while I try to shake off the icy rage that's gripped me since Travis triggered that memory.

I don't quite understand why he hates me so much. It's not like I knew who the hell he was when I slept with him. God knows I wouldn't have slept with him if I *had* known, even if he is literally walking sex on a stick. He could've pushed for my name, but he didn't, so it's not like this is all *my* fault. Was I just supposed to know who he was?

I guess to his over-inflated ego, I absolutely *should* have known who he was, and maybe if I was one of those girls who is constantly on social media and pays attention to the who's who of New York I would. But also, why try to tear me down so publicly? I'd put money on the fact that those people don't know he fucked me. They probably just think he hates me because our parents got married. Because they think I'm a gold digger. I'd bet my last twenty dollars that they have no idea about the truth of why Travis hates me so much.

They don't know me at all, otherwise they'd realize just how fucking gross it makes me feel to acknowledge that I'm using their money to survive right now.

I let out a deep breath and realize I've managed to make it back to my dorm building on autopilot. At least my subconscious is paying attention, I guess.

Buzzing myself into the building, I send up a little prayer that Penelope isn't in the room. I can't deal with a face-off with her right now too. I just want to curl up in a ball and hide for the evening, maybe do some reading to prepare for U.S. Gov and Politics, log into my online portal for my wellness class—I still love that all I have to do is wear a pedometer and upload my steps along with an exercise diary and it counts toward my credits. Best class *ever*.

After traipsing up the stairs I find the door to my room open, Penelope standing in it, talking to two girls who I think live in the room opposite ours. They appear to be some of the group of girls I saw out on the quad earlier with Travis.

Awesome, just what I wanted to round off my day.

Blowing out a breath, I keep my head high and my shoulders back, ready to face more ridicule and bitchiness. I've spent my entire life being looked down on and called trash. I'm not sure why I thought coming here would be any different.

"Hey," the bright and shiny blonde from across the hall says as I approach, her smile wide. "Are you okay? Travis is such an asshole. He needs to rein in his fan club. I'm Charli by the way."

I blink, trying to keep my expression neutral and not have the shock that floods me show all over my face. "Hi, and thanks. I'm Briar."

"I thought we'd invite Charli and Serena over for a movie night tonight," Penelope says, watching me closely. I watch her back just as intently, trying to work out what her angle is. "I didn't realize you were a scholarship kid like us. I thought you were just another rich bitch."

I bark out a laugh. "Do I *look* like a rich bitch?"

I mean, I can't complain too much. I assumed they were all rich bitches too. That'll teach me to just assume, I guess.

Serena laughs dryly. "Not at all, but you're here under the Kensington name. Like it or not, that means the rich kids will hate you, and the scholarship kids will most likely think you're one of the rich assholes anyway."

"Awesome," I say with a tight smile. Pushing past Penelope, I head into the room and pack away my few goodies in a storage tub under my bed, trying not to get stuck on the fact that I'm an outcast here to literally everyone just because of who my mom married. "Well I'm not a scholarship kid like you guys, but I am also not a rich kid, even if my mom did marry a Kensington. I am *not* one of them."

It's fine, Briar. We're good at being the outcast. It's what we've always been.

"So, movie night?" Penelope asks as the girls disappear down the hall and she shuts the door to our room. I glance over at her as I drop onto my bed.

"Does this mean you're going to dial back the raging bitch routine?"

She smiles at me and falls onto her bed. "Something like that. I was just pissed I had to share my room with a snobby prep kid. Turns out I need to reserve judgment until I get to know someone. My therapist has been telling me that for years, but people are usually assholes, so it's hard to break the habit. That said, I'm not always a raging bitch, so... truce and fresh start?"

I run my gaze over her, looking for any sign of insincerity, but find nothing. It doesn't mean I'm going to trust her with my secrets, but at least I won't dread coming back to my room every day, so I nod my head and agree to her terms. "Truce."

"Awesome," she smiles. "I'm Penelope, but everyone calls me Penn."

"Still just Briar."

"Well, just Briar, I'm probably going to call you B. It's what I do. Everyone ends up with a nickname or letter, it's just how I was raised. I'm going to order a few pizzas and the girls have gone foraging for popcorn. I'm thinking horror film. You in?"

I think it over for a second, I should really get ahead on reading, but maybe it will be nice to have friends. Even if they are just fair-weather ones to help me through the first semester. Something is better than nothing, right?

"Sounds good," I say before I can change my mind.

She grins at me and winks. "Awesome. Welcome to the poor bad bitch club."

I laugh at her as she pulls her phone from her pocket and calls for the pizza. Maybe this semester won't suck quite so badly after all. Now I just have to figure out how to avoid Travis and co. for the next three years.

Easy, right?

After the pizza is demolished and the girls have gone back to their room, I grab the pillow from my bed and hold it to my chest, trying to go over the day. I still don't really understand why Travis is being such an asshole, or why the others are just watching him act like a giant bag of dicks.

"You're thinking real loud, girlie." Penn saunters out of the bathroom and drops onto her bed. "Want to talk it out?"

I let out a deep sigh and shake my head. "I'm not sure there's much to say, I just don't understand any of it. But it's not like I'm ever going to, so I need to just keep my head down and get on with what I can control."

She tilts her head, chewing on her lip before nodding. "Okay, so you're not from here so you don't really understand how it all works, but Travis and his friends have been at the top of the social hierarchy forever. And while I'd love to say that Erica and the other whiny bitches that hover around them like flies on shit aren't the queen bees of Serenity falls... well, I'd be lying."

"I forget that you grew up with these guys."

She shrugs and crosses her legs, getting more comfortable. "I mean, kind of. I grew up here, so I know who they are, but I don't know them. Not really. They're a year ahead of us. What I *do* know is that Cole Beckett *the second*"—she puts a snarky emphasis on his name and I press my lips together so as not to laugh—"has been in the limelight since he was a toddler. His dad has been in politics forever, so the boy knows when to keep his mouth shut. He is very much his father's son. The guy has game and he rocks a set of drums like a freaking god. The guys started their little band when I was a sophomore in high school, and they were the talk of *everyone*."

I nod, but keep my mouth shut. Maybe this insight will help me understand them a little more.

"He's a Law major, which is a crazy heavy workload considering the amount of time the team takes up, but from what I can tell, he never seems to struggle. I don't know if he gets a pass because of who he is, or if he's just that good."

I have no idea what team she's talking about, but I'm not about to interrupt her since she's actually spilling the details on them all, and I'm not likely to get this info from the guys themselves.

"Travis is a whole other can of worms. I'm pretty sure he was born with a silver spoon in his mouth. Kensingtons are like, old new money, and I'm aware that doesn't make much sense, but they're not blue bloods. They've definitely got more money than I could spend in five lifetimes though. He's a Business major, probably because of his dad, and he's always been at the top of the food chain, but he's also pretty elusive. Like, I couldn't tell you what he actually does for fun, because outside of his friends and singing with them, he doesn't really talk to anyone unless it's needed. That's what the St. Vincent twins are for."

"Ah, yes, the twins. Sawyer, the bouncy people person, and Asher, the diplomat. That much I've worked out already."

"Yeah, they're actually both okay guys. Not that I've interacted with them a ton, but I think because they are new money—their mom is like, the top neurosurgeon in the country, and their dad is some hot shot defense attorney—Asher is studying pre-med, following after his mom, and Sawyer is a Business major like Travis. They don't seem to have the same pressures on them that their friends do. Oh, and Asher totally doesn't need those glasses he wears, I think he just likes the tattooed geek look. It goes with his whole guitar playing thing. But I guess Sawyer does that too, so who knows."

I laugh at her last comment. "Well, that's a little odd, but I guess we all have our own quirks."

"Something like that. They were renowned in school for their parties. Theirs were the parties you wanted to be at, and if you weren't, you were a pariah... and, obviously, I basically never went because I was an outcast and a year below them. But I know the summer before senior year they did a back to school party on their yacht, and it was all anyone talked about for months." She pauses and purses her lips like she's deciding whether or not to tell me something. "I know you're part of their family now or whatever, but do you know about Travis's mom?"

"No? What about her?"

"I don't know all the details, but I remember it being a huge thing because she just kind of... fell off the face of the earth about eight years ago. No one knows where she went, and I remember Travis not saying a word about it to anyone despite the questions and rumors."

I chew on my bottom lip. Yeah... that's not weird at all. "Do you think I need to be worried?"

"I don't think so," she says, shaking her head. "But rich people do shitty things and get away with it everyday. I'm not saying Chase Kensington killed her, she could have just run the fuck away from their life. She must have signed divorce papers, because obviously Chase married your mom…"

"Yeah, I guess," I respond, trying not to let my overthinker's brain go right off the deep end and into worst-case scenario mode.

"Anyway, that's enough about the boys. Ice cream?" She grins at me and I nod enthusiastically. I've never been the type to turn down ice cream and I am not about to start now.

My second day at Saints U was pretty quiet compared to the first. I managed to avoid Travis and his squad of sycophants. I spent more time with Serena, Charli, and Penn and found we all have a lot in common. Turns out bonding over bad wine, pizza, and a horror movie is a great way to make friends. They even helped me dye my bright red locks to a shade close to my natural chestnut, and it didn't end in a disaster.

Got to love college.

It's only day three, and, apparently, they want to drag me to a frat party tonight—yay me… I mean, who parties on a Wednesday?—but first I have my first Intro to Psych class this morning, then Abnormal Psych after lunch. It's going to be a brain break kind of day, so maybe I'll need the party tonight.

On the upside, my class tomorrow is mid-morning so I won't have to wake up too early.

I head to the same coffee cart from Monday—despite my earlier embarrassment, the coffee was too good to pass up— *Lighthouse* by Loveless blasting in my headphones, hoping that today I don't run into anyone. The coffee in my dorm was okay for yesterday, but considering my work load today, I have a feeling I'm going to need the good stuff.

The line isn't too long, I guess we'll call that a happy Hump Day win. Except I can't help but feel uneasy when I notice it's the same guy working the cart as last time. The same one from my Psych class who seemed to know I was in his class and brought me coffee.

Definitely a little weird. I mean, I totally drank the coffee because I'm not about to turn down good coffee—yes, I'm aware accepting drinks from strangers is a bad idea, but also, I was in class. It seemed safe enough.

When he notices me, he smiles and I respond with an awkward little wave. I'm not sure what it is about him—beyond the creepy class thing—that makes me feel uncomfortable, but I can't help the twist in my stomach.

You're being so weird, Briar. Get out of your own damn head. You don't even know the poor guy and you hate it when people judge you.

Nothing like an early morning shaming from your inner voice.

Oh, God, I'm so glad superpowers don't exist because I'd sound absolutely tapped to anyone who could hear my thoughts.

"Hey, Briar," the guy says with a big smile when I reach the front of the line. Lord, he even knows my name. Though, I guess he did sit next to me in our lecture.

It's not creepy, Briar. Maybe he just pays more attention to life and his surroundings than you do.

"Hey, first week going okay?"

"Yeah, just dreading today. Same as the other day?" he asks and I nod, grabbing my wallet.

"Thanks," I say with a small smile as I hand over the money for the drink. "Why are you dreading today?"

"I've got Intro to Psych and Abnormal Psych with Professor Crawford. He's a notorious hard ass here at Saints U. Giant asshole apparently."

"You're a Psych major?" I ask, realizing he's in both of my classes today, and of course the professor is a jerk. Why would I not be that lucky?

"Yeah, minor in English."

"Cool." I take my mocha from him when he hands it over. "I'll see you in class in a bit then."

See? You can be nice. Go, Briar.

"Oh, you're a Psych major too? Weird that we have all the same classes." He eyes me closely, like suddenly *I'm* the creeper here.

"I was late to sign up for classes so I basically just got what was left," I tell him, weirdly feeling like I have to justify myself, which is ridiculous, and yet… here we are.

"Oh, okay. I guess that explains it. I'll see you in a bit. Don't sit in the front row!"

I quirk my brow and he grins. "He's that bad?"

"Worse," he says with a shudder. "My brother had him two years ago and nearly dropped out."

"Well, isn't this going to be as much fun as showering a cat? Want me to save you a seat?" I hear the words tumble from my mouth and he's smiling before I have a chance to take them back.

"That'd be great, thanks! I'm Connor, by the way."

"Briar," I say with a nod and turn to walk away, grumbling to myself about being way too nice to the creepy guy just because he has the good coffee. My inability not to be super polite, even if I feel uncomfortable, causes me to find myself in situations I really don't want to be in. But can, or will I stop? Probably fucking not.

I grab my campus map and head toward the Psych building again, hoping not to get as lost today as I sip on the chocolatey coffee heaven.

"Briar!"

I pause when I hear my name, looking up from the map, and see Asher heading toward me. It takes all of my willpower not to groan out loud until I see the puppies at his feet.

Shadow yips as he runs toward me and I crouch down to catch the bundle of squishy joy in my arms when he reaches me.

I might not want to see Asher, but the puppies totally make it worth it. The others all reach me long before he does and I end up on the ground, in a puppy pile, not giving a fuck about anyone watching because this kind of joy is unmatched. I will never be ashamed about the puppy love.

Asher approaches me slowly, that cocksure strut in his step, looking like some sort of rock god that just stepped off of the main stage at a metal festival in his ripped jeans, tight black t-shirt and Converse.

God damn him for being exactly my freaking type. Right down to the artwork on his skin and plugs in his freaking ears. Stupid fucking boys.

"What do you want, Asher?" I ask as I stand. My words are acidic, but I don't care. He was there when Travis tore into me the other day and he didn't do a damn thing to stop him. Even after already apologizing for him once.

Apparently, apologies mean nothing to these people and the puppies might have me all squishy on the inside, but he doesn't get the squishy parts of me just because of my love for the little monsters. He hasn't earned that.

"I was out walking the dogs, and I saw you... and well, I want to apologize," he says, pushing his glasses up his nose, and I laugh loudly.

"Of course you do." I roll my eyes and walk around him, continuing on my way to my class, Shadow at my ankles while the others stay behind with Asher.

Little traitors.

He grabs my arm and pulls me to a stop. "Come on, Briar, don't be like that."

"Be like what?" I hiss. "Like someone who doesn't accept being treated like a piece of shit? I am not a chew toy for Travis to step on and try to tear down because he's all bent out of shape." I reach down and scoop Shadow up into my arms. I need all the squishes I can get to keep having this conversation.

"I know. He was just having a bad day. He didn't mean it," Asher says, rubbing the back of his neck.

Do not get lost in the muscle show, Briar.

"Is that supposed to be an excuse for what he did? And am I meant to be okay with the fact that the rest of you just stood there and did nothing?"

Asher shakes his head and runs his hand through his hair, like he thought this would be easier and I'm making him sweat.

Good.

"No, it's not, but it doesn't mean that he isn't—that we're not—sorry."

"If Travis was sorry, he'd be here apologizing instead of you, Asher. Don't you ever get tired of apologizing for him? Maybe if he wasn't such an asshole, you wouldn't have to clean up his mess all the time."

And maybe I should vent my frustrations to Travis instead of Asher, but he isn't here right now.

Asher takes a step back, like he really thought I'd just roll over and accept his apology as gospel. "I'm not cleaning up his mess. I came to make sure you were okay. Apparently, that was the wrong thing to do. Noted."

I shake my head, scoffing at his nonchalance. "Here I was thinking you were the smart, decent one of the four, Asher. It's not the right thing to do. The right thing is not to be a giant asshole in the first place."

He scrubs the back of his neck with one hand again. Pushing up those black-framed glasses of his with the other before shaking his head. "You're right. I'm sorry."

"Do you even know what you're sorry for, Asher?" My snark is at full nuclear levels, and I'm pretty sure people are watching, but I'm losing the last few fucks I had tucked away for safe keeping.

He just blinks at me, like he's never had to work this hard to apologize before, and I laugh again. "That's what I thought. I'll see you around, Asher." I put Shadow back down on the ground and stride away from Asher, feeling him watch me as I leave, along with a few others. Hating the yips that come from Shadow that pull at my little black heartstrings.

Travis Kensington is an asshole, but I've fought off much worse monsters than him. I just hope they all leave me the hell alone so I can graduate and get out of here and away from them.

They want me gone anyway so it shouldn't be a big ask.

I loosen a breath as I head into my Intro to Psych class, grabbing a seat in the middle of the room and putting my satchel on the one beside it for the coffee guy—pretty sure he said his name was Connor—and of course that's the moment Sawyer St. Vincent walks into the fucking room.

Someone freaking save me.

BURN

LILY WILDHART

SIX

Fuck my actual life.

I watch as Connor darts in behind Sawyer, beelining toward me, and as the realization dawns on Sawyer that Connor is heading for me... it's like a car crash happening in slow motion as that audacious, arrogant smile on Sawyer's face changes. Like someone just waved a red flag in front of a bull.

I don't even know why. He has been fully Team Travis since they discovered who I was, and he hasn't spoken to me once.

Yet... he's looking at me like I'm a toy he's played with that he doesn't really want, but he doesn't want anyone else to play with either.

I will never understand men, of that I'm positive. I used to think they were simple creatures. Turns out I was fucking wrong and all that propaganda about them being simple is just bullshit created to confuse those of us with vaginas... and dicks in some cases, but I'm pretty sure the gays have a better insight than I do right now.

Connor smiles at me as I lift my bag from the seat I saved before he drops into it. "Lifesaver. I really didn't want to have to sit up front."

"Anytime," I respond with a small smile, hoping like hell Sawyer isn't staying. Penn said he's a sophomore and a Business major so there's no reason for him to be in this class.

Right?

A man with salt-and-pepper hair walks in, dressed in a sharp gray suit that screams money with a black tie, his matching dress shoes clicking on the floor as he walks toward Sawyer. He pauses when he reaches the asshole of a blond god and they talk quietly.

I half wish I was closer so I could hear what they were talking about—especially since the two of them keep glancing at me. But on the other hand, I'm trying not to give two fucks about Sawyer or his friends, which means that really, I don't need to know what they're talking about.

"Is that Professor Crawford?" I ask Connor quietly, taking my attention from the front of the room as I pull a notebook and pen from my bag. He stares at the notebook like I'm crazy as he pulls a laptop from his bag.

"It is, and don't let him catch you with a notebook. He'll crucify you. Record the lecture on your phone if you have to. He hates 'outdated' methods." He does the whole quote marks sign thing when he says outdated and gives me an apologetic smile as I realize everyone else in the room, like him, has a laptop out in front of them.

Awesome. Another thing I need to upgrade. I have a laptop, but not one light enough for me to lug all over campus. It also doesn't work without being plugged into an outlet at all times, so that really isn't going to work.

More money I need to spend. Yay me.

I tuck my notebook away and pull out my beat-up phone. Connor's eyes go wide when he catches sight of it, but he keeps his mouth shut.

As he should.

A shadow covers my desk and I take a deep breath before looking up to find Sawyer, smirking down at me. "Can't call you Red anymore."

"You're a tall guy," I deadpan, and he looks at me, confused. "What?"

I lean back and fold my arms, smirking back at him. "I thought we were just stating the obvious."

His smile grows and his shoulders loosen before he glances at the empty seat on my other side.

"Oh no, buddy. You're not in this class," I hiss, and realize the entire freaking class is watching us. Awesome.

"Aren't I?" He grins as he moves and slides into the seat on my other side.

Connor leans over to me, glaring at Sawyer. "Are you okay?" he whispers.

I sigh, glancing over at him. "Yeah, I'm just freaking peachy."

"How do you know Sawyer St. Vincent?" he asks, and I shrug, about to open my mouth when Professor Crawford clears his throat. I lift my gaze to find him watching me intently.

"If you're finished with your conversation, Miss Moore, I'll start our class."

My cheeks flame and I officially want the floor to open up and swallow me whole. Not only is he renowned for being a hardass, I've managed to piss him off before class even starts. "Sorry, professor."

The words come out a stammered mess, and he just quirks a brow at me before glancing at Sawyer and shaking his head.

I guess Sawyer is staying.

Fun.

I also assume that Sawyer is the reason my now very annoyed professor knows my name before class even starts. Awesome.

I grab a roll of cherry Lifesavers from my bag, popping one in my mouth before setting up the dictation on my phone. I grumble lowly when Sawyer reaches over and steals one of my Lifesavers. I want to stab him in his stupid hand with my pen that I'm not allowed to have out.

He has the audacity to make kissy noises at me, but I try to just block his bullshit out and actually pay attention to my first Intro to Psych lesson.

Especially since Professor Crawford is still glaring at me.

I guess this class really is going to be an uphill battle, especially since I didn't get the chance to go to the campus bookstore yet to get the ridiculously long list of books I need for my classes.

Mentally adding that to my to-do list for after class, I try to focus as the professor starts his lecture on psychology's roots and the philosophers that helped create psychology as we know it today, but my mind keeps drifting to the blond beside me who keeps nudging my foot with his.

Fucking Sawyer.

I pull my legs and arms in as tight as I can so he can't reach me, but that just seems to amuse him even more.

"We can swap seats next class," Connor whispers to me, and I give him a small but relieved smile.

I mouth the words 'thank you' and try to refocus on Professor Crawford and his lecture. This isn't exactly how I wanted to start my time at Saints U. Especially since I have him for two classes this semester, and him hating me isn't going to help me at all.

My biggest problem is that Sawyer's presence is very distracting, even with him doing nothing but watching me— which somehow doesn't even come off as creepy, but it's more cocky than anything. Freaking asshole.

By the time the professor gives us our first assignment and dismisses us, I'm a frazzled mess. He glared at me the very few times he did look my way, but ignored me the rest of the time.

Apparently, this man isn't a fan of mine, which makes me wonder what the fuck Sawyer told him. Hopefully I can overcome whatever it is, because I can't afford to fail his class.

"Don't sweat it, Not-Red. He's a pussycat. He's just feeling you out," Sawyer whispers to me, making me jump because I hadn't realized how close he'd gotten.

"Just no." I sigh, rushing to my feet and nearly falling to my ass in my haste. Sawyer catches me before I hit the ground, his hands gripping my waist, and it would be so easy to be nice to him for helping me, especially because I believe that manners don't cost a damn thing. But then I remember he didn't help me before with Travis and that the professor likely hates me *because* of him, so I stuff down my gratitude.

Am I being a bit of a brat? Most definitely, but he doesn't get to play hot and cold and expect me to fall at his feet.

So, instead of thanking him, I pull myself out of his grasp and step around Connor. It's only when I glance back once I'm down a few steps that I notice them standing there, facing off with each other like there's some sort of pissing contest going on.

What sort of fucking world have I stepped into here in Serenity Falls? Sweet baby Jesus, this is insane. Especially since, bless his heart, Connor doesn't seem much of a match for Sawyer, even if he wasn't a slim, nerd type, meaning he's dramatically the underdog compared to Sawyer. Socially, Connor seems more my level, which means in this world, he'll never be the victor.

Instead of giving them any more attention, I hightail it from the room as fast as my feet will carry me without falling over again. The last thing I need in my life is more drama. I had low-key hoped that my mom marrying a guy rich enough to keep her entertained might mean less drama in my world.

But no. Apparently I'm a magnet for it.

Go. Freaking. Me.

It doesn't take me long to find the campus bookstore, though it does take me considerably longer to pull myself out of the fiction section than it should. Young Adult Fantasy Romance is my one true escape beyond sketching and music.

Now the Young Adult section... that one I actually have to resist using the credit card that feels like a lead weight in my pocket. Buying stuff for school? That feels weird.

I never said it made any sense.

Taylor Acorns' *Psycho* plays through my headphones as I go through my book list from the advisor, trying to get as many used books as I can, but the selection is sparse because I'm so late to get them. Which means I end up buying a ton of them brand spanking new, and it costs a small fortune.

I'm pretty sure my heart stops when the cashier rings up the total cost.

"I could put a deposit on a house with the cost of these," I grumble, and the peppy blonde girl behind the counter giggles at me.

"Don't be silly, a house would set you back millions," she says, giggling again, and it takes all of my strength not to roll my eyes at her and run the fuck away.

"Of course," I respond with a tight smile as she bags up the books. Maybe I can buy my fiction hit elsewhere. If only the coffee and cake didn't smell so good here, dammit.

This place is like my own personal kryptonite.

I'm definitely going to be back here, even with—I squint at her name tag—Amanda and her peppy disposition.

I glance back at the coffee counter, trying not to drool over the thought of an iced peppermint mocha with extra whip.

Screw it.

"Do you want to take these with you now, or have them delivered?" Amanda asks, and I swear I'm almost blinded by her bright smile again.

"You deliver them?" I ask, trying not to let my shock show.

"We sure do. Just let me know your dorm, or your address if you're not on campus, and we'll have them shipped before the end of the day. If you're on campus, they'll be with you today, if you're not, it'll be tomorrow."

"Oh. Right. Uhm, yeah I'm on campus." I grab the Abnormal Psych book I need for this afternoon and arrange to have the rest sent to my room before saying goodbye and heading over to the coffee counter. I get my cold coffee and do a little happy dance. Peppermint probably won't be around for long, because those basic fall bitches bring in pumpkin spice. And while I'm definitely a basic fall bitch, I can't stand the pumpkin stuff. Give me peppermint till I die!

Though I won't lie, if the pumpkin comes with this heat dialing back, I'll take it, because I am over this warm weather already.

My phone buzzes and I frown, wondering who the hell is texting me. I don't have many people that normally text me, no one here but Penn has my number yet and Emerson has fallen off the face of the earth since the party we went to before school started.

Mom:

Hi sweetheart! Chase and I are coming home next week.
Mandatory family dinner next Thursday. No excuses since
we're giving you over a week's notice! Love you.

I groan as I leave the bookstore. Tucking my phone back in my rear pocket, I wonder what I did in a past life to have to endure this one when I run smack into the Barbie parade that was with Travis and the others.

"Oh, look, it's the Kensington charity case," the girl who was hanging off of Travis the other day sneers, and I roll my eyes.

"Yep, that's me. Take it in. Gold digger galore, ladies, be careful of getting too close though. Poor is catching, you know? Now, if you'll excuse me, I need to go hunt down another trust fund baby to suck the life out of."

They pause, giving me just enough time to dart around them, and I think I'm home free when I get yanked back by my hair. I fall onto my ass, somehow managing not to spill a drop of my drink, but the crunch of my phone in my back pocket has despair washing through me like a tidal wave.

Yeah, that thing is dead.

Awesome.

"That's where you belong, whore. Beneath me," a brunette I don't recognize says as she steps forward. "Enjoy your shower."

I am momentarily stunned as she pours her drink over my head. They all cackle as it happens and I'm just struck stupid, unable to move. What are we, in high school? You have got to be kidding me with this petty, childish bullshit.

How is this my life?

They turn and walk away, leaving me ass down on the sidewalk covered in God only knows what the hell was in that cup of hers. It smells sweet, it's bright freaking pink, and it's cold as fuck. I wipe away as much of it as I can, refusing to let the tears that prick at my eyes fall, and climb to my feet.

Thank God I wear mostly black so whatever this is, it's not going to stain.

It's impossible to ignore everyone that's just watching me to see if I'll break down, knowing that not one of them even thought about helping. I straighten my shoulders and lift my head high, slip on my natural resting bitch face mask despite the ice and syrup still in my hair, and head toward my dorm.

These bitches think a slushie bath is going to scare me off? They have no idea who I am, or even the truth of why Travis really hates me—not that I'm sure they care about the truth of anything.

They don't know the things I had to overcome before I arrived in Serenity Falls, so if they think a little bullshit bullying is going to make me leave, they've got another thing coming.

"Briar?" I hear as I approach my dorm building.

I ignore the voice and keep walking, not really wanting to talk to anyone right now when I'm so close to being in a shower, but when someone grabs my arm and pulls me to halt, I clench my jaw. "People really need to stop manhandling me before I start fighting back."

"Woah, I didn't mean any harm," Asher says, releasing me and putting his hands up in surrender as I look up at him. He frowns when his eyes run over me, and I ball my hands into fists. "What happened to you?"

I scoff at him, because it's ridiculously obvious what happened to me. "As if you don't already know, but Travis's little sorority hit squad happened. Now, can I go and shower before I'm late for my afternoon class?"

"I didn't know. They did this?" he asks again, his jaw clenching as he folds his inked arms over his wide chest.

I let out a deep breath, realizing that trying to be a bitch just isn't going to work with him, so I soften just a little. "Asher, I really just want to shower. It's no big deal. I can handle bullies. I've been dealing with them my entire life."

"Fine," he says with a nod. "I mean, not fine, but fine. Just… if you need me, you know where I am."

"Thank you," I say, giving him the fakest smile of my life, and practically run into my building. I turn as I enter, catching him watching me while animatedly yelling at someone on his phone.

I can't help but smirk. I might not want his help, but if he's yelling at the dumb bitch with the slushie, or even at Travis however unlikely that is… well, I'm all for it.

He looks up and sees me, and my breath catches as our eyes meet. The fire in his green gaze steals my entire focus. I stumble as someone smashes into my shoulder, breaking my connection with him, and before I can even think about looking back, I run up to my room.

I don't need any distractions. I'm here for my degree.

Even if that distraction is as drool worthy as Asher St. Vincent.

SEVEN

By the time I'm done with my shower, I practically have to sprint to make it to class before I'm late. Unfortunately for me, Professor Crawford is already there waiting when I slide into the room with about ten seconds to spare.

He glares at me and I open my mouth to apologize, when he dismisses me with a look that makes me want to throw something at his head. Taking a deep breath, I glance around the room and spot Connor waving at me, motioning to the empty chair beside him.

Thank God.

I spot Sawyer on the other side of the room, but there are two girls flanking him, so I grin at him when he sees me since he can't hover over me. Though why he's in this class too is beyond me.

Moving as quickly as I can without causing any more of a scene, I slide into the chair just as Professor Crawford starts speaking.

I open my mouth to thank Connor when I feel eyes on me. I look up and find the professor staring in my direction. "Do you intend to continue to interrupt the second lesson of the day, Miss Moore, or can I actually teach *this* class without you taking it hostage?"

My cheeks flame as he calls me out. Especially since I haven't actually done anything wrong. Every single part of me wants to call him out for being an asshole, but I clench my fists and nod my head instead, keeping my mouth firmly shut. If I open it even to say yes, it's going to come out sarcastic and I'm likely going to say something I shouldn't as well.

Story of my life.

I can hide away at the best of times, but if you provoke my anger... well, it becomes real obvious that I'm a Sagittarius. I'm fiery by nature.

He quirks a brow at me before turning back to the class and I finally let out the breath I was holding. It's literally my third day of classes and my professor already hates me.

Awesome.

I wonder if he knows Travis and that's why. He was definitely friendly with Sawyer earlier. Maybe that's what he and Sawyer were talking about: ways to flunk me so I just up and leave. Unfortunately for them, I'm a stubborn ass who really hates to move because someone else tells me to.

My mom has done it plenty, but everyone else can go to hell.

I open my text book and groan when I realize I can't dictate the class because my phone is destroyed.

"You okay?" Connor whispers when he notices my despair.

"My phone is broken; I can't dictate," I explain as quietly as possible, considering Professor Crawford seems to have it out for me already. Connor points to his phone and shows it's already recording.

"I'll send you a copy. Of last class, too."

Oh, sweet baby Jesus. 'Thank you' I mouth to him, trying to draw as little attention to me as possible.

I try to focus as much as I can as the professor talks about identifying psychological disorders and what is considered abnormal. I get a little lost as he dives into the classification of psychological disorders, likely made worse by the fact that I can't take notes, and it's then that I accept the fact I'm going to have to use the credit card again.

I need a phone and I need a laptop that functions. I make a mental note to do it later, just as Connor taps my foot with his.

I glance over at him and realize a ton of people are staring at me.

Including the professor.

Fuck my actual life.

"Sorry, I think I missed that," I stammer, hating being

caught off guard.

"If you're not interested in this class, Miss Moore, maybe you should give your spot to someone more… deserving."

The professor's words, plus the giggles from the girls next to Sawyer across the room, make me wish a giant pit would open up underneath me and swallow me whole. Instead, I jut out my chin and harden my eyes. "I'm more than interested, and I deserve to be here. I'd have notes on your class and what we were talking about, but you don't believe in *archaic* methods of note taking, and since my laptop isn't quite up to scratch, I don't have notes for where we are. If you want me to focus, maybe be more lenient with your requirements. But if you're wanting me to answer whatever it is you asked me, please, repeat the question and I'll happily try to answer."

There goes my mouth again.

I wince internally while keeping eye contact with the professor. The room goes so still and silent you could hear a pin drop.

I mean, he didn't like me already. I don't really have that much to lose.

I hope.

"I suggest you stay behind after class, Miss Moore," is all he says before continuing to talk about how different parts of the world have more prominent mental disorders and the consequences of labeling.

I spend the rest of the class on high alert, waiting for him to snap back at me, but by the time class ends, he hasn't so much as looked at me again. I wait as the class empties and Connor waits with me without even saying a word.

"Mr. Berkley, you can leave now." He levels a stare at Connor, who glances at me. I nod. No point dragging this out.

"I'll wait outside for you," he says, squeezing my shoulder as he stands and leaves. Which is nice, but a little too friendly, considering I barely know him. I smile regardless, because I don't exactly treasure the thought of being alone with my new professor who seems to hate me already.

"You too Mr. St. Vincent," he says, and I realize Sawyer is still in his seat. He eyes the professor skeptically before standing, sweeping his blond hair out of his face before bouncing down the steps with that golden retriever energy of his hanging out all over the place.

"That's cool, Noah," Sawyer says with a smirk. "We'll catch up later."

I guess he really does know the professor. He must if they're on a first name basis, though from the look on Crawford's face, he isn't exactly a fan of Sawyer calling him Noah.

The door closes with a slam once he leaves, and I wince as I make my way down to the front of the class where an angry Professor Crawford is leaning against his desk with his arms crossed, glaring at my every movement.

"Miss Moore, what is the point of you being in my class if you don't want to be here?" he snaps at me, and I just blink at him.

The audacity of this man. "Who said I don't want to be here? Sawyer?" I counter, trying not to sound as defensive as I feel.

"No. Your actions, Miss Moore. They speak louder than any words could. You turn up to class and disrupt it. Mr. St. Vincent disrupted on your behalf this morning. You don't have your books or the correct equipment. From what I can tell, you have no excuses for any of this, and then you don't even have the common decency to actually pay attention during my class." He leers at me, like my body appeals to him, but everything else about me revolts him.

Elitist pervert alert.

I take a deep breath, pushing my nails into the palms of my hands as I clench my fists. "Firstly, Professor Crawford, if you knew anything about me, you'd know I only registered for classes at the end of last week, and until that time, I didn't even know I was coming here. I don't come from money like most of the students in your class, and I haven't had the chance to get the equipment or books before now, but if you paid attention, you'd see I actually have my book for this class, which I got earlier today. Now, I don't know if you're classist, or if you just have something against me personally, but if you'd allow for pen and paper, I'd have taken plenty of notes up to now."

He rolls his eyes at me and I swear to God, I've never wanted to slap the look off someone's face so bad as I do now. This jerk off might actually be a bigger jack hole than Travis.

And I didn't think that was possible.

"Are you quite done, Miss Moore?" His patronizing tone makes my teeth ache and my temper burn in my chest. I swear, if I was a supernatural type like the characters I've read about, I'd have thrown a fireball at this guy's head by now, dammit.

"I don't know, am I?" I counter as he sits at his desk.

"Make sure you're prepared for our next class. Otherwise, you'll be dropped. You can go now." He dismisses me with a wave, not even bothering to look at me. My cheeks sting with indignation as I turn and storm from the room.

Giant. Fucking. Asshole.

"Hey, Briar! Wait up!"

I barely hear the voice through the roaring in my ears, but a hand on my shoulder makes me spin around, ready to launch myself at whoever the next person to mess with me is. When I find a concerned-looking Connor, I pump the brakes on the torrent of rage that's about to spew from my mouth.

I take small mercies in the fact that Sawyer hasn't hung around.

"Are you okay?" he asks, taking a step back. He might be a little off, but at least he can apparently still read social cues.

"No, I'm far from okay, but thanks for checking."

He rubs the back of his neck, obviously feeling awkward, but *he* chased after *me*. "Okay, well, we're starting up a study group for both of Crawford's classes, and I wanted to invite you to join the group."

"Oh," I say, the wind leaving my rage-filled sails. "That'd be great, thank you."

He digs in his pocket and pulls out a crumpled piece of paper. "This is my number, for when you get a new phone. Text me and I'll send over the details."

"Thanks, Connor," I say with a small smile, trying not to look like a crazy bitch.

He shuffles his feet, and I wait for him to say whatever it is he looks like he's trying to say. "Okay, well, bye."

The words tumble from his mouth as he darts away from me, leaving me beyond confused. I turn and find Travis glaring daggers at me.

Yep, that'll do it.

I roll my eyes, because I *so* don't have the patience for Travis Kensington, and my anger spikes when he tips his head back, like he's summoning me to him.

Jumped-up rich kids, man.

Taking a deep breath, I make my way over to him, because I really don't need any more drama today and ignoring him seems like it'll just bring more stress.

His blue eyes are cold like steel as he looks down at me. I've never not liked my height until right now with him towering over me. "Ready to drop out yet, Goldie?"

"Goldie?" I ask, confused. When he smirks in response, I kind of wish I hadn't asked.

"Goldie… ya know, short for gold digger."

"Wow, aren't you original? Such a clever nickname there, champ." I sigh, my patience wearing thin. "What do you want, Travis?"

"Did you get the summons?" he asks, and I think back to the text from Mom and nod, assuming that's what he means. "Good, I'll grab you from your dorm and you can ride with me. My father never needs to know there's anything wrong, or that I fucked my whore of a stepsister."

"Yeah, because it was totally my intention to just blurt out over dinner that I rode your cock like it was the second coming of Jesus," I deadpan, and I watch as his jaw tics.

Yay. Travis has buttons to push.

He doesn't say another word, just turns and walks away, his fists clenching and unclenching at his sides as he does.

Score one to me.

I spot Sawyer across the quad, he glances at me just before Travis reaches him. I should have known that he'd run back to his keeper. Not that it matters, I won this round.

Now to work out how to stay ahead of the game.

LILY WILDHART

EIGHT

After cooling off, blasting PVRIS's *My House* in the dorm, singing at the top of my lungs to burn out the last of my frustration, and eating my favorite Peking duck ramen, I head to the library. I need to try and catch up on the reading from today's classes and actually make myself some freaking notes until I get new tech so I can listen to the recordings Connor took.

Here's hoping my Intro to Writing class in the morning is happy enough with pen and paper rather than a laptop. I have tomorrow afternoon free, so I'm going to have to suck it up and go shopping then.

I would like to think I've made my peace with it, but I know I'm going to absolutely hate every fucking second of it.

I make my way into the library, relishing the peaceful calm that washes over me as I enter the quiet space. The librarian smiles at me when I wave before trying to work out where the best place for some privacy is.

Not that I need the privacy to study, I just *really* don't want to people.

I walk through the stacks, breathing in the scent of books—one of my favorite smells—and find a group of tables where people are obviously trying to study.

Nope, this is not where I want to be.

"Briar?" I turn at the whispered call of my name to find Connor and Penn walking toward me.

Huh. Didn't know they knew each other. "Hey."

"Want to join us?" Connor asks, and Penn's eyebrows rise.

"I didn't know you guys knew each other?" she says, but it's more of a question. To be fair, I could say the same, but it's not like I really know either of them very well. I haven't even been here a whole week, and I'm not exactly the warm and fuzzy type of human that others gravitate toward. No, I identify more with a cactus. Even though we already had what she called a girls' night and she dished on Travis and co., I still wouldn't call Penn an actual friend. Not yet anyway.

Connor smiles at her warmly. "We have a ton of the same classes. She's a Psych major too."

The skepticism drops from her face and she smiles at me. "Oh, that makes sense. But yeah, you should join us."

I consider it for all of two seconds before I realize that turning them down will be considered an insult. Stupid social cues.

"Sure, thanks," I say with as much of a smile as I can muster before following them through more stacks to a small table for four tucked away, that they've obviously commandeered as their own.

At least it's quiet.

"Do you need my dictations from today?" Connor asks as I unpack my bag.

"If you have them, that would be amazing, thank you. I need to get ahead, otherwise Crawford is going to drop me." I sigh as I sit down and pull my pad and paper from my bag.

Connor frowns as he sits next to me, with Penn opposite him. "Yeah, he does seem to have it in for you."

"Yay," I utter as he hands me the printed dictation notes from today's classes. "Lifesaver. Thank you."

I groan as I realize I can't listen to music while I study because my phone is a broken mess. I still pop my headphones in, smiling at the two of them as I do before diving into my notes.

After what feels like hours of reading and note taking, Connor stands and taps my shoulder. "Coffee, ladies?"

"You know the way to a girl's heart, Connor Berkley." Penn grins. He nods before turning his gaze to me.

"Briar?"

"Sure, thank you," I say, reaching for my wallet, but he's gone before I can hand over any money.

"Not worth it," Penn says quietly. "He'll just argue with you about paying. He's a little prideful like that."

"So you guys know each other pretty well?" I ask, curious.

"You could say that," she says as she puts down her pen. "Connor grew up next door to me on the outskirts of Serenity. We were the outcasts, the poor few in a sea of rich kids because Connor's epic brain meant he had a scholarship to the private high school, and my dad worked there, so I had a spot too. We're both here on scholarship, and I'm almost convinced I only got in because of him. He's literally a freaking genius. I'd have never passed my finals or the entrance exam for this place without him."

I nod, taking in the info and the dreamy look on her face. Totally not who I pictured as her type, considering what little I know of her, but that's what I get for judging too early I guess. "Are you guys together?"

"No," she answers a little too quickly. "Why? Are you interested?"

I try not to laugh as I shake my head. I might not people well, but it's hard to miss the fact that she's definitely crushing on him. Even if he does seem absolutely clueless about it. "No, I have way too much going on to deal with guys on top of everything."

"Well, considering you have the attention of Travis and his band of merry jerks, that's not really a surprise. How, exactly, did you manage to piss them off, anyway?" she asks, leaning forward, her chin on her hands.

"I exist?" I say with a laugh. "Honestly, Travis seems to be the one with the issue, the others just follow his lead like lost puppies. But I'm not thinking about it too hard. I'm just going to focus on getting through these classes and that's it."

"Good for you."

Connor reappears with three coffee cups, and the smell alone makes my mouth water. "Penn, triple shot macchiato for you, and Briar, I just got your usual mocha. Hope that's okay?"

"Perfect, thank you," I respond with a wide smile. Coffee really is the way to this girl's heart.

I pick up my headphones again, motioning that I'm going back into the mindless ramblings of Professor Crawford and leave them to their conversation. Despite not having music to tune them out, I try not to listen in on them, even if it is kind of impossible.

From what I can work out, Penn was right. Connor does seem like a bit of a boy wonder genius type, and I'm pretty sure she's a Business major from what she's saying.

I try to refocus and tune them out, but my rumbling stomach wins out after another hour or so, and I finally call time on my study session. "I'm going to tap out for the night. I need to eat something more than ramen."

"That sounds like a solid plan," Penn says, stretching out. "Pizza?"

"Yes," Connor groans as he rubs his eyes. "I need a hit of cheesy carbs."

"Weren't you supposed to be going to a frat party?" I ask her, and she shrugs.

"I was, but I needed to study, and pizza sounds better to me right now."

I mull it over and decide that hanging with them doesn't sound so bad. Especially if it comes with pizza. And maybe then, Penn might feel a little less threatened when she works out that I'm really not interested in her guy.

A roommate who doesn't loathe my existence would definitely be a tick in the hell yes column.

"Let's do it. Take it back to our room and put something to binge on the TV?" I offer, and Connor grins wide.

"Yes, the perfect way to end this day. Come on, Penn, you know you've been wanting to binge that new zombie show."

She grumbles her agreement, and as much as zombies don't do it for me, I'm not about to rock the boat. I finish packing up my stuff, handing Connor his notes. "You're good, I've got extra copies."

"Oh, right. Thanks." I smile at him before stuffing them in my notebook and putting that in my bag too.

I follow them out of the library and across campus to a little pizza place called Rosa's, which they swear is the best one near Saints U, before we head back to our dorm.

"Did you guys leave your door unlocked?" Connor asks cautiously as we reach our dorm. I frown. I know I locked it earlier.

Penn moves in front of us and charges into the room, but stops in the doorway. I peer over her shoulder and my stomach drops.

"Holy shit," Connor utters from behind me as I take in the sight before me.

Penn's side of the room is fine. Pristine, except for some debris.

But mine…

Mine looks like a tornado ripped through it and destroyed everything.

Including my fucking bed and mattress.

The few clothes I have here are shredded, strewn across the room. Even my shoes have been torn up. The bed is in pieces and the mattress is soaking fucking wet with tears all through it, my few trinkets are smashed to dust, and my brand new books are completely destroyed too. The doors of my closet are open and it's entirely empty. Even my underwear is in pieces around my half of the room.

I close my eyes and take a deep breath.

Fuck this shit, man. All I want to do is graduate. Though maybe it's not worth all this. It's not like I ever thought I'd even get to come to college anyway.

"Who the fuck would do this?" Connor asks as he pushes into the room, putting the pizza down on Penn's bed. "We need to report it."

"Reporting it won't change a damn thing." I sigh as Penn

moves aside and we enter the room. I close the door behind me, wondering what the fuck to do from here. "This was either on Travis's say so or his little sorority bitches took their own initiative to do it, thinking he'd appreciate them torturing me."

"I'm sorry, Briar," Penn says, a look of disbelief still on her face as she takes in the complete destruction. "Let's get this cleaned up and then tomorrow we can go shopping, see what we can replace."

Awesome. My shopping trip just grew into replacing literally fucking everything I owned on top of all the shit I need for school.

"Thank you," I respond, trying not to take the rage that's burning inside of me out on her or Connor.

No, this I'm saving for Travis and his bunch of vapid little followers.

I start picking up the remnants of my life and they both help. We put everything into trash bags and Connor manages to recruit another guy from the hall to help carry my destroyed bed and mattress outside.

Once everything is in the trash, I slide down the wall on my now very empty side of the dorm.

Penn sits on her bed, watching me while we wait for Connor to return.

"I'm sorry I was such a bitch to you when you arrived," she says solemnly.

"You don't need to apologize to me again, Penn." I sigh,

resting my head back on the wall.

"It still feels like I do… you obviously have enough to deal with. If you need to talk, or ya know, drink yourself stupid, I'm your girl. We can even rope Connor into being our DD." She grins, and I bark out a dry laugh.

"He doesn't drink?" I ask, and she shakes her head.

"Not since the one and only time I got him trashed. He vomited for hours and vowed never again. He's the only person I know who has ever stuck to that vow." She giggles and I can't help but smile as some of the anger melts away. "Now, let's dig into this pizza, shall we?"

She pats the bed beside her and I move to the offered spot, taking a slice of the cheesy goodness just as Connor enters the room.

"Yes, pizza time! Let's end this night properly." He winks at us as he sits on Penn's other side and grabs the remote. "Pizza and zombies. No better way to end a Wednesday."

After what was a surprisingly easy morning with my Intro to Writing class, I meet up with Penn to go shopping for my new stuff. Advantages of her growing up in Serenity Falls is that she knows where to shop that isn't going to cost me a small fortune.

"You ready?" she calls out as she walks toward me on the quad. I lift the car keys in my hand, thankful that they were in my bag yesterday, rather than in my room.

"Ready as I'm going to be. To the Batmobile!"

"Batmobile?" she questions as she drops into step beside me.

"You'll see," I grumble as I lead her toward where I left the metal monstrosity. I click the fob and it beeps, causing Penn's eyes to go wide.

"Yep, I see. Holy shit, that's a beauty of a car. 4-liter, V8. Just stunning." She laughs, shaking her head as we climb into the thing. "Yeah, we're not going to fit in downtown in this, but if you're good with that, I am."

"Downtown is where I fit in. Not my problem that this beast of a machine isn't going to. Pretty sure the Kensingtons won't even miss it if something happens to it," I say with a shrug and pull out of the space.

"I didn't realize you knew cars," I say, more as a question than a statement as we pull up to the traffic lights, and she grins.

"Yeah, my older brother is a total grease monkey. He used to build engines for fun, race cars, all the stupid shit we're not supposed to do. He's mostly into Japanese cars, but I love a good German machine."

"Wow, so yeah, you really know cars."

"Enough to know that this Panamera is a Turbo S Exec, and is worth at least two hundred thousand."

My eyes go wide at the number. "Please tell me you're kidding."

She laughs, shaking her head. "I am not. The upsides to rich kid life."

I groan, putting my forehead on the steering wheel until the light turns green. I let Penn fuck around with the radio since my phone is dust and she directs me to the mall where I can buy everything I need without owing the Kensingtons my first-born child.

I pull into a spot outside, make sure I have the dreaded credit card in my wallet, and follow Penn inside the mall.

"Remind me what you need," she says as we enter the air-conditioned paradise. It's way too hot outside for freaking September.

Someone please tell fall that it's late, and I'm not so patiently waiting.

"Phone, laptop, clothes, bed, basically everything."

She nods, scanning the lines of stores in sight. "Let's start with the tech. Ease you in before I try to take you clothes shopping."

I nod, still thankful for the clothes she lent me for today. Though going commando wasn't on my list of things I wanted to try, I wasn't going to wear her underwear. But she's right. I am never going to be prepared for clothes shopping. It hasn't exactly ever been a hobby of mine. Thrift store bargains have always been more my style; picking up the odd piece every now and then rather than just buying a whole wardrobe.

I shudder at the thought of what I'm going to do today and

how much it's going to cost.

"Okay, yes, tech. Where to?"

She drags me around three different stores before just taking me to the Apple store and making me get the latest iPhone, MacBook, and iPad, because apparently the fact that I can sync them all up is the best thing ever and something I need in my life regardless of the cost. She even threw AirPods into the cart, because for some ungodly reason, you can't use normal headphones with an iPhone.

For someone who is a self-proclaimed poor bad bitch, she spends money *way* too easily.

I feel sick at how much I've spent already, despite knowing that I've barely put a dent in the allowance on my card. Tobias told me the limit, but I think I blacked that part out. Still, I'm fairly certain I could shop for six months and still not hit it.

"Okay, food break and then clothes?" Penn grins at me, like she's enjoying my torture way too much.

My stomach gurgles in response and I nod. "Yes, food. That I can deal with."

She leads me to a Mexican place where I order the best chicken and mushroom burrito I've ever devoured in my life— with extra sour cream and cheese, obviously. I might be lactose intolerant, but I'll accept my ticket to the bad place before I give up the good stuff—and a virgin margarita. I'd like to say we had an epic conversation over lunch, but we both just inhaled our food, her with a little happy dance with each delightful bite.

When we're done, I lean back in my chair, very much bloated from the sheer speed at which I just ate. "Okay, yeah. We can come here again."

She grins at me and nods. "I used to spend way too much money in here each week. I'm surprised I'm not a burrito at this point. You ready to continue your torture?"

I groan and drop my head to the table. "If I knew exactly who did that to my stuff, I'd shank them on principle. Not even for destroying my stuff, but purely for making me shop."

She laughs at my dramatics, but I push back from the table and stand anyway. "Let's do this. The sooner we start, the quicker it's over, right?"

"I've never met a girl who dislikes shopping as much as you do, Briar."

I shrug as she stands. "I've never had money for anything but bills. Shopping was always painful, and now that I can shop, the money isn't even mine. It just feels kinda gross, ya know?"

She tilts her head to the side, watching me closely before nodding. "Yeah, I can understand that. I've never been rich, but I've also never gone without. I've had a job since I was legally able to, and have been able to keep that money for myself. So while I don't entirely understand, I do get it. I always hated asking my parents for money for stuff. Now, let's swallow that icky feeling and go spend some of Travis's money. Seems only fair, since he's the reason you have to spend it."

I consider her words for a minute and smile. "You're not

wrong there; this is entirely his fault."

Somehow that thought makes me feel better.

"Come on, show me where to get some new clothes." My words are more of a groan, but they're playful, because I might as well at least *try* to enjoy this. Unlikely, but stranger things have happened.

She grins and claps her hands, almost vibrating on the spot. "Okay, so let's just start on this side and hit every store until we find things you like. You need shoes too, right?"

I nod, still thankful that my precious thrift store boots were on my feet yesterday. I'd have legitimately cried if they'd have been trashed, too.

"Awesome, let's do this!" she says, pointing a finger in the air and making me laugh.

I trail behind her as she drags me from store to store, throwing clothes at me and forcing me into changing rooms. I end up dismissing at least ninety percent of it, only keeping the stuff that's more me than her. I remember halfway through that I actually have a ton of clothes back at the McMansion and reel in the spending, limiting myself to a few pairs of jeans, band t-shirts, a few t-shirts with hilarious prints on the front, underwear, and a few sweaters for the cooler weather that's coming, along with a leather jacket that had a price tag that made my eyes water, but it was just perfection on me. Even if it is kind of a crop jacket. With the tee and jeans I've changed into, it looked amazing and I couldn't resist.

"Thank you for today, Penn. You're a lifesaver," I say as we head back to the car.

"Honestly, I haven't had this much fun in ages. Torturing you with dresses was possibly my favorite part of the day. I can't wait until Halloween comes around. We're going to need to come back for costumes and… well, it's going to be too much fun."

I laugh as she shrugs when she climbs in the car. "Ugh, I hadn't even thought as far ahead as Halloween. It's going to be a big deal, isn't it?"

I've always wanted to do Halloween properly. Spooky season is my favorite after all, but we've never had the house for it or the money. I get the feeling that Serenity Falls takes this stuff to the extreme from the look on her face, and I can't find it in me to be anything but excited about that.

"Oh yeah." She grins as she pulls on her belt, winking at me. "And that's after all the other costume parties that will undoubtedly happen before then. Welcome to college, Briar. It's a whole new world."

LILY WILDHART

NINE

"I still can't believe you got that wasted..." Charli giggles as Serena groans, putting her head to the tabletop. The cafeteria is absolutely jam-packed, but since I've already endured my Government and Politics class today, I need food to refuel before I do my reading for tomorrow's classes with Crawford.

"My hangxiety is still so real," Serena mumbles, and I try not to laugh around my mouthful of pizza. "I cannot believe I did that. No more tequila for me."

"Pretty sure that tequila would've been fine had you not mixed it with whiskey, vodka, and rum," Penn snorts beside me, and I press my lips together to stop myself from laughing any harder. Poor Serena has spent the last three days agonizing over the party we went to on Saturday night.

Never have I ever been more glad that I stayed sober.

She flips Penn the finger before lifting her head and taking a bite of her sandwich. "You're the one who said let's get fucked up."

Penn barks out a laugh, shaking her head. "Yeah, but I didn't mean literally fucked."

I shake my head, trying not to say a thing, considering what happened the last time I drank. Zero judgment right here.

"It could be worse," I tell her. "You could've recorded it."

Charli giggles at me while Serena looks horrified, as if searching her memory to make sure she didn't do exactly that.

"I didn't do that. I don't think. Please, God, tell me I didn't do that. No more tequila," she says, shaking her head. "Can we please talk about something else? Please? Anything else."

As if the universe answers her plea, the door to the cafeteria opens and in walks what I've dubbed my own four horsemen of the apocalypse. The royalty of Saints U, who are anything but Saints.

I turn away from them, but I can feel Travis' glare burning into my back. We have that stupid family dinner in two days, and I'm *so* looking forward to it. Not.

The crowd of princesses that follow them in with an air of hairspray and giggling is enough to make me gag. What twists my stomach more is how aware I am of them all. It's ridiculous. One drunken night and some assholeish comments shouldn't make me automatically tune in whenever they enter a room and yet, anytime they're near, I just seem to know.

"Incoming," Penn says, glancing over my shoulder, grinning at me as she wags her brows. Her laughter starts when she sees me roll my eyes. "Just the emo one, though, don't worry."

My shoulders sag a little. I caught Penn up with everything that happened on my first night in Serenity Falls over the weekend, and after her initial shock, she laughed at me for a solid thirty minutes. So she knows that Asher—a.k.a. the emo one—doesn't seem to be a bag of dicks. Well, not entirely anyway. Unlike the ones I actually had a goddamn orgy with, he seems to want to play nice.

"Hey, Briar," he says as he stops beside me at the table. "You got a minute?"

The voice in my head screams that I absolutely don't, but the people pleaser that's been beaten into me smiles and pushes back from the table while Penn smugly grins at me.

I casually flip her the bird behind my back as I follow Asher past the others. Sawyer at least smiles at me, but Cole and Travis act like I don't exist.

Better than calling me out and hurling shit at me I guess, but since I'm with Asher, apparently I get a pass.

Yay me.

We head out of the building and around the corner, where it's less crowded. "This doesn't seem ominous at all," I utter, and he smiles at me.

"Don't worry, Briar. I have zero ill will toward you. Surely you've managed to figure that out so far?" He pushes his glasses up his nose and runs a hand through his hair. I've noticed he does that when he has to tell me something I probably don't want to hear, so I'm already on edge.

"Uh-huh. If you say so. What did you want?" I ask, folding my arms across my chest, knowing I need some sort of barrier between us. He's too nice, and I need to remember that he's still essentially #TeamWeHateBriar or #TeamTravis at the end of the day, even if he does seem to be trying to keep the peace.

His smile drops a little and I already know I'm not going to like whatever is about to fall out of his mouth. He lifts one of his delightful lean, inked-up arms behind his head, rubbing the back of his neck, flexing as he does. Pretty sure he's not doing it on purpose, but if he's trying to distract me from what he's about to say, it's working.

"Thursday…" he starts, and every instinct tells me to walk the hell away from this conversation, but yay trauma, because my feet stay planted exactly where they are.

"What about it?"

He runs a hand through his dark blond tresses again and, for a second, I could swear he almost looks uncomfortable. "I know you and Travis aren't exactly on the best terms, but his dad… well, his dad is an asshole."

"And you're telling me this, why exactly?" I ask, quirking a brow. Travis's dad can be an entire santa sack full of dicks, but if he keeps my mom happy, stable, and out of my way, then

I'm happy.

"Travis has no idea I'm telling you this," he says warily. "He thinks I'm talking to you about the girls, and how he absolutely tore them apart about the slushie thing—though let's just say nothing else should happen to you, and if it does, I need to know—but I'm telling you this because Travis is going to be even more on edge than usual. I'm just asking you to play nice."

"You're kidding me, right?" I scoff. "I've done nothing but play nice. He might have yelled at them about the slushie but he's still the asshole in all this, Asher. I keep going off at you, when I should be going off at him, but he's too much of a coward to ever actually talk to me. Ever since I walked into the kitchen that morning, he's done nothing but look at me like I'm not worthy of breathing the same air as him. Like I'm less than, just because he didn't know where he was sticking his dick. This is all fully a *him* problem."

"I don't think *that* is his problem," he mutters, shaking his head. "I get it, I do. I just… we'd all usually be there, playing buffer between the two of them. Chase likes to stay in good graces with the Becketts, because having a senator as a friend is always useful for someone like Chase, but since it's a family meal, we've been asked not to come."

"I don't get the feeling you guys usually follow orders, so why now?" I ask, more than a little curious.

He lets out a deep sigh, and his shoulders drop. "Because Travis asked us not to."

Huh, curiouser and curiouser.

"Right, so play nice. Was that all you wanted?" I ask, trying to play it cool and not ask a thousand questions about why Travis wouldn't want them there since they seem utterly inseparable the rest of the time.

"No, Cole has a game Friday. I want you to come." He moves his weight from one foot to the other, almost like he seems anxious over asking the question.

"Game?" I ask, and he laughs.

"I keep forgetting that you don't care enough to know shit about us. Cole is the quarterback for Saints U. It's the first game of the season and it's against our biggest rival in the state. It's a huge deal."

I blink at him, shocked. He could've told me the sky was pink and I'd have believed that over Cole being a team sports kind of guy. I faintly remember Penn talking about the team taking up his time, but I never would've thought she meant football. "Oh."

He laughs softly, shaking his head. "Yeah, oh. So, will you come?"

I find myself nodding, while screaming at myself internally for my inability to say no to this guy.

"Great, well, I guess I'll see you Friday." He waves and walks away, leaving me staring at his back as he retreats.

Well, shit. I guess I'm going to a football game.

shudder

This day can go to hell. Yesterday was almost an entirely good day. I survived my class, even managed to do the reading for today's. My only blip was the weird thing with Asher, but overall, it was an okay day.

Today, however, Crawford has already yelled at me and fully humiliated me in front of the entire class—twice. If I thought it would make a difference, I'd report him, but all that's likely to do is draw a bigger target on my back. Which I absolutely don't want.

I can survive one semester with him.

It's *just* one semester.

I play it like a mantra in my mind as I sip my coffee and read through the chapters for this afternoon's classes again.

Penn and the girls went off campus earlier to go catch an early showing of a new film, but I declined the invite. Crawford's wrath for ditching didn't seem worth it, but I'm regretting my decision currently as I pick at the chicken and bacon club I grabbed for lunch. He was in a freaking delightful state this morning, and it doesn't exactly fill me with hope and joy for the afternoon.

The rest of my classes, so far, seem pretty chill. I mean, Government and Politics with Professor Tuscon isn't exactly the highlight of my week. Though Intro to Stats with Professor

Dotura on a Monday along with Psych as a Profession isn't how I'd have chosen to start the week either, but nothing is worse than Wednesdays.

So much for happy hump day.

It ticks me off a little, because I was actually excited to study Psych, and two out of three of my Psych classes this semester are taught by Captain Douche himself, which is making it not so fun.

Releasing a sigh, I give up on my sandwich and pull out the sketch pad and pencils I sickeningly splurged on and lean back against the tree I've been sitting beneath, trying to enjoy the last heat of the season. I smile at my own thoughts, knowing that this bitch is more than ready for fall to hit full swing.

I set an alarm and lose myself in drawing, not even thinking about what I'm doing, just letting the pencil move across the paper like my hand isn't even my own.

There is peace in losing yourself in something you love, and this, right here, is the penultimate kind of peace I've ever found, outside of reading a book.

Before I know it, my alarm sounds and a part of me almost wants to risk Crawford's fury because I haven't felt this calm and centered since I got off the plane from California just under two weeks ago.

I bark out a small laugh. *How has it not even been two full weeks since my plane touched down?*

I look down at the sketch and realize it's the horse I rode at the farm I went to over the summer with Dad. I absolutely love horses and Dad took me as a 'half birthday' present, since he won't see me for my actual birthday. It was one of the very few highlights of the entire summer.

Packing my stuff away, I make a promise to myself to at least try to draw once a week. I need this sort of escape from my life and it's been too long since I've focused on my art. Who would've thought that it was this privileged existence I'd need the escape from? Back when I was at school and working full time, trying to juggle life and keeping a roof over our head, I never had the chance to escape. I was too busy and despite all the barrels of shit my mom ended up getting us stuck in—be it with guys she brought back to the apartment or debts she racked up—I still felt more in control then than I do now.

Go figure.

If you'd have told me a year ago that I'd be in college with no job, surrounded by these trust fund types... well, I'd have laughed in your damn face.

I stand and pull my satchel onto my shoulder, double checking the time on my watch, and my eyes go wide.

Shit.

How do I keep losing track of time today?

I haul ass toward my Psych building, determined not to give Crawford an excuse to ream me out again. I make it to the building, spotting Crawford across the quad, and let out a breath of relief that I'll actually beat him. Keeping up my pace so I don't end up with a seat at the front, I glance behind me to make sure Crawford isn't on my tail as I feel eyes on me, and I walk straight into a wall of muscle before bouncing back down onto my ass.

I groan at the ache in my tailbone, hoping that somehow, in the busy halls of this building, no one saw that absolute fail.

Looking up, I find the dark god that is Cole Beckett staring down at me, not quite glaring, but he definitely doesn't look happy to see me. I let out a sigh and start to climb to my feet when a hand is shoved in my face.

I look back up and find him just watching me, disgruntled, like me not letting him help me is pissing him off. Though that could just be my existence. Cole Beckett is an enigma. He doesn't seem to speak much. Well, not to me anyway.

"Briar." My name rolls from his tongue, more of a rumble from his chest than an actual spoken word, and a part of me wants to be a stubborn asshole and just stand up my damn self, but manners don't cost a damn thing, so I take his hand and accept the help.

"Thank you," I utter, trying to ignore the tingle of my skin where it touches his, which is somewhat hard to do since he isn't letting go. I try to pull my hand from his grip, but his fingers tighten on mine as he peers over my shoulder. I turn to look behind me at whatever he's staring at, but don't get the chance when he drags me into the room beside us which is, thankfully, empty.

"Cole, what the hell?" I ask, still unable to extract my hand from his. His eyes darken to pools as black as coal as he stares down at me, stepping closer. I take a step back without thinking and the corners of his lips tilt up. We repeat the push and pull until the wall is at my back and he steps into my space, pressing me against it with the hard wall of his body.

"You, Briar Moore, are a distraction I don't need," he says, his voice deep and growly as he uses his other hand to tuck my hair behind my ear. I feel like a deer caught in headlights: frozen, breath hitched, and entirely captured by his stare.

He strokes my cheek with his thumb and I let out a shaky breath, which seems to make his eyes light up. "Your heart is racing," he murmurs as he tilts my chin up so I'm meeting his gaze.

I open my mouth to try and say something as I press my free hand against his chest in a feeble attempt to create some distance, but then his lips are on mine and it's like the world pauses. For a guy so big, his lips are incredibly soft. He gently teases my mouth with his, his tongue finding the seam, pushing through as a whimper escapes me when he releases my hand. Using both hands, he cups my cheeks as he steals my breath with his kiss.

He pushes harder against me, his kiss becoming more demanding, and rather than pushing him away, I find myself clinging to him like I don't need air as long as he doesn't stop. Fire licks up from my toes and through my entire body until

I'm sure the world has burned around us and neither of us have noticed or cared.

He pulls back and I suck in a breath, my lungs screaming at me as I look up at him, trying not to look as doe-eyed as I feel.

Resting his forehead against mine, he strokes my cheek again before pulling away. "This was a mistake. You should stay away from me. From all of us."

He stares at me for a beat before exiting the room, leaving me reeling, before I haul ass so I'm not any later for class.

What the actual fuck was that?

After arguing with Travis and coming out the victor—which I'm still not sure was the best idea, but screw it—I pull up at the Kensington McMansion in the Batmobile, *Bite My Tongue* by You Me at Six blasting loud enough that my thoughts haven't been able to plague me, and my stomach flutters with the butterflies that have taken flight in there.

Not only have I not seen my mom in months, but we weren't exactly on the best terms when I left. Not after her spectacular fuck up, but that's not something I want to dwell on right now either. Add that to the fact that Travis is a cranky asshole whenever he's in my vicinity and the warnings about Chase... I'm really not looking forward to anything about tonight.

Except for Tobias. He was all kinds of awesome when he

welcomed me to my new 'home'.

I've officially been back from California two weeks tomorrow... who would've thought my life would completely upend in such a small amount of time?

Sure as hell not me.

Taking a deep breath, I push the buzzer for the behemoth garage and wait for the door to rise before pulling the metal monstrosity of a Porsche inside and parking it where I found it before. Once I shut down the engine, I press my hands against my stomach and hope like hell that I can actually eat something tonight.

If not, there will be a ramen dash later, but still, I don't want to offend Tobias and the other kitchen staff.

I slide out of the car, double checking I have my phone and wallet in my purse. Usually I wouldn't have gone all out like this, but when Travis arrived at the dorms to insist I drive here with him and lost his shit at my jeans and t-shirt ensemble, I figured I should make a little more effort. Especially since he was in dress pants and shirt. He lost the argument of me arriving with him, obviously. Honestly, the thought of being stuck in a car with him for too long makes me feel suffocated. God knows what an actual car journey would feel like.

I smooth down the skirt of the dress for the millionth time, which is paired with a pair of shoes I borrowed from Penn since all I own are Converse and my trusty thrift store boots, but I look cute and I'm trying to remind myself this is just a simple family dinner.

Taking another breath to steady my nerves, I push my shoulders back and raise my chin before heading inside the house.

I'm definitely not wishing that Asher's merry little band of Rottweiler puppies were here tonight. Nope. Not at all.

Dammit.

I make my way up to the kitchen, because I can't remember much else of this damn maze that is the Kensington mansion, and find Tobias amidst the chaos of way more people than I thought would be needed for a simple dinner for four.

Apparently I'm Jon Snow and I know nothing—because nothing about this looks simple.

Yes I'm a nerd, so sue me. I've binged Game of Thrones at least four times at this point. Jon Snow should definitely have been king, and that is that.

"Ah, Briar, you're here. The others are in the formal dining room already. Would you like a drink?" Tobias asks when he spots me by the door looking more than a little terrified.

"Erm," is all I manage before he smiles at me.

"The gents have whiskey, your mother has wine. What's your poison?"

"Tequila," I joke, but shake my head. "Probably not a good idea, though. Maybe just water?"

"How about both? You might need the extra help getting through dinner," he says with a wink, not helping my nerves about tonight even a little before he disappears.

He comes back with a shot glass and a tall tumbler. He hands me the shot first and I decide *fuck it*. Tobias knows these people better than I do. I throw the tequila to the back of my throat and swallow, surprised at how smooth it is. I am a lover of tequila, but this must be the good stuff.

I hand him back the shot glass and he hands me the taller one. "This is called a Matador. Tequila, pineapple juice, and lime juice. Not too strong, but will help you get through tonight while still keeping your wits about you. Thought you might prefer this over the water."

"And this is why you're my favorite," I say with a wink as I take the drink from him. I take a sip and am happily surprised at how good it is. This could be dangerous. "Just how bad is tonight going to be?" I ask, my heart fluttering in my chest.

"For you, probably not *that* bad, more awkward than anything. Chase and Travis… well, they have a hard relationship. I'm not going to say any more than that, it's not my place."

"Sounds like me and my mom."

He raises an eyebrow at me and I wave him off. "Maybe Travis and I have more in common after all. Anyway, I suppose I better go face the music. Where is the formal dining room again?"

He smiles warmly and offers me his arm. "Let me escort you, m'lady."

I laugh softly and loop my arm through his. "Why thank

you, kind sir." He leads me through the maze of the house to the formal dining room where my mom, Chase, and Travis are already waiting. The tension in the room is thick enough to make me feel like I'm suffocating before Tobias even releases me.

"Good luck," he whispers, patting my arm before abandoning me in these shark-infested waters.

Traitor.

"Briar! Sweetheart! There you are," my mom coos as she swishes across the room like she's lived in luxury her entire life. She grasps my arms and kisses both cheeks before hugging me. I can't remember the last time she smiled at me, let alone hugged me. And she's sure as hell never called me sweetheart. This isn't my mother. This is a pod person. "It's so good to see you. You look beautiful."

She pulls back and runs her gaze over me, like she's assessing my choice of a little black dress paired with Penn's ridiculous stilettos that I'm still amazed I can walk in. I actually look at her properly and realize how different she looks. I guess money will do that. Her skin seems smoother, clearer, her hair is shinier and bouncier, and there's just something lighter about her. So I put on a smile and slip into the good and doting daughter role she obviously wants me to play. "Thanks, Mom, so do you."

"Let me introduce you to Chase," she says, her smile widening, and for the first time that I can ever remember, she actually looks happy.

She squeezes my arm again and turns to face who I can only

assume is Chase. He looks like an older, more distinguished version of Travis. Their likeness is almost uncanny, except there's a harshness in Chase's eyes that Travis doesn't have yet and a spattering of gray through his dark hair, though it's a shade or so lighter than his son's.

Chase's demeanor softens when he turns from his son to my mom, a smile tipping up the edge of his mouth when he looks at her, like she actually makes him happy, too.

Maybe I was wrong about the two of them. Maybe they actually do love each other. Maybe Mom wasn't just looking for a meal ticket after all.

Color me shocked.

"Briar, it's lovely to finally meet you," Chase says when we reach him, and pulls me in for a hug. I try not to be too stiff, but it's hard to ignore the coldness I saw in him a second ago and I'm really not a hugger. Plus, no one can just shut that down entirely, that quickly without it being a red flag, and I can't help but wonder which version of him is more prominent. "I trust Tobias and Travis have been looking after you."

"Oh, yes," I stutter. "Travis made me feel right at home."

Keeping the sarcasm from my words isn't easy, especially when Travis splutters on his drink, but considering the way I saw Chase looking at him, a part of me doesn't want to make life harder for him, even if he has been a bag of ass since the morning I discovered who he was.

"Tobias has been great, making sure I have everything I

need," I add on, not wanting to get him in trouble either.

I glance over at Travis, who has managed to get over his sputter and now looks unaffected by any of it. If I hadn't seen how stiff he was when he was talking to Chase before, I'd never have known something was wrong, but now that I know, I can see it in the tightness of his shoulders, in the clench of his jaw, and how he holds the glass of amber liquid as he lifts it to his lips and takes a sip.

"Oh, yes, Briar and I are well acquainted," he adds, and I bite the inside of my cheek to stop from laughing out loud.

If only they knew.

"Dinner will be served in two minutes." Tobias's voice filters through the room, and I turn just in time to see the door shut.

I take a deep breath and prepare myself for what is likely going to be the longest and most uncomfortable dinner of my life.

Chase escorts my mom to her seat, pulling out her chair, and when Travis touches the small of my back, I jump. "Just go with it," he grumbles, so quiet I almost don't hear him.

I nod, feeling more unsettled with his hands on me than I did when I discovered he was my new stepbrother.

Now if my skin would just stop tingling where the heat of his hand presses against me, that would be great.

He leads me to the table and pulls out a chair for me before sitting between me and Chase, opposite my mom. Why they need an eight person dining table for the four of us is beyond me, but I'm not about to voice my questions.

Just as he sits, the door opens and servers appear, placing a plate in front of each of us before disappearing without a word.

Is this really how the other half live? Not even acknowledging their staff?

I resist the urge to roll my eyes as Chase smiles at me. "So, Briar, how is everything going at Saints U? I trust you're settling in well?"

"I am, thank you. And thank you for getting me in so last minute."

He waves me off before picking up his cutlery. "It's nothing. The dean is an old friend of mine. I assume the dorms are to your liking? Your mom thought you'd feel more comfortable there for your freshman year. Personally, I don't like the lack of security. I'd have preferred you to have stayed here, or lived with the boys."

I balk at his last comment and take a sip of my drink to try and hide it, because absolutely not. The thought of being stuck inside four walls permanently with Travis... no, I'd rather peel the skin from my fingers.

"The dorms are great, my roommate is awesome, as are the girls across the hall. It's been a good way for me to meet people," I offer, and he smiles, nodding, seemingly happy with my answer. He turns his focus to Travis and I let out a breath, looking down at my plate of whatever the hell this is. I glance up at Mom, but she's too busy giving Chase googly eyes to notice my dilemma of whether or not I can actually eat what's on the plate before me.

"It's duck," Travis whispers to me when Chase asks my mom a question.

"Thank you," I murmur back, grateful that he seems to have dialed back his intense hatred of me for the evening, even if it's all just a show.

I manage to navigate my way through the five-course meal, trying not to groan over the delicious salted caramel and dark chocolate mousse for dessert, which I was definitely too bloated to eat, but forced myself to anyway.

Everyone knows you have a second stomach for dessert. It's the rules.

When the table is clear and Tobias comes to offer coffee, I jump at the chance. I need to be caffeinated, otherwise I'm going to go into a food coma. The guys decline, and Chase pours himself another two fingers of whiskey, but Travis declines since his glass isn't empty. He's been nursing the same one all night.

I guess Travis got his drink of choice from his dad. I swear it's the only thing I've actually seen him drink.

"If you ladies will excuse us, I just need to walk Travis through some business from this week before he takes you both back to campus, Briar," Chase announces, pushing his chair back and standing.

I open my mouth to object, but Travis squeezes my shoulder

as he stands and I shut it. Apparently, now is not the time to argue that I'm an independent woman who doesn't need a chauffeur.

Travis and I had that exact discussion earlier, so I'm not opposed to hashing it out again, but something about Travis's demeanor makes me shut up.

Instead, I nod, and Chase kisses my mom's cheek before they leave the room.

"Isn't he wonderful?" Mom sighs dreamily once they leave, and I laugh softly.

"As long as you're happy, that's all I care about, Mom," I answer without actually answering. There is something about Chase Kensington that puts me on edge. Maybe it's the warnings from everyone else, maybe it's just my read on him. Whatever it is, I'm not sure I like it.

"I am. Happy, I mean," she says with a wide smile. "This is it for me, Briar. *He* is it for me. The part of me I always knew was missing."

I nod, letting her ramble on about her happily ever after rather than speaking the retort about how a life with money definitely isn't what she was missing. When Tobias brings me the coffee I pleaded for when he came in earlier, I thank him profusely, grinning wider when I notice the huge swirl of whipped cream on top. Somehow, I resist the urge to squeal with happiness as I taste the peppermint in the chocolatey coffee delight.

He is too good to me already.

Now all I need are the puppies Asher had with him the last

time I was here and I can call tonight a win.

"Mom, where's the bathroom?" I ask when I'm practically dancing in my chair.

"Down the hall, second door on the right. Want me to show you?"

I shake my head as I stand, pressing my legs together. Stupid tiny bladder. "No, it's good, Mom. I've got it."

I dash out of the dining room and down the hall, but the sound of shouting makes me pause before I reach the first door.

"—you couldn't even get that right! Fucking pathetic, Travis. How am I expected to trust you when you fuck up something so simple? All I wanted was a smart, ruthless son to take over my empire, and what a disappointment I've ended up with."

"Dad—"

"Don't bother, Travis. I'll just do it myself, and work it out with Theodore like I should've in the first place. I should've known you weren't up to this. All you had to do was encourage her. Push them together. You've been a let down your entire goddamn life, I don't know why I'm even surprised. Get out of my sight."

I freeze for a millisecond before frantically looking for somewhere to hide, but before I can move, Travis is there, staring at me like everything his dad just said was my fault.

He doesn't say a word, just stares at me like I'm a poison in his life that he wants to eradicate. Gone is the small peace treaty from earlier, and in its place, a white hot abhorrence that I have no idea how I earned.

"Travis—" I start, and he sneers at me.

"Shut your mouth, whore. I'm leaving in five. If you're not in the car, I'll leave without you." He storms past me, knocking into me with his shoulder, and I stumble into the wall, my back hitting something hard and sharp, making me wince in pain.

What the fuck just happened?

TEN

To say the drive home last night was silent and uncomfortable is a major understatement, but that discomfort was nothing compared to how sore my back is today. When I checked the mirror after my shower this morning, there was a very prominent blue-purple stain on my skin, which I promptly covered with a hoodie.

Thankfully, I woke up to what felt like the start of fall.

Leaves are turning, the air is cool, and it's the perfect day for a hoodie, leggings, thick socks, and hot chocolate.

Downsides of the day: I had class first thing this morning and Penn jumped on me as soon as I was home last night about the football game this evening. I know Asher said that Cole is the quarterback, but I had no idea that my fiery roommate was a huge football fan—which apparently means my attendance is mandatory, despite the fact that I have no iota of a clue how the game works.

Plays.

Whatever.

Regardless, I'm being dragged to this game tonight, no matter what.

Which is exactly why I'm standing here, staring into my closet like it has the answers to all the world's problems.

I've never been *this* girl.

The one who struggles to pick what to wear.

But I've also never really been the girl who has friends either. Go figure that they go hand in hand for me. I've never worried about fitting in until now.

Plus, Penn told me we'll be going to a party after the game, either a celebration or commiseration, so I need to dress appropriately—mostly because I've stopped trying to fight her about dragging me to parties—both for the game, the party, oh, and the gnarly bruise on my back.

I grab a pair of ripped jeans, a new set of black Converse, and a black crop top covered in tiny tears that's ridiculously 'gothic cute'. Since my first foray into crops, I've decided I actually kind of like them. Go figure.

I'm just about to start changing when Penn bounces into the room and launches a top at me.

"For you," she coos and I pull the black, blue, and silver material from where she flung it onto my head.

"What is it?"

She rolls her eyes at me as she drops onto the bed. "It's a jersey for the team. I got you the tight end's number. Something tells me he's your type." She winks at me and I laugh.

"I highly doubt *football player* is my type."

She pushes up to sitting, a wicked grin on her face. "He's tall, inked, muscles on muscles, a washboard of abs enough to make a Greek god weep… also kind of gross to talk about him that way since he's my cousin, but I've heard enough girls simp over him to know what they think."

I burst out laughing and shake my head. "Your cousin is a tattooed Adonis?"

"Exactly." She grins. "Precisely what a little emo cutie needs in her life."

I roll my eyes at her, wondering if this is her way of making sure I don't go after Connor, but I don't say anything, because one, Connor is definitely not my type, and two, I'm not about to call her out on it.

"I'll wear the stupid jersey, at least it's soft, I guess," I say with a shrug, and head behind the divider she put up in here to get changed. Not because I'm weird about showing off my body, I actually kind of love the way I look, but mostly because I can't deal with questions about the bruise.

It hurts just pulling my t-shirt off over the top of my head, so God knows how bad it looks now.

I change quickly, pulling the jersey over the top of my

ensemble, and laugh when it floats down past my ass. "Just how tall is your freaking cousin?" I ask, laughing as I come out from behind the divider.

"Tall," she answers with a grin, wagging her eyebrows. "Just how we like 'em."

"You're terrible." I laugh again, grabbing the front of the jersey that is way too freaking big. "What am I supposed to do with this?"

"I mean, you look hot. Your hair is falling in those beautiful natural waves of yours that I'm definitely not jealous of, and you look kind of amazing, so I'd just go with it."

I quirk a brow at her, but she just shrugs and I take her at her word. "When are we leaving?"

"As soon as you're ready."

"That would be now," I respond, and she jumps to her feet.

"Then let's go pre-game, bitch. That's half the fun!" She claps her hands together, practically bouncing on the spot. I grab my phone, keys, and wallet, stuffing them in the pockets of my jeans because I can't be bothered to carry a purse tonight.

"After you." I grin at her as she practically pushes me out of the door. "So, my cousin, Dante—"

"Wait, his name is Dante?" I interrupt her, and she looks at me like she's got secrets for days.

"Yes, Dante…"

"Dante Reed?" I clarify and die a little on the inside.

"Yes," she huffs, like I'm losing my mind. "Why?"

"Oh, nothing," I say and head out of the dorm building.

Of course her cousin is Dante fucking Reed. Fuck my actual life.

"How do you know Dante?" she asks as she catches up to me outside the building, looping her arm through mine.

"I don't. Not really." I don't tag on that I fucked him before I went away for the summer and definitely didn't ghost him while I was gone.

Ah, Karma is a sneaky bitch.

"Uh-huh," she grunts, side-eyeing me. "I guess I'll find out in a few minutes since we're sitting in his family seats and he's got our tickets."

I swallow the groan and give her a tight smile, regretting my decision to cave and come to this stupid game.

We head to the stadium and the sound of the crowd is already insane. I don't think it starts for another hour, but it's like there's a full party already going on inside. She leads me away from where most of the crowd is lining up around the side of the enormous building.

How I didn't notice this place before is beyond me. Though, in my defense, I haven't exactly had a reason to come to this side of the campus.

"Dante!" Penn calls out, waving over to where a few guys are standing, and I see him turn to face us. He smiles at Penn, but when he sees me, that smile turns smug as fuck and I kind of want to die.

"Penn, good to see you. You didn't tell me your friend was Briar Moore." He smirks at her before pulling her in for a hug.

"So you do know each other?" she asks, her gaze bouncing between us.

"You could say that," he says with a laugh. "How you doing, Briar? You kinda disappeared over summer."

"Yeah, sorry. I was in Cali. New phone too," I say, awkwardly waving my phone in my hand. "Last one was kinda destroyed."

"That means you're actually going to call me back this time if I get your digits again?" His grin matches the one on Penn's face, and I can feel the heat blaring from my red cheeks.

"Yeah, maybe," I say with a shrug, pretending not to be mortified. It's not like Dante wasn't a fun time, but I was dealing with some shit and he was a very pretty, very convenient escape. He did seem nice though, maybe I should give him a chance.

He laughs at me and shakes his head as he runs a hand over his buzzed black hair. "I do like it when you're mean to me, Briar."

"Okay, enough. Gross," Penn interjects. "Give me the tickets and I'll give you her number."

"Hey!" I groan, and she flips me the bird, which just makes Dante laugh again.

"Got yourself a deal, Penn."

She takes his phone and puts in what I assume is my number while I grumble under my breath about consent issues before taking the tickets from him. "Kick ass tonight."

"There is no way we're losing to those knuckle-dragging Neanderthals," he says with a wink. "See you at the after-party?"

"You know it," she answers and links her arm through mine again.

"See you later, Briar Moore," Dante calls out as we walk away. I just lift my hand in a weird wave, the sound of his laughter haunting me as we keep walking.

"So you fucked him, huh?" Penn asks, giggling when I groan.

"Remind me why I'm going to this stupid game?"

She grins and tugs me to move faster. "Because I'm your new bestie and this is what besties do."

After three hours of having no idea what was going on, but getting swept up in the energy of the crowd anyway, my legs ache, my throat is sore, and the electricity in the air from the win is so hyped that I'm bouncing as we head toward the party Dante was talking about earlier.

Even the awkwardness of knowing he'll be there isn't enough to turn down my hype. Maybe he'll be fun to fuck around with this year. God knows I don't want anything serious, and Dante doesn't seem the type to want to be tied down.

It could be a win-win situation.

Connor is walking just up ahead with Penn—he met us

after the game. Apparently, despite being her bestie, *he* wasn't subjected to the actual game.

"Has Cole seen you wearing that?" I turn to find Sawyer walking behind me and roll my eyes. He catches up in an instant and drops into step beside me.

"Seen me wearing what?"

"Dante's number," he responds, like I'm stupid.

"Dante is Penn's cousin. That's all." I sigh. Boys are ridiculous sometimes.

"That's far from all," he says with a smirk. "But then, I'm good with sharing."

"So you're actually talking to me now, then?" I ask, which sounds way more needy and dramatic than I meant it to.

"Oh, Beautiful, I was always talking to you. Travis just has his panties in a bunch about fucking his new stepsister. That whole forbidden fruit thing is a vibe, mix that with the potential fallout with daddy, add a touch of taboo fuckery, and it has him all kinds of twisted. He's a lot of fun usually. You already learned that." He winks at me and I roll my eyes again.

If I spend too much time with these guys, I'm going to end up seeing the inside of my skull at some point.

"So... what? You've decided to break rank for the night and pretend I exist again? Or did you just get jealous that Asher has been stealing my attention?" I prod him, knowing full well Asher hasn't had any of my attention, not really, but Sawyer seems like he's the competitive type.

Especially with his twin.

"Maybe, or maybe I just decided to go after what I wanted rather than toeing the line like a good boy." He drapes his arm over my shoulder and pulls me into his side. "Plus, you're coming to the house. Someone has to make sure you behave."

"Wait, what?"

He chuckles beside me as we walk. "You didn't know the party was at our place?"

"No, I freaking didn't," I grumble. Of course Penn left that bit out. That girl and I are going to be having words about boundaries.

He just laughs harder and tightens his arm around me. "Just stick with me. I'll look after you."

I don't say anything, because what can I say? I have no idea where the hell I'm going, but I decide to just go with it. He talks with several people walking in the direction of the house. Apparently everyone knows who Sawyer St. Vincent is. It's like the four of them are freaking celebrities on campus.

It's kind of absurd, but I guess this is how rich people function.

"Wait, does this mean I get to see Shadow and the puppies?" I ask hopefully, and he chuckles at me, shaking his head.

"I'm afraid not, hot stuff. The mini monsters are at Mom and Dad's for the night. Puppies and drunk college kids don't really mix.

"Dammit," I grumble, trying not to sulk while he laughs at

me some more.

After a few minutes, the sound of music reaches my ears and he leads me up the drive to what looks like a mini mansion. It definitely doesn't have anything on the Kensington McMansion, but I wouldn't exactly call this a house either.

Who even needs this much space?

"Did you bring a bathing suit?" he asks, wagging his eyebrows at me, laughing harder when I shove him.

"No, I didn't. You guys have a pool here?"

"Of course we do. Cole needs somewhere to do hydrotherapy. The pool on campus is always too busy." He answers like I'm the crazy one for thinking otherwise.

"But of course it is," I mutter.

"I'm sure you can have plenty of fun without a swimsuit on." He grins at me as we enter the house, and the sound of his voice is drowned out by the music and the insane number of people packed into the open space.

From what I can see in the dimly lit room, the entire ground floor is open, the kitchen to the right, a sitting area to the left, and the back looks like an open area. I can see a band setup on a raised platform—I guess they're playing again tonight. Definitely not getting flashbacks.

Nope. Not at all.

The staircase in the center of the space is the only thing that breaks it up, but it looks like it's roped off, with guys standing guard so no one goes up there.

"Don't want people in our space. Advantage of freshmen wanting to impress Cole," Sawyer shouts in my ear when he notices where I'm looking. "You want a drink?"

I nod and he takes my hand, pulling me toward the kitchen. As we enter, the area clears of people.

Like I said, freaking royalty.

Sawyer pulls out his phone and a few moments later the music lowers a little. But of course. At least I can hear a little better.

"What's your poison?"

I look up at him, wondering if drinking is a great idea, knowing what happened the last time I drank around him, then decide fuck it. I'm at college. We're supposed to make the best mistakes of our lives here. "Tequila."

His eyebrows rise and he smiles like he's almost impressed. "Let me see what we've got."

I lean against the counter while he rummages around in the fridge and cupboards. He turns back to me and grins. "I've got white rum and pineapple juice?"

"It'll do." Rum would be my third choice, but with pineapple juice, it just tastes like juice.

He smiles and fills me a red cup before grabbing a bottle of Bud from the fridge. "Thank you."

"So, you know Dante?" he asks, motioning to my jersey.

"Kind of. Is it really going to be an issue if I wear it?" I ask, biting my lip. I have no idea why it would be, but I also don't want to deal with any drama tonight.

I look up and find the man in question sauntering toward us. "Briar Moore, you really are here, slumming it with the St. Vincent scum no less."

I freeze, wondering if this is an actual thing, or if it's stupid boy shit. So when Sawyer laughs, I let out a relieved sigh.

"I told you I'd be here," I say with a shrug before leaning against the counter.

"Where's Penn?" he asks.

"No idea. She disappeared with Connor."

His grin widens and his dimples make an appearance. "I guess that means you're all mine for the night then."

"I don't think so," Sawyer interrupts, stepping up beside me.

"It's my jersey on her back," Dante says with a shrug before moving to the fridge and grabbing a bottle of beer too.

"Stupid fucking jersey," I mutter and lift it over my head. I wince at the pain and realize too late that my back is on show as I throw it at Dante.

"What the fuck happened to your back?" Sawyer asks, and I freeze for a moment before turning to face him and rolling my eyes.

"I fell," I deadpan. "Calm down, caveman."

"Who's a caveman?" I turn and find Asher standing on the other side of the island with Cole and Travis flanking him.

"Your brother," I say with a sigh.

"Why is he a caveman?" Asher asks, quirking a brow at Sawyer.

Sawyer grabs my shoulders and spins me, lifting up the bottom of my crop top, showing them the giant bruise between my shoulder blades. "That's why."

"Sawyer, will you please stop manhandling me?" I hiss and push him off of me. "Dante, do you want to dance?"

"Sorry, Briar. I'd like to know how you really did that too," he says, and I swear the testosterone in here is freaking suffocating.

I turn and face Travis who has a face like thunder. Asher seems to notice where I'm looking first, but it only takes a second for Sawyer to catch on.

"Travis did that?" Sawyer asks, pulling me back a step and moving to almost stand in front of me, creating a barrier between me and my supposed stepbrother.

"I didn't know," Travis says, his gaze traveling back over to me. For a second, he almost looks sorry, but then that stony facade of his returns.

"Fuck that noise, bro," Sawyer yells, and Asher and Cole move back, herding the crowd away from the kitchen with Dante's help. "You did this to her?"

"It's not like I meant to," Travis says with a shrug.

"Sawyer—" I start, trying to dial this back before what is essentially nothing explodes into more than something.

"Briar," Sawyer says, turning to me, eyes blazing. "He

doesn't get to fucking hurt you like that."

"It's done," I tell him with a sigh. "Doesn't make it right, but you can't change it."

"The fuck I can't," he rages before turning back. "I am done with your bullshit, T. I'm done with her being off-limits. If I want to spend time with her, I'm fucking doing it. You can shove your bros before hoes bullshit up your ass."

"I'm a ho, nice," I mutter, but Sawyer grasps my hand and intertwines my fingers with his.

"Don't take it personally, Beautiful. You're *my* ho," he says with a cheeky wink, somehow masking his rage for a moment.

Travis turns to me, glaring at me with that icy rage of his again. "I knew you'd tear everything apart. Nothing but a whore spreading her legs, just like your mother."

Sawyer dives forward, his fist connecting with Travis's cheek, and I let out a scream as they fight out their frustrations on the ground. Cole and Asher rush back over and drag them apart, and Penn appears with Dante and Connor in tow.

I look from the guys over to her and sigh. "I'm going home."

Penn's face drops, but I shake my head. I put my hand out to Dante for his jersey and pull it back over my head. "I'll see you later, Penn."

"Are you sure?" she asks, biting her lip. I can tell she doesn't want to leave, especially with Connor holding her hand.

"I'm good. Too much excitement here for me. Have fun," I tell her and head out the door.

"Briar," I hear Dante call behind me and I groan. "Just let me walk you back, okay? Those hot heads need to calm down, and I'll feel better knowing you got back safe."

His reasoning is pretty sound considering the stories of what happens to girls at college parties, and I almost kind of know Dante. He doesn't seem the type to hurt me.

"So I'm guessing that asking you out is a bad idea," he jokes as he drops an arm over my shoulder, and I groan at him.

"I don't know why it would be. I'm entirely single."

He smirks down at me and shakes his head. "Yeah, it seemed like it."

I pull out from under his arm and shrug. "I am. They're just idiots."

"Guys usually are when it comes to girls," he says with a small smile. "Come on, let's get you back, and I promise not to ask you out again unless you ask me to."

I smile up at him, trying not to laugh at the stupid face he's pulling. "Thanks," I say, rolling my eyes.

Freaking idiots. All of them.

But at least this one makes me laugh.

ELEVEN

I wake up to the sound of my phone ringing on my nightstand and groan into my pillow. Whoever is waking me up at—I lift my head up and glance at the giant clock above Penn's empty bed—seven in the freaking morning has a death wish. I plant my face back in my pillow and pull the duvet up over my head, letting out a sigh of relief when my phone stops.

Until it starts again.

"I swear to God," I mutter as I reach for my phone. "What?" I snap, without even looking at the screen.

"Well, good morning to you too, sunshine child." Sawyer's teasing voice sounds through the phone and I moan again.

"It is too early for your pep, Sawyer. What's wrong?"

"Why would something be wrong?" I swear, I can hear his fucking smile through the goddamn phone. Someone should not be *that* cheery at this time in the morning, at least not before I've had coffee.

"Because you're calling me at the ass crack of dawn, that's why," I whisper-shout down the phone.

"I mean, it was better than me pounding on your door, right? That was my initial plan, but Asher talked me down."

Oh thank God for Asher.

"You're outside?" I ask, lifting my head from the pillow before padding over to the door and looking through the peephole. "Of course you're freaking outside."

I hang up the phone and yank open the door, ignoring the fact I'm in an oversized t-shirt and a pair of panties. "Why are you here?"

"I brought coffee," Sawyer grins, pushing the cup of java toward me before entering the room, and Asher follows.

"Puppies?" I ask, hopeful, looking out into the hall, my hope instantly disappearing when there's no Shadow and they both laugh at me.

"Dog's aren't allowed in the dorms," Asher explains and I pout.

"But puppies," I grumble before Sawyer shakes the cup of coffee at me again, stealing my attention as I close the door.

"We'll sneak him over at some point," he says with a wink. "Anywayyyyyy, I wanted, sorry, *we* wanted to spend the day with you. To hang out. To kind of apologize for last night, but mostly, I wanted to see your cheery face."

"At least you brought coffee," I say, taking the cup and padding back to my bed. "So why, exactly, did you want to come so early?"

"This isn't early," Asher says with a smile. "We've already been up with Cole for over an hour, and finished our morning workout."

"You guys are insane." I take a sip of the coffee, kind of amazed that he got my order right. I glance up and see his wide smile, and I hate it just a little that it makes me smile back. "Thank you."

"You're welcome," he nods, winking at Asher. "Totally out here racking up these points, bro. Best catch up, otherwise the girl is mine. Unless you want to play sharesies." He wags his brows and I ignore his ridiculousness, because there's no way I'm walking into that conversation.

"So are you going to tell me what the plan is?" I ask with a yawn, stretching out before realizing they're both staring at the spot where my t-shirt rode up. "My eyes are up here."

"Oh, we know," Sawyer teases. "But as for the plan, you need a bikini and not much else."

I roll my eyes and turn my focus to Asher. "What's the real plan?"

"We thought we'd take you out on the boat."

"Of course you have a freaking boat," I mutter. "Fine. I like the water, I prefer horses, but I like the water. I can deal with a boat day." I shrug, trying to embrace the fact that I'm surrounded by wealthy people these days.

I can honestly say I've never just had a weekend surprise of 'oh yeah, let's hang out on the boat' before. "Give me twenty to look somewhat presentable," I say with another yawn. "I might need more coffee though."

"Coffee can be provided," Asher says with a smile as Sawyer gets up and opens my closet.

"Come on, Sunshine, let's do this. Where are the bikinis at?"

I laugh and shake my head. "I don't own a bikini, Sawyer."

"Well, that's going to change. Get dressed." He playfully slaps my ass and I scowl at him when I spill my coffee, but he's too excited to take me seriously. "*Vamanos*!"

"Tell me to hurry one more time…" I threaten, idly, and his grin turns to a smirk.

"Oh, Sunshine… this is going to be too much fun."

After a trip shopping for a freaking bikini—or six because Sawyer refused to pick just one after making me try them all on—we finally pull into the marina. I thought Asher might level out Sawyer's playfulness, but it turns out they're a whole sunshine and grumpy trope all on their own.

The book nerd in me can't help but smirk at the thought, but neither of them questions the rare smile on my face.

Asher pulls the car into a spot, and we climb out into the sunshine.

This place is almost obscene. I don't even want to think about the sheer amount of money that's moored up here.

"Brunch before we head out?" Asher suggests, and I swear my stomach rumbles in response. "I'll take that as a yes."

I'm of two minds, because I'm ridiculously curious about their boat, especially now that I'm looking around and there isn't anything smaller than a freaking yacht here. But I'm also literally starving to death.

"Yes! Let us feed you. I didn't warn the crew to prep for food," Sawyer says with a wince. "My bad."

Asher rolls his eyes and shakes his head, but the smile on his face tells me he suspected as much. "There's a place around the corner that does the most amazing lobster rolls," he says, and I shrug.

"Yes! Gino's is amazing! Lobster rolls!" Sawyer bounces on the spot, his excitement contagious.

"I've never had them," I offer. "So sure, why not."

Sawyer looks at me like I have two heads. "You've never had a lobster roll? Oh, my God. You're about to have a life-changing experience."

He takes my hand and practically starts dragging me down the sidewalk. Asher takes my other hand in his, calling out to Sawyer to slow down a little so that we can all walk together.

It should feel weird being flanked by the two of them,

especially since I'm holding hands with them both, but it doesn't.

I'm not about to examine it too closely. Before I have a chance to get in my head too much, Sawyer is pushing through the door of Gino's.

"Gino!" he calls out as he saunters through what looks like a closed restaurant and heads back into the kitchen.

"Erm, is he allowed to do that? Are we even supposed to be here?" I ask Asher, biting my lip as I take in the chairs still stacked on the tables.

"Gino is like an uncle to us," he says with a small smile, taking off his shades. "We've been coming here since we were about three. Gino would be more offended if Sawyer didn't burst in here like he owns the place."

"Oh, well, okay then." I nod, trying to take in the quaint little seafood restaurant. It's exactly what you'd expect a waterside tourist spot to look like. All done in a nautical theme, whites and blues, even the tablecloths are in sailing stripes with little anchors.

It's actually kind of adorable.

"Gino, this is Briar!" Sawyer calls out as the door swings open, and he returns with an older Italian guy who doesn't look much older than Tobias. He has to be late thirties at most. "Briar, meet Gino. He makes the best lobster rolls in the entire world!"

Gino smiles at me as they head toward us before opening his arms for a hug.

One day, these people will realize I am not a hugger, dammit.

Reluctantly I step into his arms and hug the smiling man. "She's beautiful, boys. Which of yours is she?"

"Neither," I respond before either of them can, pulling back from the hug. His smile widens.

"Oh, I like this one." He chuckles. "Sit, sit, I'll bring you out some fresh rolls. Gino will look after you, bella." He winks at me and laughs as he heads back to what I assume is the kitchen while Asher pulls down a few chairs for us to sit.

"Old guy is trying to steal my girl," Sawyer says, almost put out.

"Not your girl," I remind him, shaking my head.

"Not yet," he responds with a wink.

Asher's phone starts to ring and he frowns at the screen. "Sorry, I have to take this. I'll be back in a few minutes."

He answers the phone with a hello and Sawyer frowns as he watches his twin leave the restaurant.

"Everything okay?" I ask, feeling confused.

Sawyer shakes his head, but smiles through it. "I'm sure it's fine."

He keeps up his inane chatter about the boat and heading out onto the water until Asher returns.

"Sorry you guys, I need to go."

Sawyer's face drops. "What's wrong?"

"Dad needs some help."

"He need me too?" Sawyer asks, but Asher shakes his head.

"I got it, you enjoy your day with Briar," he says before

turning to me. "Don't let him corrupt you too much, and if he gets to be too much, just call me."

He takes my phone from the table and taps his number in. "I've put us both in there; Travis and Cole too. Not that you need theirs, but just in case."

"Just in case doesn't even sound ominous…" I say cautiously. "Does your dad really need you? We can go out on the boat another time."

"Not a chance," he says, smiling down at me. "Have fun, just not too much."

He leans down and kisses the top of my head. "I've got to take the car, but use the service to get home if I'm not back."

"Will do," Sawyer responds, bumping fists with Asher before he leaves.

Soon after he's gone, Gino appears with the lobster rolls, and after a few minutes, Sawyer is back to his playful self. We finish eating and I concede that the rolls really are amazing, despite having nothing to compare them to.

"To the boat?" Sawyer asks hopefully. I nod, wanting for some reason to keep that playful joy in his eyes.

"To the boat."

We've spent the day out on the water, sailing to nowhere, and we're finally heading back now that the sun is setting. Sawyer got a call from Asher about half an hour ago and only just returned, but since I've been standing here staring out over the water in a trance, I can't complain.

"Thank you for today," I sigh softly, smiling back at Sawyer as he presses against my back. Leaning against the railing, looking out over the water, I find a little bit of peace once again. "It's a shame Asher had to leave so quickly. Is everything okay?"

"Mhmm," he murmures into my ear as he wraps his arms around my waist. "Everything's fine, Beautiful. But thank you."

He presses his lips against the soft skin behind my ear before making his way down my throat, and I tip my head to the side, giving him better access. Should I be questioning this new side of him? Probably, but I saw him go toe-to-toe with Travis, I've seen the way he's been with me today, and there's something so genuine about him that I don't *want* to question it.

I just want to be and let it be.

His fingers trail up and down the bare skin of my ribcage, my bikini and denim cutoffs giving him plenty of access to my skin.

"Do you want me to stop?" he asks quietly, and I shake my head. Maybe I should, but I don't. I've spent the last few weeks walking on eggshells around him—around all of them—and I'm ready to let go.

"Good." He smiles into my neck.

I let out a squeal as he bends down and picks me up, caveman style, tossing me over his shoulder.

"Put me down, Sawyer!" I squeal through my giggles. All he does is laugh in response and spank my ass.

I adore how playful he is, even when I'm hanging upside down, apparently.

"Sawyer!" I squeak when he tickles the bottom of my feet, but his mischievous laughter keeps any seriousness out of my voice as I squirm in his grip.

"Captain, no disturbances!" he calls out, and I cover my face with my hands. I'd almost managed to forget about the crew since we left the dock. I bounce on Sawyer's shoulder as he walks across the deck, but I keep my face covered because the heat in my cheeks has to have me looking like a freaking beet.

The sounds of doors opening and closing are all that accompany the slap of his feet against the floors until I'm being flung from his shoulder. I bounce on the soft bed, letting out another squeak, hating that I'm obviously becoming *that* girl, because apparently that's the version of myself that Sawyer brings out.

It must be that excited golden retriever energy of his. It's infectious.

Enough to even make me forget about the twinge in my back from the bruising.

Except, when I look up, he looks anything but playful.

His light-green eyes have darkened to emerald and he looks at me like I'm his prey. My mouth waters as I take in the sight of him in nothing but his board shorts, his blond hair pushed back, and every chiseled inch of him on show for me.

"Tell me to stop, Briar. This is your last chance."

My heart pounds in my chest and I shake my head. "Not going to happen."

"Don't say I didn't warn you." My shorts and bikini bottoms are a thing of the past, discarded somewhere across the room, before he spreads my thighs and his hot mouth lands between them. I'm achy and needy for him already, his tongue working a kind of magic over me that's enough to make a girl lose her mind.

Pumping my hips up and down, seeking out Sawyer's tongue as he teases me, silently begging for more, I clutch his blond strands with one hand and the now-crumpled sheets with the other. My entire body is on high alert as he sucks on my clit, flicking the swollen nub with expert precision.

He pushes me until I climb so high that I tremble on the edge of a precipice, and there's no mistaking how close I am to losing any semblance of control. He's pushing me harder, sucking on every inch of skin, and just when I think his teasing will be the end of me, he takes both of my thighs in his big, strong hands and pulls my pussy as close as he can to his mouth, his tongue fucking me as he feasts on me like he hasn't eaten in days.

"Fuck, Sawyer, I'm go—" My words die on my tongue as he pushes two fingers inside me, fucking me as his mouth sucks on my clit.

My torso arches off of the bed as I thrust my hips up and down, my movements lacking any sense of rhythm as my body aches for release.

It's torture.

Delicious and exquisite torture. It's as if making me come is his own type of pleasure.

"Give it to me, Beautiful." He punctuates his command with a curling of his fingers and everything behind my lids explodes into bright colors as the world becomes little more than muted sounds. I can't hear a thing as my senses freeze with the onslaught of the orgasm that travels from my core to the very tips of my fingers and toes.

"Fuuuuck!" The word is more a silent scream than anything coherent, and I slowly come back to myself.

"That's my good girl, coming all over my face. Now give me more."

I look down at him to find his green eyes watching me, alert and on fire, from between my legs. A grin curves his delicious mouth.

It's intoxicating how eager he is to please me.

As he slowly pulls out his fingers, I fall back onto the bed and try, in vain, to catch my breath.

"One day, soon, Briar." I feel a hint of pressure sliding from my slit to my ass and gasp, holding my breath as his wet finger circles me. He watches me as if gauging my reaction.

I have no idea what he sees, but when a wicked grin spreads

across his face I know I'm in for a whole world of trouble. "Oh, yeah. One day *very* soon."

Quicker than my mind can process, Sawyer climbs to his feet, his hands at the waist of his board shorts and a glint of mischief in his bright green eyes.

My eyes drop to his cock—standing proud and eager—as he steps out of his clothes and pounces on me.

"Your scent is driving me fucking crazy, Briar." I don't think I've ever heard his voice so low, so gravelly and determined. I'm sure a normal girl would be afraid of the filthy things his eyes promise me, but I never claimed to be normal.

Caging me in with his folded arms at the sides of my head, he brings his mouth down on mine, kissing me like it's the last chance he'll get, licking and sucking on my lips and sharing the taste of my orgasm with me.

He teases me with his dick. The head of him rubs against my clit and somehow I'm already desperate for him. Though, no matter how hard I try to move my hips so he slides right in, he averts me. I should probably ask him about a condom, but I somehow trust him, and while it might be a stupid move, I'm on birth control, so I let the thought drift away.

With a grunt, he's off me again, sitting on his haunches, catching his own breaths coming in a ragged rhythm.

"I want you on all fours, Beautiful. Show me that delicious ass of yours."

I don't hesitate, turning swiftly onto my hands and knees

and looking over my shoulder at him. He's feral, his eyes boring holes into my skin as his big hands grasp my hips, fingers squeezing like he's trying to reel in his own control.

I realize that I don't want him to control himself. I want him wild and unhinged. I want him to forget there's even a world outside of this room. This yacht.

"The things I want to do to you right now are illegal in forty-nine of the fifty states."

I suppress a giggle because this is neither the place nor the time. "In which one of them is it legal?"

A feral grin slowly transforms his entire face as his gaze finds mine. His words make my pussy clench for more.

"My state of mind." In one swift, powerful thrust, his dick is buried right to the hilt inside me. My lungs empty with the force of it, making it hard to take in a single breath. "I want to own you, Briar. Every fucking piece of you." Pulling out slowly, he digs his nails into the skin of my hips and thrusts back inside me. My arms give out and my head falls to the mattress. The only part of my body still in the air is my ass, and that's only because he's holding me up, the muscles in his arms flexing with the effort he's exerting.

"I want to fuck you so hard you break into a million pieces just so I can put you right back together again."

Faster this time, he pulls out again and slams back in so hard that I can barely breathe and somehow, it's not enough.

I need more.

I want more.

As though he can hear my thoughts, Sawyer slowly moves over my entire body, his hands seeking out my hands, his torso covering my back, his dick sinking impossibly deeper until I can't feel anything except him.

But it's when he moves that my entire world begins and ends with him.

Entwining his fingers into mine, he brings his mouth to my ear and whispers his own version of sweet nothings.

"I'm about to fuck you so hard you will see stars, and when you come all over my cock, you'll know that you belong to me."

I don't have time to register his words fully before he's already sliding out and pummeling back in with a rhythm that erases everything from my brain, except for the unparalleled pleasure he's giving me.

Thankful the bed is bolted to the wall, I realize he's folded over me to protect me from hitting my head with the force of his every thrust.

We're fucking so hard and fast that we don't have time for words or even thoughts. We're all moans and grunts and empty lungs.

Completely consumed by his keen focus on my pussy, I let him bring me to orgasm over and over again.

Just when I think I can't take it any longer, Sawyer sinks his teeth into my shoulder and releases one of my hands to slide under me and pinch my clit.

Everything stops.

My very existence is frozen in time as my body convulses—my pussy squeezing the life out of his cock—as I come all over him in an almost painful orgasm.

"That's it, baby. I can feel your cum all over my dick. I can't wait—"

Then I feel it. His cock pulsing inside me, thrusting once, twice, and stilling as he pumps me full of his own cum.

It takes a minute for my brain to turn back on but when it does, I let out a sigh as he presses his full weight against me.

"Holy fuck, Briar." He shudders before pulling from me and lying next to me, rolling me onto his chest.

"Uh-huh," is all I manage to say, feeling entirely boneless as he strokes my hair.

He kisses the top of my head and I feel as his lips move against my hair. "I'm not going to ever be able to let you go."

And while that should be terrifying, I'm not sure that I want him to.

LILY WILDHART

TWELVE

The paper drops onto my desk with a big red F and my heart sinks. I glance over to Connor, who has an A, and shake my head. We worked on the paper around anxiety & phobic disorders together, from Sunday through to last night. He read through mine, because I figured his genius brain would pick up on anything I'd missed, but he said it was good.

He glances over at me and frowns at the F, so I flip the paper over before Sawyer can see it too. Especially since he's still coming to all of my classes with Crawford, despite doing none of the work. And despite me asking how he's keeping up with his own classes since he keeps sitting in on mine.

"Some of you exceeded my expectations. Others, well..." Crawford says before turning his gaze to me with that pissant smile of his on his face. "You did exactly as expected."

I clench my fist under my desk and take a few deep breaths. I have no idea what Crawford's problem with me is, but I'm going to find out.

He is not going to fail me just because he hates me. It's utter crap.

Right now I'm glad for my fancy tech recording his lecture, because I'm too distracted to pay attention to his lecture on dissociative disorders and how the real world views them. His voice drones on and it occurs to me how hard passing this class is going to be.

I've never been a massive fan of Christmas, but for once, I'm looking forward to the end of the year. Purely because it symbolizes my classes with Crawford being over.

I'm three weeks into college and he's making me hate it.

Go figure.

I never thought one professor could mess with my entire schooling experience. Turns out I was really freaking wrong. I'm almost positive I didn't deserve the F, but I have no idea how to prove it. How to prove that he's purposely tanking my grades.

I shake my head and try to focus as he deep dives into dissociative amnesia and fugue states, but I'm too emotional. It's ridiculous. I've always been able to regulate myself pretty well, I've always been really self-aware of my issues and triggers, but something about this man pushes buttons I didn't know I had.

To say it's frustrating me might be the biggest understatement of the year. Almost as big an understatement as saying Travis isn't a fan of mine.

I snort a laugh at my own ridiculousness and smother my mouth, trying to play it off as a cough, because the last thing I need is more flack from Crawford. He sneers at me from the front of the room, but continues as if I didn't just laugh mid-lecture.

I'm going to take the win, no matter how small. Especially when I'm already going to have to speak to him after class about this F. I can't afford an F. I have too much to do to retake credits, and there is no way in hell I'm retaking his class.

When class ends, I shut off the recording on my phone, making a mental note of the new paper we have to write before next week—goodbye social life—and wait for the class to empty.

"You coming?" Connor asks, and I shake my head.

"I need to speak to Crawford," I tell him, and he frowns.

"You want me to wait?"

I smile at him as I finish saving the recording on my phone. "I'm good. You're off to dinner with Penn, right? Don't keep her waiting on my behalf."

"Yeah, it's all good, Berkley, I've got my girl covered," Sawyer interjects from behind me, and I roll my eyes.

Connor glares at Sawyer before looking back to me. "You sure?"

"I'm sure. I swear. Go, have fun. Make her bring me home

a burrito."

He smiles at me and runs a hand through his hair. "Chicken with extra mushrooms and sour cream, I remember."

He gives me a weird one-armed hug before darting from the room. These people really need to learn I am not a hugger.

"You can go too," I tell Sawyer as the last few stragglers leave the room.

"Oh no, I'm not leaving you alone with him again."

I quirk a brow at him. "Firstly, it wasn't a request. Secondly, we're going to unpack your presence here and your reluctance to leave me alone tonight."

"So you're coming to the house tonight, then?" he asks with a grin, and I drop my chin to my chest.

This freaking guy.

"If you're both finished dawdling, I have places to be," Crawford snaps from his desk at the front of the room.

"You can wait for me outside if you insist," I say to Sawyer, who reluctantly agrees and heads out of the lecture hall.

I lift my head and roll back my shoulders before making my way down to Crawford. "Actually, Professor, I wanted to speak to you about my grade."

"What about it?"

"It's unreasonable. There is no way I deserved that fail."

He raises his eyebrows at me as he leans back in his chair and folds his arms. "Is that so? You think you know my class better than I do, Miss Moore?"

"Of course not," I snark. "But I do know that I worked with Connor on it, and he got an A."

"His work was obviously more up to par than your substandard efforts."

I take a deep breath and try to remain calm. "My efforts were far higher than substandard. I don't understand what issue it is you have with me, but if you refuse to take another look at it, I'm going to have to speak to the head of the department about someone else assessing my work and grade."

Total bullshit. I don't even know if that's a thing, but the reddening of his cheeks tells me that I must've hit my mark.

He pushes his chair back and stands, leaning forward before laughing in my face. Rage boils in the pit of my stomach, to an almost unreasonable level.

"Feel free to attempt it, Miss Moore, but you'll get no handouts from me and zero extra credit. I still don't believe you deserve to be in my class, but please, attempt to prove me wrong. Breaking you might be my new favorite sport."

I see red, but somehow manage to keep my mouth shut and storm from the room, sweeping past Sawyer as I leave the building while I try to temper the rage inside of me.

Oh yeah, that ass really knows how to push my buttons.

"Hey. Briar! Wait up! What happened?" Sawyer calls out from behind me, but I can't stop, because if I stop, the rage is going to boil over and I'm going to scream very loudly in front of a ton of people.

I really don't want to be branded the freshman weirdo, so I keep my legs moving and my lips clamped together to keep it all inside. It doesn't take long for Sawyer to catch up, and I let him steer me away from the people to the parking lot and into his car. Once the doors are shut, I let out a frustrated roar and hit the dash a few times.

I don't feel entirely better, but at least the edge is gone.

"Are you going to tell me what happened?" he asks, watching me warily.

"Are *you* going to tell me why you're in my class and didn't want to leave me alone with him?" I counter, and he remains quiet. "That's what I thought. I've got to go and start on this new paper because I can't afford to fail this class."

"You still coming by the house later?" he asks with a sad smile on his face as I reach for the door handle.

"I don't know, Sawyer. I'll text you. Sorry," I say, deflated, knowing he doesn't deserve my bitchiness. I lean over and kiss his cheek before climbing from the car.

Determined, I make my way to the library. I am going to nail this freaking paper if it kills me, and if I get a chance to try and work out why Professor Crawford hates me so much, then that would be awesome.

Until then, I'm going to look into whether the whole head of department thing is something I pulled out of my ass, or if it's something I've read somewhere. Because I want out of his class.

Turns out the life of the privileged really isn't one I'm suited to.

"Maybe he's just into you and is playing the 'treat 'em mean, keep 'em keen' card?" Charli says while dipping her fries into her shake. "Boys have being doing stupid things for all of existence."

"Oh yeah, Professor Crawford is totally into me," I deadpan. "That's why he's an ass."

Serena and Penn laugh at me while Charli just shrugs. "It's a possibility. Especially since there's no other reasonable answer that you know of."

"She's not wrong," Serena adds, and I groan, dropping my head into my hands.

"Whatever his reasoning, it's asinine."

"Ooooo, big words!" Penn teases before taking a bite of her gigantic burger. "Maybe drop some of those on him and just bewilder him into being nice to you."

"Or you could just show him your tits. You've got real good tits," Serena tags on, and I can't help but laugh.

"I do have good tits, but I'm pretty sure flashing them isn't going to help me."

"Who are we flashing? Please say it's me." Sawyer grins as he slides into the seat beside me, and I swear Charli and Serena just go slack-jawed staring at him.

I knock into him with my shoulder, and he drags me onto his lap. I let out a squeak as he manhandles me, and Penn just laughs at us while Serena and Charli continue to stare. Which gets worse when Asher takes a seat in the chair I just vacated. "Will you please tell your brother that he doesn't need to be my seat?"

Asher grins at me wide, his eyes sparkling with mischief. "I dunno, I think he looks pretty good as your seat. I mean, I'd look better, but second place never hurt anyone."

Sawyer laughs and I drop my chin to my chest, realizing just how alike these two can be sometimes. "I didn't hear her calling me second place over the weekend."

"Sawyer! I swear to God!" I screech while the twins just laugh. I look to the girls for help, and while Penn looks like she's having way too much fun to intervene, it occurs to me that Serena and Charli maybe didn't realize that I'd smoothed things over with the twins.

"Serena, you've got some..." Penn says, pointing to the corner of her mouth, and Serena turns red as a beet while Charli giggles at her.

"You guys know the twins, right?" I say casually. "Guys, this is Serena and Charli. You already know Penn."

"Ladies," Sawyer says with a grin, and Asher gives them a weird boy wave thing. "Are you done with classes for the day?"

"I am," I answer him, and the smile on Asher's face at my

answer to Sawyer makes me a little apprehensive. "But we're going to catch a movie."

"Oh! I love a good movie date. What are we watching?" Sawyer asks, and I shake my head.

"No, we, as in the girls, are going to catch a movie."

Sawyer grins at me as he wraps his arms tighter around my waist. "You trying to tell me there's no room for us?"

"That's exactly what I'm saying," I deadpan when Serena and Charli start giggling.

"You're so funny, B. Of course there's room for them," Serena chirps up, and I roll my eyes before giving in and leaning back on Sawyer to rest my head on his shoulder.

"I knew you'd come around," he murmurs in my ear as Asher strokes my thigh.

"Incoming," Penn says, grabbing my attention back from the twins, and I look up to find Travis and Cole staring at us from across the room.

Fuck my actual life.

They start making their way over when Asher stands up, and Sawyer tightens his arms around me.

"Asher will deal with whatever that is, Sunshine. You absolutely don't need to deal with Sir Grumpalot, especially considering his obvious lack of concern with hurting you," Sawyer murmurs to me, and I let out a sigh.

"I don't want to come between you guys. You're like family."

He turns me in his lap so I can't watch the tension between Asher and the other two, and grips my chin so I'm looking at nothing but him. "You are not the problem here. Travis and his daddy issues are. He was all for us sharing you on day one, I'm pretty sure you remember. It was just after that he got his panties in a wad. That's on him. And Cole... well, he's like Travis's loyal dog. Asher and I have actual puppies for that. But Cole is already on team Briar, even if he doesn't show it. He just won't make a move without Travis's go ahead. For the son of a politician, he's surprisingly pliant. Just don't tell him I said that. He could crush my skull with one hand without breaking a sweat."

I laugh softly and his eyes crinkle at the side. "There she is. See, the big rain cloud is already leaving, so you don't need to worry." He releases me and I turn to Asher heading back in our direction, a little tension in his shoulders, but nothing major.

"So, Care Bears or the Scooby-Doo movie?" Penn asks, breaking any remaining tension, and Sawyer chuckles beneath me.

"You totally seem like a Care Bear kind of girl to me," Sawyer teases her, and she flips him the finger. "You're totally a Cheer Bear fan, aren't you? All pink and fluffy. You can't lie to me, sweet Penn."

Asher sits back down just in time to stop Penn from launching at his twin, while Serena and Charli seem just a little star struck by the boys.

Which definitely doesn't make me feel awkward or anything. Nope.

Not at all.

"So, movie?" I put forward, trying to bring the conversation back around to the original topic. "There's that new monster movie that looks fun," I suggest, and Asher grins.

"Our girl wants to watch a monster movie? Absolutely up for that." I shut down the shock at this very open declaration about being their girl, especially since I haven't so much as kissed Asher, but I'm definitely not opposed to fuckery with them both.

Though Penn is still pushing for me to go out on a date with Dante, too. This definitely isn't a problem I thought I'd have when I started here.

The mean girls, on the other hand, were like a set-in-stone problem. Girls rarely like me, but it's not something that's ever bothered me.

"I'm up for a monster movie," Penn agrees, looking over at Serena and Charli. Neither of which look particularly excited about the prospect, but they both nod anyway, side-eyeing the twins.

"We'll go get the cars," Asher says, standing, and Sawyer slides me off his lap and follows suit.

"I'm calling shotgun for our girl in my ride," he coos, and Asher rolls his eyes.

"See you in a minute," Asher says, basically dragging

Sawyer from the cafeteria.

Penn stands and loops her arm through mine and we follow them out, Charli and Serena right behind us. "You caught those two salivating over the twins right?"

"I did," I say with a shrug as I glance back at them. "But I'm not worried. The twins aren't mine, and I'm not really the jealous type anyway."

Her eyebrows rise and she shakes her head. "If you say so. Maybe I'll be territorial enough for the both of us, cause if I catch so much of a hint of them moseying on in, I'mma throw hands."

I can't help but laugh at her. "You're a good friend, Penn."

"Eh," she says with a sly smile. "I nearly threw hands at you when I saw you with Connor for the first time, but I've since realized you're good people."

I shake my head, chuckling at her. "Don't worry, P. I'm not about to steal your man."

She winks at me as we approach the twins' cars idling at the curb. "He's not mine either. Not yet, anyway."

I laugh as I fall through the doorway into the boys' house, trying to escape Sawyer and his demonic tickling ways, and land straight in Cole's arms.

"We've got to stop meeting like this." He smirks down at

me, and I groan as the twins enter behind me, laughing.

"Yeah, falling into your arms isn't exactly my idea of happily ever after, either," I quip back at him.

"Oh, I don't know," he teases. "There could be worse endings."

His eyes sparkle as he holds my arms, despite the fact I've found my feet again.

The puppies rush toward us and I drop down into a crouch to fuss over them, leaving the boys to say their hellos. After getting their ear scratches, the other three head over to Asher and I scoop up Shadow, who always stays with me, as I stand, rubbing his belly as his tongue lolls out of his mouth, making me laugh quietly.

He's so freaking cute.

"You finally shaken the collar, Cole? Boarding the Briar Express?" Sawyer jokes as he puts his arm around my waist, and Cole's hands fall from my arms.

"The only type of express here is my Hot Mess Express," I deadpan. "Zero boarding for any of you guys."

"That's not what you said last weekend," Sawyer murmurs in my ear, and I feel my cheeks heat.

Travis descends the stairs and tension threatens to suffocate me as he reaches us.

"I should probably be heading home. It got late," I say quietly, not wanting to deal with him and the broody assholeness I know is coming. Shadow lets out a yip, and I realize I've held him a little too tight, so I kiss the top of his head as an apology before I put him down on the floor.

"Oh, look, the trash can take itself out," Travis sneers as he heads into the kitchen area.

Yep, that assholeness. Right on cue.

"Turn down the douchebag status, Travis," Sawyer barks, his grip tightening on my waist.

Travis barks out a dry laugh and turns his narrowed stare back on me. "I see we're letting the whore come between us again. You see what you're doing? You're nothing but poison, slowly killing my family. Tearing it apart. Just like your mother."

I open my mouth to respond, but Asher steps in front of me, the puppies crowding at our feet. "You don't get to talk to her like that, Travis. The only one causing problems here is you, not her. You need to apologize to her."

"I'm not apologizing for shit. You all want to chase pussy, put it ahead of your family. I can't stop you, but when shit gets real and she runs away—because they all run away—don't come crawling back to me." He pauses for effect before turning and heading back upstairs.

Cole glances at me before running a hand over his buzzed hair, then leaves the house without another word.

"Fuck me, they're both such giant buzzkills," Sawyer groans as I bite the inside of my cheek, trying to keep my emotions locked down.

Travis's words should roll off me. I've been called much

worse. Heard worse. Experienced worse. And yet… coming from him, it seems to cut deeper than it should.

Maybe because on that first night we met, he looked at me like I was the sun and he was the moon, lighting up because of me.

Whatever it is, I want off this rollercoaster.

"I'm going to head back to my dorm," I say quietly to the twins before taking a deep breath.

"Briar—" Sawyer starts, but Asher cuts him off.

"Let me walk you back."

I chew on my lip as I wrap my arms around myself. I'd rather be alone, but I also know that's a stupid idea. "Sure."

He nods while Sawyer just looks deflated.

"I'll see you tomorrow?" I say to him, trying to apologize without uttering the words I know he won't accept.

"You bet your fine ass you will," he growls and pulls me in for a hug that is so goddamn good, it threatens to tear down the walls I've built up to hold back all of my emotions. He kisses the top of my head before pulling back and glancing at his brother. "Get her home, then get your ass back here. I'm calling a family meeting."

Asher nods and holds out his hand for me, which I take. I could be confused about them and what we're doing, but I decided earlier that I would just roll with it and see where it takes us. That's how I've lived my entire life and I'm still here, so it can't have been the worst idea.

"Come on, Beautiful. Let's get you back," Asher murmurs, and I nod. "Wait a second, I'll grab the leashes and we can take the monsters out for their walk."

He disappears into the kitchen and when he comes back the puppies go crazy, yipping like he's dangling fresh meat in their faces. He hands me a black leash and motions toward Shadow as he handles the rest. Shadow instantly sits when I look down at him, and I swear my heart melts a little. Screw Travis and his shit. Shadow is the only guy I really need.

"Ready?" Asher asks as he opens the door into the brisk night air, the puppies already pulling to try to get outside.

I nod and head out first with Shadow, and he follows behind.

One day I'll get to just have a good day. One entire day without someone trying to shit all over my happy.

Or maybe I won't and the Travis Kensingtons of the world will always win.

LILY WILDHART

THIRTEEN

I walk out of my Intro to Writing class and find the twins leaning against the wall opposite, wide grins on both their faces.

"Surprise!" Sawyer says, jumping forward and waving a piece of paper in my face.

"Surprise?" I ask, laughing at his obvious excitement.

He wraps me in his arms and spins me around while Asher watches on with amusement. "Sawyer, put me down!"

"Yes, Mr. St. Vincent, put the poor girl down," Mr. Hamilton, my Intro to Writing professor, says sternly as he steps into the hall.

Sawyer, obviously, doesn't put me down, he just grins at the professor cheekily. "But her poor legs need a rest, sir. I'm just being chivalrous."

"I'm sure," the professor deadpans before looking back at me. "However, this is a place of education. Put the girl down, Mr. St. Vincent."

Sawyer sighs before sliding me down his body, and my cheeks flame at the obvious grope he gets as he does. "Spoil sport."

"Yes, Mr. St. Vincent. You're not the first to call me it. I'm sure you won't be the last. Have a good weekend, Miss Moore," he says before walking down the hall, the sound of his shoes clicking on the wooden floor.

"Is he always such a buzzkill?" Sawyer pouts.

"Not always. Now then, what is this surprise?" I ask, trying to distract him.

He grins at me before glancing at Asher. "I don't know if she's ready for it."

"You might be right, little bro," Asher teases, and I pretend to pout, folding my arms across my chest.

"Now who's the buzzkill?"

Asher clutches his chest like I've wounded him and I can't help the giggle that escapes my lips.

"I guess we can tell you," Sawyer murmurs as he hugs me from behind, nuzzling into my neck, and laughs when my stomach growls so loudly that heat spills across my chest. "But first, let's feed you."

We head out to Asher's car, and I spot Penn walking back to the dorm on the way. I wave her over, and she eyes us with that curious smile she gets whenever I'm with the two of them. "Where you three heading to, looking all happy and shit?"

"Food," I say with a grin. "Way to any girl's heart."

"Same, I'm thinking ramen or sushi."

"Ooooo ramen," I sigh dreamily. "There was a place in the city that did the *best* Tonkotsu. I miss that shit."

"You want ramen?" Asher asks as he unlocks the car. "I know a place."

"Of course you do." I smirk. "Want to join us?" I ask Penn, but she shakes her head.

"Oh no, you enjoy your little threesome. I'm meeting up with Connor anyway. I'll see you later?" She looks at Sawyer with a coy smile before turning back to me.

Weird.

"Yeah, I'll see you later." I wave as she heads back toward the dorm, turning when Asher opens the door for me and I slide into the front seat. "So where is this place you know, and do they have Tonkotsu?"

"You'll see," he says with a wink, shutting the door while Sawyer jumps in the back of the car. I turn to ask him the same question but he does that whole zip lip, throw away the key bullshit and so I turn back around in my seat and call on the well of patience that I absolutely don't have.

I mess with the radio until I find a station that has Carrie Underwood playing—because while I love pop punk, country is the second love of my life—and enjoy how much neither of them like my song choice but don't say a goddamn word.

We've been driving for roughly half an hour when we pull up at what I'd call a mega mansion, and with a click of a button, the gates swing open. "Erm, Asher, where the hell are we?"

Sawyer bounces forward from the back seat, and grins at me. "Welcome to Casa St. Vincent, Sunshine. Where Red, our chef, makes the best, most authentic ramen you've ever tasted in your life. We spent two years in Japan and he came back with us, bringing all of his family recipes." He does the chef's kiss thing as Asher pulls the car up to the house and my stomach flip flops like I'm on a rollercoaster.

This is soooo not okay.

Are their parents here?

We are definitely not even close to meet the parents. Hell, I barely even really know them, which I'm aware is something I should probably work on if I'm fucking Sawyer—fucking both of them, I'm a little unsure how this is going to work—but holy crap.

"Calm, Briar," Asher says, squeezing my thigh. "Our parents aren't here, they're in the city visiting our little sister. She started at Juilliard this year and our budding ballerina has a show tonight."

I let out a sigh, but the tightening of my chest doesn't quite release. "Warn a girl next time."

"So you'll come back then?" Sawyer asks with a cheesy grin.

I shake my head as I unbuckle myself. "No questions when I'm hungry, it's against the rules."

"You heard the lady,"Asher says with a grin, hopping out of the car. He rushes around and opens my door before I get a chance to and helps me out. "Let's eat!"

I pull up at the spa hotel and look up at it in awe. "I still can't believe the twins got you a spa weekend." Penn sighs.

"Got us a spa weekend," I correct her. "You might have forgotten, but you're here with me."

She rolls her eyes at me and I laugh softly. "They got it for *you*. Just because. I mean, I know money isn't really a thing to them. They may not be Kensington rich, but they're still St.Vincents. Besides, they only paid for me because they knew you wouldn't come alone."

"So when did they ask you to come with me?" I ask her, curious.

She bats her lashes at me and grins. "A week ago, after your little boat outing with Sawyer. Asher came to see me, said they wanted to do something nice for you and would I be up for riding along."

"So you didn't help them?"

"Nope," she says with a grin. "Not even a little, I just got told to keep your weekend open and to pack bags."

An older guy with graying hair appears at the door of the car and opens it. "Miss Kensington, welcome to Waldorf Spa. We've been expecting you."

Shock floods me, but he offers me a hand as Penn's door opens and someone helps her out of the car too.

"If you'll follow me, someone will get your bags," the gray-haired man says as he leads me inside to the biggest foyer I've seen in my life. There's marble everywhere, and I'm sure the temperature just dropped a dozen degrees.

Freaking rich people, man.

"Holy shit, this place looks like something out of a movie," Penn whisper-shouts when the doorman leaves us at the check-in desk.

She's not wrong though. My skin is crawling with the outright show of wealth. This was definitely a nice gesture by the boys, but this really isn't my scene. And I'm guessing I'm not doing the best at hiding it because Penn starts laughing at me.

"Girl, you should see your face. You look like you want to get all Wile E. Coyote on this place and run the hell away."

I shrug, because, yep, I absolutely do. But I also don't want the guys to think I don't appreciate their gesture.

Even if I still don't know the whys of it all. I hate that I'm so distrusting, but I've learned that it's rare for people to do things just out of the kindness of their heart. So I can't help but feel a little... off about this whole trip.

"Stop overthinking it. They're just being nice. This is how rich boyfriends are nice."

"They're not my boyfriends," I respond, rolling my eyes.

"Miss Kensington?" A woman appears behind the check in desk, calling my name, "My name is Marie, I'll be looking after you during your stay. Mr. St. Vincent has requested we take care of your every need."

"It's Miss Moore," I correct her, and her response is no more than a tight smile. I am *so* not using the Kensington name.

"Of course, Miss Moore," she responds, though it definitely seems like more of a sneer. "You're staying in our presidential suite. An in-room massage has been arranged for yourself and your guest, and then someone will show you the rest of the facilities. Your bags have already been taken up to your suite."

Her snootiness is all kinds of obscene, but I paste a fake smile on and tell myself I can fake it till I make it. Even if just so as not to offend the boys.

Though I'm still suspicious about why they gifted me this weekend.

Penn opens her mouth to say God only knows what, so I loop my arm through hers and drag her toward the elevators on the far side of the lobby.

"That stuck up—"

"Oh I know, Penn. But you're supposed to be used to the rich bitch parade. I'm meant to be the hotheaded poor bitch."

"Says the new Kensington dating the St. Vincents," she

snarks, rolling her eyes. "I know, I know, but still. You know I don't hold it against you really, bitches like that just get on my last nerve."

"Well," I start, with a wry grin. "Take solace in the fact that she's *our* bitch this weekend."

Penn barks out a laugh and pushes the button to call the elevator. "I am going to make her hate us before the weekend is over."

I cackle with her as we enter the car.

I might not trust the whys of this weekend, but maybe I can learn to enjoy it. Just this once.

FOURTEEN

"**Y**ou have got to be kidding me," I scream into my pillow after checking my phone. There was me, thinking that maybe it was actually getting better. That this new life of mine, despite its few bumps, would be survivable for the three years I've crammed getting my associate and bachelor's into.

Sure, I have a douchebag professor this semester, but that's just one ~~two~~ of like nine classes, and sure Travis is a giant prick, but I can avoid him for the most part.

At least I *would*, if my mom would stop arranging these ridiculous sham family dinners like the one she just texted me about.

"You okay?" Penn asks as she pokes her head out of the closet she's been sitting in for the last thirty minutes, pretending like she isn't having a panic attack after Connor texting her last night saying they needed to talk.

Things had gone so well after our weekend away. That was two weeks ago, and I've managed to avoid Travis since. Asher and Sawyer have been nothing but adorable, and neither of them has pressured me to do anything but chill with them and the puppy squad which isn't exactly a hardship. Unsurprisingly, Cole has stayed MIA along with Travis.

What *is* surprising, is that Professor Crawford seems to have climbed out of his own ass and hasn't been a dick to me for the last two weeks.

Not sure what prompted the turn around, but I'm also not going to look a gift horse in the mouth, or even question it.

Contrary to Crawford's belief, I'm not stupid.

I should have known that *something* was coming because these two weeks have been so good. Nothing in my life is ever hunky dory for long.

"Family dinner. Apparently, Chase has something to tell us." I flop onto my back and groan while staring at the ceiling. "Because obviously he can't just tell us in a text or phone call. Like a normal person. I swear to God, if they're pregnant…"

She bursts out laughing, clutching her stomach as she bends in half, laughing at me so hard that she actually starts to cry. "Oh, God, I needed that," she says, sucking in air like it's going out of fashion. "But for reals, what if they are?"

"So freaking gross." I shudder at the possibility, but at least her crazy outburst of laughter lightened my mood just a tiny bit.

"At least I have a car so I don't have to get a ride with Travis."

"I thought you gave the car back…" she says as she drops onto her bed opposite me.

I nod, because I did, and had that insufferable trip back to campus with Travis, but after doing that once, I decided having the Batmobile was the lesser evil. I tell her exactly that and she pulls a face at me.

"So the twins bullied you into going back and getting a car?"

I can't help but laugh at her deduction. "They very much encouraged it. Especially since I wouldn't let them drive me everywhere. *But* I did get puppy time, so it was a win-win."

"I want to play with those squishums. Pictures aren't enough, ya know."

"Oh, I know. I don't like that I barely get to see them as it is. Stupid Travis and his bullshit."

"So when is this dinner anyway?"

I groan again, remembering the stupid text from my mom. "Tonight. Apparently late notice is her thing now."

Penn chuckles quietly. "At least tomorrow is Friday and you can let off some steam at the party you promised me you'd go to."

"Not the toga party." I groan, covering my face with my hand. I agreed to that shit under epic protest.

"Yes, the toga party," she says, rolling her eyes. "We only get to do college once, B. Lap up the experiences. All of them. These are supposed to be the best years of our lives."

"Whoever said that was old and sad, you know that, right?" I deadpan.

"Who cares," she retorts with a shrug. "It's still true. So let's live it up. Ya know, *after* you know for sure there's not a baby in your immediate future."

"Never have I ever been more glad for birth control," I say, tapping the little rod of genius under the skin of my bicep.

"Amen to that." She looks at her phone and her eyes go wide. "Don't you have class in like, twenty minutes?"

What?

I look at my phone and freak the fuck out. "Oh, shit," I screech as I scramble off the bed, barely avoiding falling flat on my face when I get tangled in the sheets.

One day, I won't live aboard the Hot Mess Express, but apparently, today is *not* that day.

I take a deep breath as I approach the dining room of the McMansion, trying to prepare myself for whatever the hell is going to happen tonight, but it's not enough and I stop dead in the doorway when I start to enter the room.

What in the name of all that is holy?

I mean, of course I expected the same pomp and opulence that is always here. I expected to find my mom, Chase, and Travis—despite not hearing from Travis about the dinner. I knew I wasn't going to be the only one summoned—but what I did not expect to see before me was Asher, Sawyer, Cole, and what I can only assume are their parents.

Yeah, that was shocker number one.

"Briar, you made it," Travis says with a giant smile on his face, moving toward me, almost with a bounce in his step. I freeze, wide-eyed, waiting for someone to yell PUNKED. Instead, he hugs me tightly, lifting me until my Converse-covered feet leave the ground.

"Smile and pretend like this is normal, for fuck's sake," he hisses in my ear before putting me back on the ground. I let out a dry laugh and put on the mask I perfected long ago.

I've always known how to pretend like nothing's wrong. It's something I learned at a young age.

Pressing my hands down the skater-style dress I grabbed from the closet in my room here after arriving an hour ago, I'm fully regretting not asking Tobias if he knew what was going on tonight.

Sawyer bounds up to me once I'm back on the floor, lifting me and spinning me before kissing me smack on the lips then putting me down once more. "Sorry, Sunshine. We didn't know the folks were coming until we got here, otherwise we'd have sent up a warning flag."

"You didn't even tell me *you'd* be here, and now you're kissing me in front of your freaking parents, Sawyer," I whisper-shout at him, becoming very aware that everyone is watching us.

Sweet baby Jesus, let a hole open up beneath us and make me freaking disappear.

"Well, isn't this lovely?" my mom coos as she glides across the room toward us. "Briar, darling. Why didn't you tell me?"

She hugs me tightly, but Sawyer doesn't release my hand, which I can't decide if I'm thankful for when his mom stares at the joining of us like she just saw two pigs fucking.

Oh yeah, the disdain is real.

"Just smile," Mom murmurs in my ear before squeezing me and letting go. I glance over to Asher, who looks pissed at Sawyer, but also like he wants to rescue me.

Oh, fun.

That really fills me with joy.

"Briar, this is Erica and Thomas St. Vincent," Mom says once she's back at Chase's side. I take a deep breath and release Sawyer's hand, preparing myself for dealing with his parents. "And this is Senator Theodore Beckett."

Senator Beckett gives me what I would call a politician's smile as I approach and holds out his hand, which I take and shake. "Lovely to meet you, Senator."

"The pleasure is mine, I'm sure," he responds, his eyes raking over me before he glances at his son.

I turn to the St. Vincents, my gaze locking with Asher's before I turn to his parents as Sawyer joins them. "Mom, Dad, this is Briar," Sawyer says cheerily.

His mom glances over me quickly, giving me a tight smile.

"Lovely to meet you both," I say, trying not to sound as awkward as I feel.

"Lovely to meet you too, sweetheart," Thomas responds. "I've heard so much about you."

"Oh, God," I say, before covering my mouth and looking at him wide-eyed.

He chuckles before taking a sip of his drink. "Only good things, don't worry." He winks at me before turning to Chase and the senator, starting up whatever conversation they were having when I entered.

I head to the other side of the room to pour a glass of water from the jug, trying to compose myself. Any thoughts of apprehension I had about why I was summoned here swiftly departed upon seeing who was in this room.

"Deep breaths, Beautiful," Asher murmurs in my ear, squeezing my waist from behind. "You've got this. Tonight is all about them, so don't stress."

I finish my drink, placing the glass back on the cart before turning around and realizing the four of them have formed a barrier around me. I just kind of blink at them, trying to work out what the hell is going on.

"We need to put on a united front against whatever this charade is tonight." Travis's eyes bore into mine as he speaks. "You're new here, but this is a game we're used to. We don't have to like each other to be on the same side, you understand?"

I raise my brows, wondering why the hell he'd think I'd

side with him after him being a colossal bag of douchery since I arrived here at the start of the month, but then I realize he's right. Whatever this is tonight, they have more experience with it, and chances are that not only am I out of my depth, but I'm probably not going to like it.

Especially after my mom's whole 'just smile' warning earlier.

"What do you think they want?" I ask quietly as the low hum of the conversation on the other side of the room picks up.

"No fucking idea," Travis complains. "But when they gather us like this outside of a holiday function or party to pretend we have an awesome family dynamic, it's usually because they want us to play show pony for whatever new money grab they've dreamed up."

His snark isn't lost on me, but I'm too freaked out to really grasp it fully. This is a side of my new life that I knew would happen at some point. Money never comes without strings, and now it's obviously time to pay the piper.

"Dinner will be served in five minutes." Tobias's voice is like a soothing blanket as he interrupts the room, but, if anything, his presence calms my nerves. Which makes absolutely zero sense, but I never claimed to make any sense at all.

"Let's get this show on the road," Travis says, gulping down the remnants of his drink, which smells like whiskey. He and Cole make up the front of our little pack, with Sawyer at my side and Asher behind us.

Yeah, this is weird.

It's like we're gearing for battle and I am so not here for it.

But I let myself be led, like a lamb to the slaughter, to my seat at the table. At least this time, with this many people, it doesn't seem so obscenely big.

I end up seated between Travis and Sawyer, opposite Senator Beckett.

Yeah, this isn't awkward at all.

Never have I ever wanted to run away as much as I do right now.

That's actually a total lie, I've definitely experienced worse than this, but god, do I feel awkward.

We eat, and while it looks beautiful, I struggle to enjoy the five courses because, well, anxiety is a cruel mistress and I feel like I'm sitting on pins waiting for Chase to get to the freaking point of his dinner.

Once the dessert bowls are cleared away and Tobias brings out coffee, Chase finally clears his throat and stands. "Thank you all for joining us here today, as you know, I brought you here to bring you in on some news."

He pauses and squeezes my mom's hand and my stomach flips in direct response. "We actually have two pieces of news. The first is that we're pregnant, and we couldn't be happier."

I glance at Travis and his jaw clenches. I feel like I'm going to be sick.

"And second, is that I am going to be running for mayor of

New York. The current mayor has their sights set on stepping up, and after talking with Theo, we agree that this is a great step for me. With his backing, of course."

He pauses again and I glance around the table to see exactly what I'm supposed to do here.

"What this means for you is, obviously, campaigning and keeping yourselves out of trouble. We will need you available for appearances when called upon, zero exceptions." Chase glares at Travis with his final words.

"Congratulations, Mr. Kensington," Cole says with a smile on his face that I haven't seen before. Oh yeah, he was definitely raised by a politician.

"If you'll excuse me," Travis says, standing and leaving the room before another word can be said.

Everyone gets up and starts to talk while I sit, dazed by the fact that my mom is pregnant. She eventually comes to sit beside me and smiles. "I know this is a surprise, Briar…"

"A surprise? Mom, you've never even been able to look after yourself, how do you expect to look after a baby? I have school and I want to have a life. I can't just raise your kid the way I raised myself."

Her eyes go wide, like she hadn't considered that I wouldn't be happy for her. Maybe that makes me the asshole here, but after my childhood, how could I be happy for her?

"Briar—"

"No, Mom," I say, cutting her off and standing. "Don't ask

me to be okay with this. Not after everything."

Her mouth closes, and I see when it registers with her just how fucked up it is that she told me like this.

After everything…

No, I am not going down that rabbit hole of despair. I survived too much to go back there.

Without another word, I leave the room and head to the car.

They can have their baby and their campaign, but they can leave me the hell out of all of it.

I throw back another shot of tequila before lifting my hands and becoming one of the woo girls I usually roll my eyes at. I barely slept last night, and what sleep I did get was wrought with nightmares. Thanks to Mom's lovely baby bomb, more than a few unwanted memories tried to rise to the surface, so I squashed them down with coffee, and now I fully intend to drown them in tequila.

Serena hands me two Jell-O shots and I swallow them both down, chasing them with a beer. It tastes gross, but I also know that there is a fuck ton of it at this party.

I might not like or approve of sorority life, but these girls can throw one hell of a party. Even if it is a toga party.

Penn's reaction to my enthusiasm over tonight's party was laughable. There was bouncing, clapping, and squealing, but it was the exact energy I needed. Her concern for the dark bags under my eyes was noted, but definitely muted by my willingness to get blackout wasted.

Emerson would be proud I'm sure.

The music is a throwback to before we were born, but the DJ looks about thirty. I'm not complaining when Katy Perry's *Last Friday Night* starts playing and cheers go up around the entire room. Apparently, I'm not the only one enjoying the cheese fest of vintage music tonight.

Give me enough tequila and I'll woo to just about anything.

I grab my red cup of cocktail from the table, take Penn's hand, and drag her to what seems to be the dance floor. Serena and Charli join hands with her and we make a train through the crowd of people until we become one with the writhing masses.

Losing myself to the music, I finish my drink and let my hips sway. I don't ever really pay attention to who is around me or what is playing. All I want is to forget. To escape the onslaught of horror that's been threatening to overwhelm me since last night.

Serena and Charli tap out first, but Connor continues to bring Penn and I drinks so we don't need to leave our spot.

I lose track of time and how much I've had to drink. My eyes closed, my body swaying like a feather on the wind without a care in the world, I keep dancing.

When I open my eyes, I realize Penn and Connor aren't anywhere near me. In fact, I don't know any of these people;

not the girl grinding against my front or the guy with his arms around my waist.

I manage to untangle myself from them and stumble from the dance floor.

Reaching under my flimsy toga to the pocket of my shorts, I pull out my phone and try to text Penn.

Me:

Where did you go?

I send the same thing to Serena and Charli before deciding to try and find a bathroom. This much tequila on my tiny bladder has suddenly become a problem.

Trying not to stumble through the house, I smile at people as I pass them, a few guys from the football team saying hello as I breeze by.

I momentarily wonder where Travis and the guys are. I haven't seen them tonight, and it's not like them to miss a party.

I haven't seen Dante either.

Weird.

The thoughts are fleeting as I find a line for what I assume is the bathroom and groan.

There is no way in a house this big there is just one bathroom, so I head for the stairs. I'm pretty sure the higher levels are supposed to be out of bounds, but there's no one watching the stairs here like there are at most of the parties I've been to, so I cling to the rail and hope to God I don't fall flat on my face as the world tilts a little.

There's still a ton of people on this floor, so I carry on up the stairs to the next level and find it quieter. There are six doors, three on each side of the staircase.

One of these has to be a bathroom, right? There's no way this many girls live together with just two baths.

The first two doors I try to the right are locked, and after face planting the first, I'm a little more careful with the second.

But when the third opens into a bedroom, hope sparks in me. I open the door on the left side of the room and fist pump the air.

Hell yes for an ensuite.

I mosey into the bathroom, happy that I found a place to pee in peace without waiting for an hour in line, and speed-pee in case whoever this room belongs to decides to come back.

Once I'm done, I put the room back how I found it and creep back into the bedroom.

I freeze when I notice that the lamp isn't on anymore and try to find my phone again for the flashlight. It's pitch freaking black, so bad I can't even see my freaking hand.

I try not to panic, but my body doesn't listen as my heart hammers in my chest and my hands shake rather than focusing on grabbing my phone.

Hot breath on my cheek makes me freeze as my heart stops beating.

Hands grasp my biceps so tight I already know through the tequila fog that I'm going to have bruises. All I want to do is run, but I'm paralyzed, and my eyes start to droop as the male voice whispers in my ear.

"I knew I'd get you alone at some point if I was patient. Looks like I was right."

FIFTEEN

The voice spurs me into action and my fight instincts take over despite the tequila. I throw my head back, the crunch followed by a scream as my arms are released. The darkness is blinding, but I run for the direction I think the door is in.

A laugh sounds in the room, turning my blood cold. "You crazy bitch, I kind of like it."

I search frantically for the door as the laughing gets closer and my heart pounds so hard I think it might actually stop.

My hands skim the wall when I feel his hand in my hair and I'm ripped backward, slamming to the ground so hard that I'm momentarily winded. The toes of his shoes press up against the side of my ribcage before he stomps on my stomach, and any air I thought I'd regained whooshes from my lungs.

"Silly little gutter whore, thinking she can play here. This is my world, bitch."

He moves away from me, and I hear the unbuckle of his belt. Panic slams through me and despite the pain, I know I have to move. I scramble onto my hands and knees and notice a small beam of light from what I'm hoping is under the door.

I try to move as quietly and quickly as I can. I make it a few paces when he grabs my ankle and twists. I let out a scream from both shock and pain, kicking back at him despite the agony I'm in, taking the win when I hear his groan followed by a thump and a mumbled, "you bitch."

Moving quickly, I stand and rush to what I hope is the door, trying not to sob as I attempt to escape. When my hand wraps around what I think is the handle, relief floods me as I rip the door open, throwing myself out of it and running straight for the stairs.

The sound of the music assaults my ears, but I almost don't hear it over the noise of my rushing blood.

I fall into someone and trip into someone else before I end up falling down the rest of the flight of stairs. I look behind me to see if there's anyone following me, ignoring the pain that rips through my ankle as I jar it on top of whatever he already did to fuck it up. I can't see anyone specifically that looks like they're chasing me, and everyone around me seems too wasted to be much use.

The crowd is my ally and my biggest enemy. I can hide in it, but so can they. Whoever they are.

"You okay?" I look up and I nearly cry when I find Dante staring down at me.

I open my mouth to speak and a sob rips through my throat as my eyes start to water.

"Briar?"

I shake my head and cover my mouth while I try to keep my shit locked down. He reaches down and helps me up, but I wince when I try to put weight on my ankle. He frowns at me and, without a word, lifts me into his arms before walking us out of the house as tears run silently down my face.

Once we're outside, he walks me to the end of the drive where there's a bench that he sits me on before pulling his phone from his pocket. I try to tell him to stop because I already know who he's calling, but before I can make my voice work, he's speaking.

"Yeah, man, I'm at the Delta house. You need to get here, now. Something happened to your girl." He keeps the phone to his ear for a few seconds before hanging up. "You going to tell me what happened?"

"I—" I start, but my voice cracks as I think back through it. The tequila is still very much in my system, because I've definitely experienced worse than this and cried less, but holy shit.

I know people talk about shit happening in college, but I thought I was safe here.

Stupid me, I guess.

Tires screech as a car comes to a halt in front of the house and Sawyer basically flies from the passenger seat.

"Briar!" he calls out, stress lining his face as he runs the few feet to reach us. "What happened?"

He picks me up from the bench and cradles me against his chest. This shouldn't feel so comforting. I should definitely not be leaning on him to make me feel safe. I've always done that myself, I don't rely on people.

But this has shaken me worse than usual. Maybe because I thought I was safe here. My mind is way too tequila soaked— not to mention the hit of adrenaline—to make sense of anything right now.

When I don't answer, Sawyer turns to Dante.

"I don't know, man, I found her on the stairs, crying, looking like she'd just seen a ghost. She looked fucking terrified." Dante scrubs the back of his neck, as if he wishes he knew more.

"Okay. Well, thank you. For getting her out here and for calling." Asher joins us as he finishes speaking, looking more than a little frazzled.

"Hey, Beautiful. Let's take you home, shall we?"

Fear roots through me again. I don't know who was in that room, but it sounded like they were looking for me. Maybe I shouldn't go home.

Oh, God.

Penn.

"My phone," I mutter, trying to find the stupid block of

technology. "Call Penn."

"On it," Dante says, hitting the screen of his own phone and handing it to me.

It rings twice before Penn answers with a huff. "What do you want, Dante?"

"It's me," I say, my voice sounding smaller than usual. "Stay with Connor tonight. Don't go to our room."

The minute the words are out of my mouth, the three of them stare at me with a mix of anger and confusion.

"B, stop fooling around." Penn laughs, but her voice is sharp, like she's rattled.

"Not messing, Penn. Please, just... don't go to the dorm."

I hear Connor's voice in the background and let out a sigh of relief that she's not alone. She tells him what I said to her and then his voice fills the line. "Briar, what happened?"

"It's not safe. Just please keep Penn at your place," I stress, and whatever he hears in my voice seems to make him relent.

"Fine, but tomorrow you explain what the hell is going on."

"Okay," I say quietly before saying goodbye and hanging up. Dante takes his phone back and pockets it.

"Dante, get in the car. We'll take this conversation somewhere a little more private," Asher suggests.

Sawyer stands and loads me into the back of Asher's truck, letting Dante take shotgun as he climbs in beside me. The drive to their house is made in silence, and it doesn't take long.

The house is dark when we arrive, and I'm both relieved

and disappointed that Travis and Cole aren't here.

They wouldn't have done this to me as some sick joke, right?

The puppies come bounding toward us as Sawyer walks me toward the sofa. Asher heads to the kitchen with Dante, before rejoining us with a bag of ice. He puts it on my ankle and I wince at the chill of it, but I know I need it so I don't complain.

The cold plus the pain actually helps to clear my mind a bit, and I suddenly feel a little… foolish.

I freaking cried.

"Let's get you comfortable, shall we?" Asher says, taking off his hoodie and handing it to me before helping me unpin the makeshift toga. I slide into his hoodie. His scent and warmth flood me and I snigger internally that he's obviously never getting this back.

The puppies sit around us on the floor at Asher's command, but he scoops up my little friend and places him in my lap.

Yay, puppy.

The now-not-so-little ball of squish snuggles up to me, putting his head on my shoulder, and I melt.

Once I'm snug in his hoodie with Shadow, Asher hands me a cup of coffee that Dante brings in before they both settle onto the couch opposite the one Sawyer put me on. Sawyer's sitting on the coffee table, watching me, looking as serious as I've ever seen him. "You ready to tell us what happened?"

I bury my face in the puppy before telling them everything

I remember, from leaving the party, finding the bathroom, and everything I can think of, up to Dante finding me.

"Sounds like what happened to Katie last week," Asher says. I look up at them, confused, as Sawyer nods. "We should report it to campus security."

"Wait, this happened to someone else? Why don't I know about it? Why doesn't everyone know about it?" I ask incredulously.

"Katie didn't want to tell anyone. She felt... foolish. We only know because she's dating one of the guys on the team who told Cole," Sawyer explains, and Dante nods, agreeing.

"Oh," is all I say, because well, I get it. Entirely. Because I absolutely want to just forget this all ever happened. "Maybe she was right, maybe it's just some stupid prank?"

Asher looks at me like I've lost my mind. "You don't want us to say anything?"

I bite my lip and scratch between the puppy's ears. "I mean, what if we say something and people don't believe me? I drank a *lot* tonight. What if it was some stupid prank?"

"Then they shouldn't have played it on you," Sawyer growls. "Not on my girl. We're telling campus security, Briar. What if it happens to someone else and it wasn't a prank and you didn't say something?"

I pick at the skin by my thumbnail, not looking up at him because I know he's right, but it's been ingrained in me from a young age that we do not snitch. Even when it's really fucking bad.

"Briar?" Dante asks, and I look up at him, avoiding both of the twins' faces. "What do *you* want to do? This happened to you, and no one is going to force you to do anything."

He glares at the twins before looking back to me.

I chew on the inside of my cheek as my anxiety ramps up to the point it feels like there are bubbles under my skin. I rub at my arms to try and get rid of the sensation. "I don't want to say anything," I say quietly. "But how about I sleep on it? I don't have to decide right this second, right?"

"If that's what *you* want, Briar, then that's what we do," Dante says firmly. I have no idea when he became the guy in charge in this room, but neither of the twins have said anything.

Moments later, the door swings open and Travis and Cole enter the space, and the tension racks up again.

Travis pauses, taking in the scene before glaring at me. "What the fuck did she do now?"

"You going to be okay in here?" Asher asks as I walk out of his bathroom in nothing but a towel.

After Sawyer and Dante nearly flipped their shit at Travis being an asshole, Asher managed to calm everyone down and explain everything. It's fairly obvious that Travis would think I was lying if my version of events wasn't so similar to Katie's, but he's still skeptical of me.

I wish I knew why he bounces between hot and cold so much, but knowing the inner workings of the male mind has never exactly been my forte. Most men I've known were more monster than man and the few who weren't monsters... well, they never stuck around.

Amid everything else going on, it was decided I would stay here. Dante is crashing on the couch because, apparently, he trusts Travis as much as I trust a fraying rope to swing me across a river. Then Sawyer and Asher played rock, paper, scissors to see whose room I ended up in. Sawyer lost. He's been pouting ever since.

I realize Asher is still watching me as I stand still, dripping water onto the floor. "Yeah, I'll be fine."

It's a lie, but being alone and afraid isn't a new sensation for me.

"As long as you're sure," he says, eyeing me suspiciously. "I'll bunk in with Sawyer for the night. If you need anything, he's just across the hall."

"You really don't need to give up your room. I can sleep on the sofa, or you can just share the bed. I promise to keep my hands to myself," I joke, motioning to the sofa opposite the bed because it's the only defense I have left at my disposal, all things considered.

"If you don't want to be alone, I can stay." He watches me closely as I wrap my arms around myself. "I got you a pair of sweatpants and a t-shirt. They're going to be too big for you, but I figure they're better than nothing."

"Thank you," I say quietly, trying to balance so as not to put pressure on my rolled ankle. I hobble over to the bed before I start toweling off my hair. There's nothing like a night of fear and panic to sober a girl up. Top it off with that shower, and well, I'm now frightfully sober and my usual wit and snark seem to have dried up along with the remnants of the tequila that was in my system.

"I'll give you some privacy," Asher says as he stands up from the sofa opposite the bed, but I shake my head.

"You're fine. And honestly, the thought of being alone in another bedroom tonight really doesn't appeal," I say, before shimmying into the sweats and hoodie then removing the towel. "See, no privacy needed."

He smiles at me, concern crinkling the corners of his eyes. "Let me take care of the towels, you climb into bed."

He takes the towels and heads into the bathroom. I hear the shower turn on and decide to do as he said and climb into bed. Sighing as I sink into the marshmallow cloud of a mattress, I snuggle down, pulling the duvet up to my chin. I'm probably going to overheat like crazy, but screw it. Comfort is key right now, and being surrounded by the smells of fresh linens and all things Asher sweeps a settling calm through me.

There is something about him that feels like the safe harbor in a storm. Despite my initial reservations about him, there's something that makes me feel relaxed. Safe. I could say the same thing for Sawyer, but it's a different kind of feeling. Sawyer is the playful one, the one who will fight any battle to save me from having to. Asher? He's the guy who would stand at my side and cheer me on, knowing I could fight my own battles, but would step in if I needed him to.

It's strange to compare the two of them.

Hell, everything about my life is strange since I came to Serenity Falls.

Especially when it comes to the four guys who live in this house, and Lord, do not even get me started on Dante.

None of it makes sense.

Way to distract yourself from the fear, Briar. Focus on the penis parade. That always works.

I shake my head, but thinking about the boy situation in my life is a lot more manageable than trying to work out if I recognize the voice from earlier. A shiver runs down my spine at the thought and I wriggle in the bed as if trying to expel it.

Yep, focusing on my boy dilemma is definitely the easiest thing to occupy my brain right now. Except, I don't know that I even have a dilemma as such.

I mean, yes, I fucked Travis and now he hates me, and also, he's my stepbrother.

Cole kissed me, but he told me to stay away from him after finding out who I was.

Sawyer... well, he acts like he's my boyfriend, but we've

said exactly zero about *what* we are, and Asher, he calls me his—to be fair they both call me theirs—but beyond that, he hasn't pushed for anything.

Hell, he hasn't so much as tried to kiss me.

Yet, he fought Sawyer for me to stay in his bed tonight.

See? Confusing. And a much better way to distract my brain than any other in existence.

"You look like you're concentrating pretty hard." Asher chuckles as he crosses the room with a towel wrapped around his waist.

Holy freaking libido, down girl.

Watching water drip from his dark blond hair and down his painted skin is enough to make my mouth dry.

He turns and catches me basically devouring him with my eyes and smirks. "Like what you see, Beautiful?"

I try to swallow, to find my voice, while nodding. "I mean, what isn't to like? You're carved like a freaking painted Adonis, plus you have that whole geeky vibe thing going too. You're like tacos and margaritas... a girl's wet dream."

He barks out a laugh at the ridiculousness that falls from my lips, but not one word of it was a lie. I didn't think guys like him and Sawyer existed outside of the pages of my books.

"Well I'm glad you like what you see," he says with a wink. "But shouldn't you be sleeping already?"

I sit up in the bed, wincing a little when I put pressure on my ankle. "Can't sleep, my mind is too loud."

He roots around in his dresser before pulling on a pair of shorts and a t-shirt. Opening his bedroom door, he whistles and I hear the thuds as the dogs rush up the stairs. "Let's see if I can help with that."

The puppies storm the room and jump up onto the bed with us, and I let out a squeak as Shadow basically attacks me, licking my face.

"Calm," Asher commands, and the puppies dial back their excitement instantly. He points to the end of the bed and they follow the command, curling up in the most adorable puppy pile.

Seconds later, he climbs into the bed and drags me toward him. "Lie down, Briar."

I curl up into his side, my head resting on his chest while his fingers play with the strands of my drying hair. I feel movement at the end of the bed so I lift my head, smiling when I see Shadow moving to curl in the crook of my knees.

Such a cutie.

"You know," he starts, the murmur of his voice rumbling in his chest. I lay my head back down and my eyes flutter closed as he goes on to tell me a story of his and Sawyer's first-ever sailing lesson. Before I realize it, a smile plays on my lips as I drift off to sleep. His voice is no more than a whisper when he kisses the top of my head. "Sweet dreams, Beautiful. Don't get ideas of going anywhere, I could get used to this."

LILY WILDHART

SIXTEEN

I fling the door to the dorm open as dramatically as I can manage before sauntering into the room. "Hello, friend, it is the return of I, the great conductor of the hot mess express. Destination: insanity."

I flomp face down onto my bed with the sound of Penn's laughter ringing in my ears.

"I see the dramatics are back. Glad to see you haven't lost your sense of humor in all of the madness," she retorts, and I flip onto my side, propping my head up on my hand.

"They are, and obviously I can finally walk on my stupid ankle again. Life is looking up." I grin at her and she rolls her eyes.

It's been a week since the weird encounter at the toga party, and I've managed to shove it in a little box, which is firmly on a shelf in a locked closet in the back of my mind. Along with a ton of other stuff that I'm sure a therapist would have a field day with. But we're not thinking about that.

"Travis backed off your ass yet?" she asks before slurping a mouthful of her ramen.

"Ugh," I grunt as I sit up. "Yes and no. Yes, in that I've barely seen him, but no, in that when I *have* seen him, he stares at me like I'm some sort of super spy sent to infiltrate his life and blow it up. Honestly, if you'd seen how he looked at me that first night… you'd think he'd been replaced by a pod person or something."

"Maybe he has," she says with a shrug, and I smirk.

If only.

"At least if he's back to avoiding you, rather than questioning you about what happened, it's a bonus. You decide to report it?" she asks, and I can hear the conflict in her voice. She's made her opinion on me not telling anyone very clear. Connor agreed with her and there was a whole thing once I came back here on Sunday, but she mostly hasn't asked about it since then.

"Nope. I honestly think it was just some dumb guy being stupid and the tequila made me not see sense."

She rolls her eyes at me but nods. "I still think you're being that stupid white girl in horror movies. You know, the one who always checks the basement? But I love you regardless."

"I love you too." I laugh. "You got any plans for the weekend?" I ask as my phone beeps. I pull it from my pocket and see Asher's name on the screen.

"Connor is taking me out on an official date tomorrow."

My head whips up and my wide-eyed gaze meets hers. "Are you shitting me?"

"I am not, as it turns out, shitting you, my friend." Her grin is insane as she puts down her bowl and chopsticks.

"Holy crap! Where's he taking you?"

"I have no idea." She sighs dreamily, and I can't help but giggle at her. "Isn't that perfect?"

"I love it when a guy actually makes a plan," I agree. It's not entirely true, though. I've never really actually dated anyone, but I've read enough to know that *that* guy is the one you want.

"Me too. All I know is I need to dress up. I'm so excited."

"I'm excited for you, friend." And I really am, I'm so happy she's happy. I like Connor. He's been nothing but nice to me and the initial creeper vibes I got from him disappeared pretty quickly. A vibe which, realistically, just came from me being an untrusting wench anyway.

"Means you need to find company for tomorrow so you're not here alone, though."

I nod, because that was the condition I agreed to. Not just with her, but with the twins too. I wouldn't report it, but neither of us would be in the dorm alone at night. Not until there were no more instances of it happening, and with the twins' network, they'd know if there was.

My phone beeps again and reminds me of Asher's message.

Asher:

What you doing tomorrow night?

Me:

Nothing yet, why?

Asher:

You have plans now. With me. Be ready for 8. Dress nice… but not too nice ;)

Me:

Oh I do, do I?

Asher:

Don't be a brat, you know you want to be a good girl.

Oh, hot damn. A text message shouldn't make me squeeze my thighs together.

Asher:

Now, do as I asked and be ready for 8.

Me:

Yes, sir ;)

I grin as I hit send, and Penn clears her throat. "And who was that smile for, huh?"

My cheeks heat as I laugh a little. "Turns out I have plans tomorrow night now too."

I check my reflection in the mirror, wondering how Penn convinced me this outfit was a good idea. My dark tresses have new streaks of red flashed back through it after our trip to the salon earlier. I have a black crop top with a dark pair of ripped jeans, finished with a pair of heeled boots borrowed from Penn and a black blazer with lace arms.

My makeup is dark and smokey with red lips to match my hair and my newly painted fire-truck-red nails.

I look nothing like myself, but I'm pretty sure I fit the requirement of nice, but not too nice. Especially when I look at Penn in her little black dress, cute slingback shoes, and her red hair, which now has blonde highlights, pulled back from her face with a few strands left loose to frame it.

"You look smokin'," she tells me, and I smile.

"Maybe, but have you seen you? Freaking stunning. Connor isn't going to know what hit him."

She opens her mouth to respond but a knock sounds on the door. "Right on time." She grins as she moves to the door and opens it.

"Holy…" Connor's voice trails off and I put my head round the door to take in the look on his face. His jaw is slack and his eyes are wide. "Penn, you look… phenomenal."

"You clean up nice too," she says, coyly clasping the lapels of his jacket. "Shall we go?"

"Yes," he says entirely too fast, and I clamp my lips together to hold back a laugh. "I mean, sure, let's go."

"I'll see you later, B."

"Have fun, you guys," I say with a finger wave, closing the door behind them. Seconds later, there's another knock.

I check the peep hole and see Asher on the other side. Damn, that boy is way too freaking hot. I open the door and he whistles as his gaze rakes over my body. "I am a lucky guy."

"Yes, yes you are. I'm freaking awesome," I say, sticking out my tongue.

"You won't find me saying otherwise," he retorts with a grin, and I take in his shirt, jeans, and shoes look.

"Am I overdressed?" I ask, suddenly nervous. Especially since I'm wayyyy out of my usual comfort zone clothes-wise, yet again.

"Not even a little, come on. The car is waiting."

"The car," I mutter, rolling my eyes. I make sure I have my phone, wallet, and keys before locking up the room and letting him lead me outside to where a black luxury sedan idles at the curb.

He actually meant a car was waiting.

Fucking rich people, man. I will never get used to this.

He waves off the driver and opens the door for me. It takes a second to move, but then I slide into the back before he drops in beside me. Once the car pulls from the curb, I turn to Asher and ask, "Are you going to tell me where we're going?"

"Not yet," he says with a coy smile and intertwines his fingers with mine. "But I will tell you we're heading to what you say is your favorite place."

"We're going into the city?" I ask as excitement floods my veins. I miss New York so freaking much.

"We are," he says, grinning. "But the rest, you have to wait for."

I lean over and kiss him. Probably a little too enthusiastically, but he cups my cheeks and kisses me back with as much vigor. We spend the journey into the city talking about not much at all. He tells me funny little stories about him and Sawyer as kids. I tend to just laugh and encourage him to talk because I don't have stories like that and I am absolutely not telling him about my childhood right now.

Once we're in the city, I feel like a kid again. I've only been in Serenity for about a month, but since I was in California for the summer, it feels like forever since I've been back.

It takes almost as long to drive through the city as it did to get here, but when the car pulls to a stop, my jaw drops.

"Shut up."

"You like?" Asher asks as the car crawls forward, and I

just blink at the sight outside the window. The red carpet. The paparazzi. The glamor of it all.

We're at the opening of the new Demi Hawke installation at the Gagosian Gallery.

Holy shit.

"How did you know?" I ask, trying not to sound as emotional as I feel right now.

"I saw your sketchbook on your desk in your room. You had a ton of Demi's work and when I saw the invite in the mail at Mom and Dad's, I snagged it because I had a feeling you'd like it." He squeezes my hand and I turn to face him, trying to put everything inside of me into words.

But I can't find them, so I settle for, "Thank you."

"There isn't anything I wouldn't give you," he says, tucking my hair behind my ear. "I thought after this, we could go for a ride through the park. I've never done it, and I know you like horses."

Holy shit, this guy actually fucking listens.

"This is all incredible," I say wistfully as the car pulls to a stop and the driver jumps from the car. "It's almost unreal."

"Oh, it's real, Briar," he whispers as the car door opens and the shouts flood my ears. "And this is only the beginning."

We enter the darkened house and Asher takes my blazer from

me, hanging it up on the coat hook, though how he can navigate in the darkness is beyond me. He takes my hand again and kisses me softly. I hear the puppies in the back room and half want to go to them, but Asher tugs me along with him and there's no way I'm not going to follow.

He leads me up to the second floor and to the end of the hall, to his room, before pausing.

"You okay with this?" he asks, and I squeeze his hand.

"Yeah," I say softly. I kinda love how he keeps making sure I'm okay. Sure, we had a rocky start, what with him being Travis's go-between, but we've come a long way since then. Especially after last weekend. Waking up to him wrapped around me the morning after everything happened was the safest and most content I've felt in forever.

So I think we've come pretty far from our first meeting. Or at least it feels like it. Even if we have only known each other about a month, it almost feels like I've known him my entire life. I still can't get over this whole night. Especially since his 'ride in the park' was actually pre-planned, and we even had a starlight picnic.

Everything about tonight was just perfection, and everything he's done up to this point is exactly why I'm not doubting this decision. We'll work out the finer details later.

He ushers me into the room, closing the door behind him as I try to take in the details from the dim lighting from the lamp in the corner of the room. I spot his guitars on their stands in the corner, smiling at the thought of him looking like a rock god, strumming away on his acoustic guitar. It's an easy vision to have of him.

He spins me and pulls me toward him, kissing me softly as he pushes his hands into my hair and holds me in place like he's worried I'm going to run away. I slide my hands around his waist and under the hem of his shirt, unable to stop the smile as he shivers beneath my touch. "You keep doing that, you're going to learn that you shouldn't play with fire."

"Maybe a girl likes to get burned every now and then," I murmur back against his lips, and he nips my bottom one, making me jump, his hands still firmly in my hair.

"You sure about that?" he asks, and I nod, my breathing increasing in tempo. I move my hands to his fly and pop the button on his jeans before undoing his zipper. His breath hitches and I drop down to my knees, his hands staying in my hair.

I look up at him and smile when I see the look on his face. Like I'm the only thing he's ever seen. Like nothing else exists.

His cock bobs free when I pull at his jeans and boxers, and I suck in a breath.

Holy freaking monster dick.

It's fine. I've totally got this. Blow job super powers activated.

"Briar," he groans as I wrap my lips around the head of his cock, and he tilts his head back against the door with a thud. "Fuck."

I hum in delight, which makes him moan again, before taking his dick down my throat and holding once my chin touches his balls, delighting in the expletives that fall from his mouth. That's before I stick out my tongue and lick his balls before pulling back.

He pulls my head back, tilting it so I look up at him, and he gazes down at me in wonder. "Holy shit, Briar."

"I know," I say with a wink and take him in my mouth again, wrapping my hand around his base and loving the sounds that fall from him as I enjoy pleasing him. I take him to the back of my throat and hold him there for a beat before coming up for air and repeating it, enjoying myself as curses stream from his lips as I lick his balls while pumping his shaft with my hand.

"You need to stop, otherwise I'm going to blow my load already, and I am not ready for that." I laugh as I lick the underside of his dick, watching him take deep breaths as he closes his eyes like he's trying to calm himself down. "Stand. Strip and on the bed. Now."

His command shocks me, but adds to my excitement. He releases my hair and I do as he says, pushing down my jeans and thong, making sure to bend over and give him a show before pulling off my crop top and undoing my bra.

"You are fucking stunning." He groans as he watches me, dick in hand. "Now, on the bed. I want to watch you."

I move up the bed, positioning myself so he can see me without obstacle. I want him to see just how much he turns me on. How his thoughtful gestures make my body come alive for him.

Spreading my legs, it takes every ounce of willpower to keep my hands on the bed as I wait for further instruction from him. He may be attentive and gentle, but beneath that polished exterior lies a rough diamond ready to cut through my walls.

"Such a pretty pussy. Spread those lips for me. Show me how wet you are." Without taking my eyes from him, I slide my hand down and use my finger to open myself up for his viewing pleasure. His nostrils flare, his tongue peeks out his mouth, the top row of his teeth sinks into the plump flesh of his bottom lip, and I know he's just as turned on as I am.

Slowly, he wraps his long, thick fingers around his shaft, his thumb spreading the precum across the head of his cock.

"Play with yourself, Beautiful. Be a good girl for me. Show me what gets you off."

I bring my fingers to my mouth and suck on two digits. There's something inherently erotic about Asher standing over me, watching as I bring my wet fingers to my clit and draw out slow, sensual circles. He strokes his dick in rhythm with my movements, slowing down when I do, speeding up when my excitement gets the best of me.

"Fuck, you're dripping." His gaze sears a path across my skin until we're staring at each other once more. "Is all that for me, Gorgeous?"

"Yes." The word is little more than a breath that escapes

from between my lips. Watching him jerk his fist up and down his shaft is like real life porn. I don't know how long I'll last before coming all over my fingers, and I'd much rather come over his.

Asher takes a step closer then brings his free hand to my pussy, one finger sliding through my wetness, and I groan and I watch, seemingly in slow motion, as his finger goes up to his mouth and he sucks—hard—moaning and groaning at the taste of me.

"Fucking delicious, just like I knew you'd be."

My hips rock uncontrollably as I rub my clit, chasing that high, needing to come so badly I can practically taste it.

"That's it, baby, I want to watch you come all over my bed. Then, I want to feel you all over my dick."

Fuck, that dirty mouth of his will be the death of me.

But the faster I circle my clit and the more I fuck myself with my fingers, the slower he jacks himself until he's squeezing the base of his cock, pain etched on the perfect features of his face.

"I'm not coming until I'm inside you."

With my hips rising off the mattress, I cry out my release. Pumping my fingers in and out until all I can do is press my throbbing nub as my cum slides down the inside of my thighs.

"Good girl. My turn."

Like a predator, Asher climbs onto the bed with me, straddling my hips before dropping to carry his weight on his forearms. He's caging me in, his breaths tickling my mouth and chin.

"They all got to touch you when I wasn't there." He places an open-mouthed kiss on my temple, tracing a sensual path down the line of my jaw before biting the tip of my chin.

His cock is nestled between my legs and I want it. I want it so fucking bad that I try to move my pelvis just so…

"Quit moving, Beautiful. I want… no, *need*, to kiss every single place they touched before I make you mine."

With my breathing elevated and my body burning with want, I force myself to give him the control he demands.

"Hmm, right here, between your neck and your jaw? It smells like fucking heaven." His tongue teases me in that exact spot, and it's all I can do not to wrap my legs around his waist and impale myself on him.

As he licks a hot, wet trail down the column of my throat, I realize he's actually going to kiss and lick and bite every part of me before he gives us what we both want.

Holy hotness, I don't know if I'll survive this sweet torture, but I'm sure as hell down to try.

Once he reaches my nipples, I moan, the touch of pain from the pressure of his teeth automatically sends my hips to grind against his. My hands slam against the mattress, fingers grabbing at the sheets so hard they immediately ache.

"Look at these perfect tits." He lavishes them with attention until I can't speak.

By the time he reaches my pussy, I'm a mess. A barely-functioning, lust-ridden mess who can only think of one thing… feeling him inside of me.

"Asher, God, please, please, please…"

I practically shake with my need for him and when his eyes meet mine, I know he knows it.

Keeping his gaze on me, he lowers his mouth and licks a path from the bottom of my opening all the way up to the clit, like he's feasting on an ice cream cone and I'm his favorite flavor on a hot summer's day.

"Damn, you really are perfect."

"Asher, please." I'm reduced to begging and I'm not sorry about it.

"Anything for you, Gorgeous."

In one smooth move, he rises up and slides his cock into my wanting pussy as he grabs hold of both of my hands and places them above my head, pinning them with one of his.

He starts off gentle, pulling out just enough to allow me to breathe before pushing his massive cock back inside, filling every inch of me. But when his lips touch mine, his rhythm accelerates.

In a matter of moments, we're nothing but tongues and teeth, one of his hands holding me steady at the hip as he controls our movements, fucking me with determination that makes every cell in my body sing with pleasure.

I'm on a sex high, reeling from the taste of him and the feel of him and the power he exudes. He's everywhere, fucking me, kissing me, holding me down. My legs wrap around his hips, my heels digging into his ass cheeks as he begins to slam into me, over and over again.

"Oh, God, Asher... I'm—"

"Wait. Hold on just a little longer."

It's fucking hard, but I do as he says, somehow compelled to follow his orders.

He slows his thrusts, languidly sliding in and out like he can do this all fucking night. At this speed, I can feel every inch of him as the agonizingly slow pace ignites every fiber in my body.

"Faster, Asher. Harder. Please."

"I don't want this to end, Briar. I want this to last an eternity."

He continues his slow torture and, just like before, my body begs for more.

Asher must reach his breaking point because his rhythm gains speed, his thrusts just a little harder, a little less calculated.

"Fuck, yes! Now, baby. Come all over my cock. Squeeze me, hard."

The permission to come is like freedom I've never known.

My chest expands with the deep inhale, the muscles in my legs freeze, and everything goes still. My entire world is held prisoner in this moment of utter bliss.

He groans above me as he comes, his forehead pressed to mine, his breath ragged.

"Holy fuck," I say, sucking in oxygen that fills my poor

lungs.

"Yeah, that," he responds, and a small smile tugs at the corner of my lips before he softly kisses me. "Don't think I'm done with you, Briar. Because I'm not even close to done."

LILY WILDHART

SEVENTEEN

Sometimes I'm not sure how I've survived two months in Serenity Falls. Especially times like tonight, where my mom and Chase think it's fun to keep summoning us back home for family dinners. Like we're one big functioning unit. Like we don't have better things to do.

I'm still not sure what makes it worse. The tension between Mom and me—we've barely spoken since her baby bomb—the tension between Travis and Chase, or the weirdness between Travis and me.

Whichever way you flip it, tonight is a big ball of awkward, and despite the amazing food Tobias keeps hurling our way, it just isn't enough for me to want to be here.

I've barely said ten words all evening beyond please and thank you to the servers when the food and drinks have been brought out. If it wasn't for needing to drive back, I'd have definitely taken the wine refills that keep being offered.

One advantage of parents who don't really parent: the rules are super lax. Well, about some things anyway.

"So, I need you both to come to the city this Saturday," Chase says out of nowhere, and I just kind of blink at him before darting my gaze back to Travis, whose jaw looks so clenched, I'm kinda worried for his teeth.

"I've got stuff going on, Dad. We're hosting the Halloween party this year. You wanted me to keep up with the younger demographic and keep them on our side. In order to actually do that, I need to be here, engaged with those exact people."

Chase puts down his cutlery and glares at Travis while I sit and watch the battle of wills between them. "It wasn't a request."

"But—" Travis starts, but Chase slams his hand down on the table, and I let out a squeak of surprise, mixed with a little fear.

I've seen enough violence to know when someone is walking a tightrope, and my shaking hands in my lap are enough of a sign to know that this could get real bad, real quick.

"But nothing." Chase's raised voice is firm and accepts no argument. I try to shove down the ridiculous response my nervous system is having to being shouted at by an authority figure, even though, technically, I'm not the one being shouted at. "This is what is needed, so you will do it. Both of you."

"Yes, sir," Travis says through his gritted teeth. Chase just nods like nothing happened and resumes eating his steak while Mom giggles.

"Well, now that that's all sorted... Briar, I wanted to talk to you about planning a baby shower."

And just like that, it's as if a bucket of icy water was poured over my head. The nerves, the shaking, all of it is drowned in numbness.

"And I'm out," I say as I push my chair back and stand.

"Briar—" my mom starts, and I hit her with a stare as cold as the shivers running down my spine.

"Absolutely not, Mom. I already told you, just no. You want to have this baby, fine, but I will not have anything to do with it." I glance at Travis, who seems to be almost angry on my behalf, but there's no way he knows the truth behind my anger.

Without another word, I put my napkin on top of my plate, grab my bag, and leave the room, ignoring the sniffles coming from my mom.

Fuck her and her fake tears.

It's only when I get down to the garage that I notice the footsteps behind me, but I ignore them and continue to the Batmobile.

"Briar, are you okay?" Travis asks as I go to open the car door. I spin to face him, wiping away the tears that have fallen down my face. He takes a step forward then stops himself, like he's remembered that he actually doesn't like me anymore.

Or maybe that he never did.

But his pause is all I need to open the door and get in the car. I pull out of the spot and drive away, leaving him standing in the rearview, watching me go.

Fuck all of this bullshit, I need happiness and puppies.

I don't even care if that means I'll probably see Travis again. I pull over to the side of the road and drop Asher and Sawyer a group message.

Me:

Can I come over?

Sawyer:

Hell yeah you can, hot stuff, you don't even need to ask.

Asher:

You know you're always welcome. What's wrong?

Me:

Just need some time with Shadow and the pack ;)

I feel the corners of my lips tilt up because I already know they're both laughing at me.

Sawyer:

Of COURSE she likes the puppies better than us.

Asher:

Hell, I *like the puppies more than us.*

Sawyer:

Fair point.

Asher:

Drive safe, we'll see you soon.

Me:

See you soon.

I put the phone away and continue the drive back to Saints U, trying to shove off the memories that try to overwhelm me on the way. Before all this, I thought I'd just about managed to deal with my grief. With my guilt.

I keep this trauma locked tight in a box way, way back in the recesses of mind. It's a box I don't prod, that I avoid touching at all costs, because even just thinking about it absolutely destroys me. After everything, I just can't.

Why did she think this was a good idea? Why would she tell me the way she did, and after everything that happened with Iris… She had to know that there was no way on this fucking earth that I was going to be okay with any of this.

I turn my music up loud enough to drown out the thoughts and focus on not crashing on the way to see the boys.

Anything to stop the memories resurfacing.

By the time I pull into their drive, my throat is a little hoarse from singing so loud, but I feel a little lighter. Like the rain cloud that loomed has gone back off into the distance.

I don't even make it out of the car before Sawyer is at the front door and bounding down the steps to see me. He has the door open before I get a chance and grins at me before pulling me from the car.

"I can walk," I say with a laugh as I clamber to get my bag. He closes the door once I have it and kisses my cheek.

"You can, but you're not going to. If I have to give up cuddle time to those damn dogs, I'm going to get some where I can."

I laugh again, snuggling into his neck. "Makes sense, 'cause once I cross this threshold, I need to be in a puppy pile."

He gallops up the stairs, making me laugh louder and cling on tighter to him, before bursting through the front door.

"Honey, I'm hoooooome," he calls out, and the dogs all rush at us.

"Put me down," I complain when he keeps me held hostage in his arms. "I already told you the rules."

"Fine, fine. Freaking woman." He kisses me softly before placing my feet on the ground. I head over to the sitting area, smiling at the lyric and music sheets scattered on the coffee table, with the guitar propped up in the corner and drop onto the giant bean bag. I glance around the space, taking in the drum set behind the stairs where it always seems to be—I guess moving a drum set isn't all that easy. It's nice seeing the small parts of their personalities spread around the house. It makes them all seem a little more human, like the guys I met that first night.

Once I get comfy, Shadow is the first to jump in my lap. He slobbers all over my face, and while it's totally gross, I kinda love it.

This is exactly what I needed.

"You guys really need to tell me the others' names," I say as Asher comes down the stairs, and three other puppies jump on me while Mom and Dad stay lying down on the other side of the room. They almost look relieved to have the puppies climbing all over someone else.

Asher drops onto the sofa closest to me, resting his leg against mine. "Well Mom is Fi, Dad is Hellion, and the little monsters around you are Shadow, Phoenix, Maverick, and Goose. Guess which two Sawyer named."

He winks at me as Sawyer calls out something undeterminable from the kitchen and I giggle.

Yep, this is definitely what I needed.

Sawyer heads in my direction and throws something at me, which I flinch and totally miss, while he laughs at me. "Sorry, should've given you a heads-up," he says with a smirk.

I look over at the package that is wrapped in some sort of halloween gift wrap, which is weird but okay. "What's that?

"Open it and you'll find out," he says as he sits down next to Asher who looks as confused as I am. "I just saw it and thought of you."

Tell me why that one line makes me feel a little nervous.

I reach over the puppies and grab the gift, which is squishy on its own, but the paper is so pretty I almost don't want to tear it. Starting tentatively to try and preserve the paper doesn't go too well, mostly because Sawyer is practically combusting. Instead, I tear into it and start laughing when I see what it is.

Pulling the black t-shirt from the paper, I lift it to show Asher.

"Holy shit, that's hilarious," he says, laughing.

"I thought so," Sawyer says proudly.

The giant ramen bowl with the most adorable little smiley face on it, with the caption that reads 'Send Noods' is possibly my new favorite funny.

"Thank you," I say to him, grinning widely.

Yeah, time with these guys was definitely what I needed.

I stir and realize I've been asleep on the beanbag with the puppies for God only knows how long, but when I hear their voices, I decide to keep my eyes closed.

"So you were what was up with her earlier, huh?" Sawyer asks, and I realize that Travis must finally be home.

"Probably, but it was most likely her mom bringing up the baby again." He sighs and I hear them all shuffle around before everything goes quiet as one of the puppies adjusts in my lap.

"Do you know why it's triggering her so badly?" Asher asks, and a part of me wants to stop this conversation right the fuck now. The other part of me, the part that's keeping my eyes closed, my breathing steady, and my body still, wants to know what he knows.

I wonder if Mom told them about her?

"I know bits," Travis says. "But that's her story to tell."

Huh… who would've thought that Travis was going to be the one to keep my secrets?

"I can appreciate that," Asher says as my heart races in my chest.

"Does she know you know?" Cole asks, and I hear someone take a drink of something before glass touches down on something hard.

"I doubt it. We're not exactly best buddies."

"And whose fault is that, dick bag?" Sawyer chastises Travis, and I dare to crack open one eye, just a smidge, because I want to see.

Curiosity really is going to kill this cat one day.

The four of them are standing around the island in the kitchen space. Travis's shirt is ruffled, his hair is a mess, and he looks the messiest I think I've seen him. Cole looks exhausted, wearing nothing but gym shorts, and the twins are still just casual like they were earlier.

Fi is sitting at Asher's feet while Hellion stands by Sawyer.

They definitely paint a picture, and just like that my fingers itch to draw this scene out. The four of them looking as relaxed as I've seen them since the first night I met them.

"I'm aware it's on me," Travis grunts, running a hand through his hair. "But could you imagine if my dad knew I'd banged her? That I want her just as bad as you idiots? He'd fucking string us all up, bleed us out, and then make out like his rivals did it, just to cash in on the sympathy vote. It's better this way."

"You're an idiot," Sawyer argues, but Cole steps in.

"Just be thankful that your parents accept the two of you dating the same girl for now. But you know this can't last. We agreed that night to share her, but then everything changed. And then *you* fucking claimed her in front of everyone at that dinner. Now none of us get to have her. Not really. So Travis is right. This way is better."

Sawyer scoffs at him, but Cole shakes his head. "Better for her, dickhead, not for us."

"Oh," is all Sawyer says, like he hadn't considered the consequences. Considering the way his mind works, I doubt that's true, all of them always seem to be four steps ahead of everyone else on campus, but I guess everyone has blindspots.

I feel a little gross eavesdropping on their conversation after that little revelation so I make a show of waking up and stretching. The puppies do not seem happy with my movement, but by the time I'm sitting up, they're all looking at me.

"Oops?" I say with a shrug, wiping at my mouth as discreetly as I can in case I drooled in my sleep. "What's going on? You all look so serious."

"I was just telling them about Dad's mandated trip for us to the city. The boys are going to come with us so we don't kill each other," Travis says with a grim smile, that cold stare that he seems to reserve just for me back on his face.

But now I know that it's little more than a mask, and I'm not sure how I feel about that.

"Oh? I guess you need as much security as you can get," I tease, and he rolls his eyes.

He puts down the bottle of beer he's been drinking and runs a hand through his hair. "I'm crashing," is all he says before he walks away and heads up the stairs.

"Me too," Cole adds. "I've got practice at six."

He follows Travis up the stairs, leaving me with the twins. "I suppose I should get back to the dorm," I say, checking my phone to see a message from Penn saying she's staying with Connor tonight.

"We should talk before you do," Asher says seriously, and the two of them come and sit on the sofas near me.

"Sure, what's up?" I ask, my stomach churning.

"It was brought to our attention that Sawyer claiming you in front of our parents might have made you uncomfortable, especially since we haven't actually discussed anything," Asher says, and Sawyer rolls his eyes.

"I was excited, so shoot me."

"Don't tempt me," Asher teases.

"Ash…" I start bringing their attention back to me.

"Right. So our parents are aware that we both like you, and for some reason, since we're twins, they don't seem to object to us being with the same girl. That is, if you want that. I know Sawyer told you that the three of them agreed to share you that first night when I wasn't there… but Travis and Cole… well, that's for them to input. What I'm trying to say, and saying very, very badly, is that we want you to be ours. Publicly. Nothing hidden."

My eyes go wide as my heart beats in my chest.

Is this what I want?

Yes, stupid, say yes.

It might not be conventional, or even close to what I was expecting them to say, but I nod. "Yes," I say, the word little more than a breath.

"Good," Sawyer says before pouncing on me as the puppies scramble. "I say we make this official."

He kisses me and I swear I see stars. He pulls back and jumps to his feet, holding out a hand for me. I take it as Asher takes my other. I should probably hesitate when they lead me upstairs, but I don't.

I'm not going to run from this, even if it means I eventually run head first into a brick wall. Being with them makes me feel things I never thought I would, and if that means that I get burned at the end of it…

Well, so be it.

Today's trip to the city has been something of a nightmare, except for the fact that Travis seems to have dialed back his douchebaggery to almost-zero levels.

We left his dad's campaign office after having a million and one photos taken, and the guys and I have been out exploring the city since.

It was supposed to just be me and the twins, but I think the other two needed the escape and I'm not about to be queen bitch and tell them no.

To be honest, it's been fun just being back in the city and knowing that I'm faceless here. Even the guys are. Cole, less so, thanks to his dad, but people have left us alone for the most part. Darkness has fallen and there is just something magical about the city at night.

We're heading to get my favorite Tonkotsu when I hear a phone ringing to my right, followed by what sounds like a struggle from the alley we're walking past.

Normally I'd walk on by, because well, single girl in the city. But I have four burly guys with me and I'm not about to keep walking this time.

"Hey! What's going on down there?" I call out when Sawyer

pulls out his phone and turns on the flashlight. I spot a girl on the ground, bruises already starting to form around her neck.

We rush forward to help her, but Sawyer reaches her first.

He crouches down in front of her and I follow suit, 'cause if she was just attacked, me bringing four guys with me probably isn't going to make her feel better.

"Holy shit, are you okay?" Sawyer asks her, and she nods, but I don't believe her at all.

"We heard a phone ringing by the entrance then noticed you down here. What a fucking scumbag. Are you okay? Can you move? Do you want us to call anyone?" I ask, taking in just how messed up she looks, but then she gazes at me like I'm her freaking guardian angel.

"Thank you. So much," she says, her voice hoarse, her smile tight. I know that smile. I wear that smile. She's hurting but she doesn't want the world to see. Especially five strangers who found her in this position. "Honestly, thank you. The fucker's gone now, but I can't tell you how grateful I am."

She pushes against the wall to stand, and I stand with her, realizing the four of them have formed a sort of semi-circle at my back. Like my own wall of protectors.

If I wasn't so focused on her, I'd think back to the conversation I overheard on Thursday, but right now, there are more pressing issues.

I try to make sure the woman is okay, but it's hard in the dark. That's when I see the mess of her face and reach forward to push some of the hair from her face. "Holy shit, your face!" I blurt before I can stop myself. "Sorry, that was rude, you're bleeding."

"You might need some stitches," Asher says from behind me. The joys of having a second year med student with us.

"Is it bad, Ash?" I ask him, and he frowns at me before looking her over more closely and shaking his head. I loosen a breath, because thank God. "He's right though, that looks nasty. Can we help?"

"I just need to find my keys and phone so I can get home. I've got a first-aid kit," she says, rubbing a hand across her forehead, wincing when her fingers brush against her bleeding eyebrow.

"Are these yours?" Sawyer asks, holding up a phone and keys. I didn't even see him disappear to find them. I guess I was too focused on the girl.

"Yes! Oh my God! Where did you find them?" she asks, taking them from him and clutching them against her chest like they're her dearest possessions. Something in me resonates with her. She might be older than me, maybe by like five or six years, I'd guess, but that darkness in her, the pain in her eyes, the desperation wafting from her in waves...

That much I understand.

This city is beautiful, but it's also dark and fucking disgusting, and if you let it, it will take everything from you.

"The keys were a few feet from the ringing phone that

caught our attention. Good thing it did and that we aren't the kind of assholes who'd just walk on by," Sawyer responds, and she nods. I step back to give her some more space and the guys all seem to follow my lead. Travis and Cole have been surprisingly quiet, but then, they're probably chastising me mentally for running down a dark alley.

Fun times. Pretty sure I'll hear about that later.

"Thank you, guys. Really," she says, moving to head out of the alley. I follow, which means the brooding hulk of man meat behind me follows too.

"Do you want us to walk you back to your apartment?" Cole asks, his voice low, and I realize he's been quiet because he's angry. He probably doesn't want to scare her, but I know what he sounds like usually, and right now, he's almost menacing even though I'm sure he's not trying to be.

"No. I'm good. It's only two minutes from here. I want to stop at the store on the way before it closes," she answers as we reach the alley entrance, and I realize we're at Broadway Alley.

And here was me thinking this part of town wasn't the worst.

"Are you sure? We don't mind, we've got time," I say, putting my hand on her arm and regretting it instantly when she winces. "Sorry, I didn't mean…"

"It's fine," she responds too quickly, but I get it. I've been her.

"Do you want to take my number for the police report?" I ask, pulling my phone out before she can say no.

Silence stretches between us as I watch a feast of emotions run riot on her face.

And before she says anything, I already know she's not going to report this. Which, again, I understand. I just hope she has a decent circle to lean on rather than struggling alone.

Her tight smile reappears on her face, that mask of hers firmly back in place. "Sure. Here's my card. Send me a text with your details and I'm sure they'll be in touch once I've reported it."

Her words are cold, but I don't hold it against her. I put a hand back to keep Sawyer quiet when I feel him bristle behind me. Apparently, he doesn't get her being so cold. I can't imagine any of them can, but they haven't been her.

They haven't lived this life.

I have.

"Are you sure you're okay?" I ask again, a little more firm because she really should get checked out. She nods, some of the coldness falling away.

"Just a little shaken up. But I'll be fine, I promise."

With an awkward wave, she thanks us again and walks away, and I can't help the twist in my stomach that something terrible is going to happen to her if she doesn't report tonight.

"Well, that was an interesting end to the day," Sawyer says, his laugh breaking some of the tension. Then he winces, as if realizing what he said. "I didn't mean it like that."

"It's fine," I tell him, trying not to smile. "You didn't mean to be an insensitive dick about a girl getting attacked."

"I swear I didn't," he stresses, and I kiss his cheek.

"I know." I turn to face the others and notice Travis's face of thunder.

"What the hell were you thinking? You could have gotten yourself killed running down that alley like that!" he chastises—and there it is as predicted—running a hand through his dark hair. It's almost like he cares.

"But I didn't, and we helped her. It seems like it was worth it to me," I say with a shrug. "Now, are we going to get food? I'm starving."

I don't wait for them to answer me, I just turn and head in the direction we were going before, knowing that I definitely haven't heard the end of it when Travis's voice sounds behind me. "Briar, for fuck's sake…"

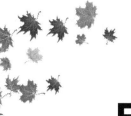

EIGHTEEN

"You sure it's okay for me to do this?" I ask Asher for like the fifteenth time.

He laughs at me, pinching the bridge of his nose before putting his glasses back on. "Yes, Briar. You can add stuff to the house. You're staying there often enough, but also, I want to see you more even when you're not there, so add whatever the fuck you want if it means you can come back more."

Since I've been spending so much time at the house, he wanted to add some touches of comfort... Which I've decided mostly consists of making sure there is real food in the fridge that isn't leftover take out and some actual hot chocolate. Except, I still kind of feel like I'm overstepping.

We walk through Target—which is hilarious because I'm convinced Asher has never stepped foot in a Target in his *life*—

him pushing my cart, while I *uhm* and *argh* over every single thing I kind of want.

But he keeps saying it's fine, and I'm getting a little better at using the money Chase made available to me—especially after a phone call from my mom telling me he was offended I had barely touched the allowance set up for me, which is apparently a thing.

I stare dreamily at the different syrups that are available, and decide to splurge. I grab a peppermint, because duh, and a cherry one, dropping them in the cart before adding marshmallows, whipped cream, and chocolate curls, along with a cute little tray to make everything look pretty on and jars for storage.

Apparently, today I'm really embracing my basic bitch self.

Once I grab the few things I want, we browse, because I've always said you don't come to Target knowing what you want, Target tells you what you need. So obviously I get things to make s'mores too, because ever since I saw the fire pit out in their backyard, I've been craving them.

When we reach the fall decorations, I swear my heart about stops.

Yes, yes, I know… but I love fall. It adds to my basic bitch self, but I've never been able to decorate for fall before… and there's that huge fireplace in the lounge at their house… and so much counter space.

I stare longingly at it, but keep moving.

"Briar…" Asher starts, holding the cart still. "Do you want

to decorate?"

His eyes are crinkled at the edges where he's trying not to laugh at me and I feel my cheeks heat.

"No, it's fine," I say, wistfully staring at the adorable freaking little ghost display that is practically calling my name.

"Briar. Do. You. Want. To. Decorate?"

"I mean, kinda. I've never been able to before, but it's not my house."

He rolls his eyes at me and turns the cart back to the start of the decoration aisle. "Well, it's mine, and I say we decorate, so let's do it."

"Really?" I ask, not wanting to get my hopes up, but really, on the inside, my inner child is screaming with excitement.

Not to be all woe-is-me, but I've never been able to decorate for anything. Well, except for the odd Christmas, but after everything that happened… yeah, Christmas is not a fun time. But decorating for fall, and Halloween, and enjoying spooky season?

I am *here for it.*

"Yes, really. Honestly, I don't think I've seen you this excited about anything other than the puppies, and I like that I've been the one to give you that joy twice, so if this is what you want to do, we'll do it. I'll even rope Sawyer into helping us actually decorate once we're home." He pulls his phone from his pocket and I assume he shoots Sawyer a message when he taps on his screen, but I'm too excited trying not to bounce up and down about the prospect of what we're going to do.

Asher laughs as I coo over garlands, string lights, little ghosts and pumpkins. I even find ghost and pumpkin outfits for the puppies, which are absolutely happening on Halloween.

"We should've grabbed a bigger cart," Asher laughs when we're at the point where I realize I've gone overboard.

We have wreaths, jars, a centerpiece for the dining table, as well as just a *ton* of other stuff, and when I look at the cart, I chew on my bottom lip.

"I should probably put some of this back, huh?"

Asher raises his brows at me before he realizes I'm serious. "Don't you dare. This is fun. I've never decorated anything. Mom and Dad have always had people do it for us. I'm looking forward to this."

"Are you sure?" I hate how weird I feel about doing this when it's something I really want to do. Guilt shouldn't be a thing, especially when Chase *wants* me to spend his money, and Asher *wants* to decorate, yet, it floods me.

"Yes, I'm sure, you crazy woman. Come here," he says, looping his fingers in my belt and pulling me flush against him. "I want you to be happy. And this makes you happy. So it's happening. Stop fighting it. You haven't told us much of anything about your past, but I see the sadness in your eyes way too often. Today, I've seen you smile more than I have in the entire time I've known you and it's beautiful. So this is happening."

"Okay," I say breathlessly before he gently kisses me.

He releases me and takes hold of the cart again. "Now, are we missing anything?"

"Probably," I say with a small chuckle.

He shrugs and takes my hand, putting it under his as he pushes the cart to the check out. "Well, if we did then we'll just have to come back. Shopping with you is the most fun I've had in ages."

And just like that, I fall a little bit harder for Asher St. Vincent.

"Girl, you look FIRE!" Penn squeaks as I exit the bathroom, trying not to look as self-conscious as I feel right now. Don't get me wrong, I love my curves, and I've been expanding my wardrobe choices since starting at Saints U, the occasional crop top has been odd but fun.

But this...

"Penn, I am never letting you be in charge of our Halloween costumes ever again."

She rolls her eyes as she toddles over to me on the stilts she has for shoes. "Don't be so dramatic, B. You look amazing. And look, we match. Zombie cheerleaders for the win. Now let me finish your freaking makeup so we can get going."

I'm not going to deny that she looks amazing, but having

this much skin on show at a party, especially after the last one just makes me feel a little gross. But the party tonight is at the guys' house, and ever since Saturday, Travis and Cole seem to have called some sort of ceasefire on their douchebag status.

I wonder if Travis knows I heard what he said.

Or maybe it's because I'm technically now official with the twins and he doesn't want any more issues with his friends.

Whatever it is, I'm not going to question it, even if it does have me at a disadvantage. Grumpy asshole Travis I know how to deal with. Kind of. But this new, not-quite-friendly Travis... nope, definitely have no clue how to deal with him.

And Cole, well, he's a little easier. He was never outright cold or cruel, just distant. Now he's just a little less distant than he was before, and he'll actually acknowledge my existence.

Though I think a lot of it has come from the trip on Saturday. I got some insight into their world, more so than I have up to now at least, and the pressures that Travis and Cole must have lived with their entire lives...

It's different for the twins. Sure, they're from money, but their parents' expectations are a little different. They didn't push Ash into medicine like his mom, or Sawyer into business, despite the fact their dad is a high-flying defense attorney.

But Travis has been in the limelight his entire life, the same as Cole. From what I can make out, their futures have been laid out for them since they were born. Asher told me the music thing is just something they do for fun. Which, considering how talented they are, blows my mind. He said it's the same with football for Cole. It's what he wants to do, but he knows he has no real future in it because his dad has other plans.

I can't imagine growing up with that sort of pressure.

"Yo!" Penn squeaks, snapping her fingers in my face. "Earth to Briar."

"Sorry, just a lot going on in my head with this party," I say, giving her a small smile before popping a cherry Lifesaver in my mouth, savoring the sweetness. My little anchor to reality.

She frowns at me, her hand dropping from her hip. "I didn't even think… are you sure you'll be okay going tonight?"

"I'm fine," I say, waving her off. "Just being dramatic like always. Zombie me up."

I give her the best, biggest grin I can muster and drop onto the stool at the dresser she's set up for all this makeup. "Just not too much zombie grossness," I say, and she rolls her eyes, back to her bright self.

"As if I would. We're going for hot undead, not gross undead."

I laugh as she practically attacks me with her makeup kit, but I don't complain. Penn's been nothing but good to me since that first hiccup of ours, so I vowed to myself to be nice. A girl needs a friend, even if it's just one.

And the boys don't count, because well, penis parade.

Once she's done, my phone is blowing up every few minutes from Sawyer asking how much longer I'm going to be.

Anyone would think I was late. And I mean, I am, but who turns up to a party before ten anyway?

"Your boys have it bad, girl. Did I give you props again yet for managing to bag them both after the way you all met?" She wags her brows at me and I laugh at her.

"You did not, but noted. You joker."

"Why thank you," she says, doing a weird bow thing. "Now get your shit so we can go."

"I've got everything," I tell her, sliding my phone into my bra and zipping my keys into the tiny skirt of this freaking cheer outfit.

At least it has the tiny shorts underneath. It's not much, but it's something. My ass feels like it's hanging out of the skirt, and don't even get me started on how obscene my boobs look in this top.

"Good," Penn responds, pushing a set of pompoms at me. "Then let's go rock the shit out of this Halloween. Get us some sugar." She winks and I bark out a laugh.

One thing is for certain, at least when Penn is around, life isn't dull.

"Not going to lie, you're rocking the dead cheerleader look," Sawyer murmurs in my ear as he leads me up the stairs of the house, Asher just a step ahead of us.

The tequila I drank tonight has me a little tipsy and more than a little brave, but the thought of a threeway with these two has butterflies taking flight in my stomach. I mean, don't get me wrong, I totally made out with them both the last time they got me in a bedroom, but it didn't go any further than them getting me off. This is definitely more than that and I'm not sure if I'm more nervous or excited.

The music is still playing and the house is packed, but one of them has been at my side all night to make sure I'm not alone. They've encouraged me to let loose, to prove to myself that I can and that things would be okay.

I trust them, so I decided why not? And now I'm tripping over thin air.

Go figure.

Not going to lie though, I am so ready to get these torture devices off of my feet. I don't know where Penn found them, but never again.

Her and Connor left a while ago, so I don't have to feel guilty about ditching her either. I don't have to worry about anything except what I've agreed to. Not like this is my first group session, but it's my first with both of them, and since they're my, like, kind-of-boyfriends I guess, it just feels like... more.

Asher leads us down the hall to his room, and I can't say that him dressed as Sam Winchester isn't doing it for me. Though Sawyer dressed as Dean Winchester isn't exactly hard on the eyes either.

When they found out about my love for Supernatural, they thought this would be fun.

Not going to lie, it totally is.

Sawyer closes the door once we're all inside and I swear my heart stops when I find them both staring at me like I'm the answer to all of their prayers.

"Strip for us, Beautiful," Asher demands, and I bite down on my lip as they both take a seat on the sofa opposite the bed.

I pull down the zipper on the barely-there crop top and drop it to the ground at their feet, before reaching up and loosening my hair from its confines until the waves drop down to my mid-back.

"Fuck," Sawyer groans as he leans forward, elbows on his knees. "So freaking stunning. Every goddamn inch of you."

His words bolster my wavering confidence and I turn to give them my back, showing off my ass as I bend over and push down the skirt and tiny shorts, leaving my lacy thong in place. I kick off my stilettos and lift one leg to the bed before taking off one stocking, then the next.

"Fuck this," Sawyer grunts, jumping to his feet. Before I can blink, his hands are on my waist and his lips are on mine. "You taste like cherries and tequila," he groans without really stopping the kiss.

He tastes just like he looks, fun and untamed. Our kiss is wild with want as our tongues battle for control and our teeth nip at each other without a second thought. My arms wrap around his neck as his body comes flush against my practically naked one.

I should feel off balance being the only one of us naked, but they make me feel safe so I don't. I also know that if I said stop, they'd stop.

But no fucking way am I doing that.

Especially when my skin heats with Asher's presence as his lips trail down the back of my neck. One of his hands slides from behind me, up my stomach, and lands on my hardened nipples.

"I think our little vixen is eager for us, brother." Asher's breath tickles my shoulder as he speaks, my skin erupting with goosebumps with every touch of his hot mouth.

"Well, who are we to deny her?" Sawyer says playfully as his lips brush against mine, before dropping to his knees and kissing his way down my body.

Asher moves his free hand onto my other breast, squeezing and pinching my nipples as he peppers me with kisses from shoulder to shoulder, occasionally biting down, and I know I'm going to have marks but I can't find it in me to care. It feels too good.

Meanwhile, Sawyer's gaze is fixed on mine as he runs a finger through my wetness and brings it to his mouth, moaning his approval. "Hmm, I could eat your pussy all fucking day long, Beautiful."

Grabbing his t-shirt at the back of his neck, he pulls the cotton over his head and throws it to the side, his torso and abs on display for my viewing pleasure. How can a man be this perfect? More importantly, how is it possible there are two of them?

"Sit on my face, Briar. Time to get my fill." Asher rips my thong right off just before Sawyer's mouth latches on to my pussy, his big, strong hands cupping my ass cheeks as he licks and sucks my clit, and I swear I see freaking stars. His tongue prods at my opening as his pinky fingers slide across to the crack of my ass, playing with my hole without actually entering.

I reach back to wrap an arm around Asher's neck while my other holds on to Sawyer's blond strands. I control his movements as much as I can with my fingers tightly wrapped in his hair as I ride his face.

"Make her come, Sawyer." Asher doesn't need many words to spur his brother on, and Sawyer doesn't need telling twice. His tongue laps at me in the best way, his teeth nipping at my clit, his fingers pushing just a little inside my asshole. All the while, Asher's fingers are pinching my nipples harder and harder, his kisses turning to sucking, my skin burning with the heat of them both.

"Oh, God. Yes, yes, yes!" I hurtle into my orgasm, but Sawyer doesn't let up.

"That's it, baby. Give it to him. Come all over his face," Asher encourages, and just as my pelvis rocks into Sawyer's mouth, he pushes both pinkies inside my ass deep enough to make my orgasm erupt even harder. I'm a shaking, trembling mess as Sawyer's fingers pull out, and in their place I can feel how fucking hard Asher is behind his jeans, rubbing against my ass.

It's all too much, yet, not nearly enough.

"On the bed, face down, ass up." Asher whispers the command in my ear before turning me to face the four-poster and gently guiding me to the mattress.

Behind me, I hear the rustling of fabric and, without even looking, I smile, knowing I'll get to see them naked again.

Oh no, what a shame… twin nakedness. Yeah, my life is the worst.

On my hands and knees, I lower my chest to the mattress and present them with my bare ass as high as it'll go, wiggling it just to tease them a little, thanks to the liquid courage that is tequila. I peek behind my shoulder and almost come again at the feral look in their eyes.

I can't help but wonder what it is they're thinking and a wave of self doubt hits me.

My attention is refocused on this moment when a hand connects with my ass cheek, making me yelp in surprise.

"Your mind doesn't wander, Gorgeous, it stays here with us." It's Asher's voice I hear, firm with a hint of tenderness, like he knows exactly where my mind went.

Sawyer kneels at the head of the bed, right in front of me,

lifting my face off the linen, and positions it mere inches from his insanely hard cock.

I lick my lips, the urge to taste him overwhelming. "Soon, baby. Soon." His promise only makes me want him more.

Behind me, Asher runs a hand down the expanse of my back, over my hips, and across my ass cheeks before spearing my pussy with two fingers.

"Fuck, she's wet." He groans as he slides his fingers in and out of me and I whimper at the touch.

With my thighs on either side of Asher's legs, he removes his fingers and positions himself at my core, his cock leisurely gliding up and down my slit, the tip playing with my clit. When Sawyer fists my hair and pulls my head back, I look up at him and have zero doubts that what he sees is unbridled need. It's exactly what I see reflected back at me in his vibrant green eyes.

"Take me."

His grin is devilish at best, pure heat at worst. Nostrils flaring, I can tell he's barely holding onto his control. His gaze darts to his brother behind me and without a single word, they both enter me at once.

Sawyer's cock slides into my mouth as Asher pushes his dick into my pussy. It's like they're inching inside me at the same speed, making sure I get the full effect of every inch that rubs against my flesh. Once they're both filling me to the brink, I moan around a mouthful of cock and revel in Sawyer's grunts.

"Keep doing that, baby, and I won't last long enough for

you to gag on my dick."

"Fuck, her pussy is so hot and tight. It's gonna be torture not to come." Asher's words only spur me on. I want them both to lose control. I want to be the reason they lose their fucking minds.

Asher is the first to pull out while Sawyer only pushes deeper, testing my gag reflex and holding my head steady with a fistful of my hair, keeping my mouth on his dick and cutting off my air supply until my eyes water.

"That's it, baby. Choke on it." I blink, letting the tears fall down my cheeks, the salty liquid landing on my lips and mixing with the musky taste of Sawyer.

Asher thrusts a little harder, and a little deeper, while his brother slides out of my mouth except for the very tip, giving me time and space to breathe—to suck in much-needed air— before slamming back in.

"Goddamn, her throat is tight." I gag a little, but smile around his cock as he curses my deviant little move.

Asher fucks me like it's the last time he'll get the chance, and the only thing keeping me from falling over are their strategically placed hands holding me in place.

Sawyer's holding my head, my hands braced on either side of his knees, while Asher's fingers are crushing bruises into my flesh with every thrust of his hips.

When Asher leans in, two fingers on my clit, I realize just how close I am to climax, just how much these two have me ready to lose all control.

My eyes widen and my throat expands as my fingers clench the sheets and bliss rips through me. I silently scream around Sawyer's dick while my pussy contracts around Asher's cock.

"Fucking hell."

"Jesus fucking Christ."

They both curse at the domino effect their actions are causing. And just when I thought things couldn't get any filthier, they both pull out at the exact same time and give me more.

Sawyer's pumping his cock, once then a second time, before he aims the tip at my face and covers me with his cum. Behind me, Asher is thrusting two fingers inside of me while he empties himself all over my ass.

My arms and legs shake as I struggle to stay upright after everything, and I hear Asher disappear before coming back with a wet cloth, which he uses on my face, then my ass. Sawyer pulls me into his arms and cradles me against his chest moments before I hear the shower.

"Shower before sleep, Beautiful," Asher murmurs, and I realize my eyes have drifted closed. I let him pull me from the bed to the bathroom, with Sawyer close behind me.

"Don't think we're done with you yet, Sunshine," Sawyer smiles wickedly at me as I step beneath the spray, the chill of it shaking the sleep from me. I grin back at him as the water glides down my body and I run my hands over my bare flesh.

"If you think you can go again, then show me."

Their eyes flash and they stalk toward me at once. I let out a squeal when Asher reaches me first and pins me against the tiles, his hand on my throat with the best kind of pressure. "Oh, you are going to regret that, Beautiful."

My eyes brighten with challenge. "Oh, I doubt it."

I wake up to my phone pinging like crazy, and it takes me a second to get my bearings from being wedged between the twins.

Yeah, definitely not the worst way I've woken up.

When my phone starts ringing again, Sawyer groans loudly. "If someone doesn't fuck off, I'm going to murder them. Don't they know it's a Saturday?"

"Sorry," I mutter as I try to extract myself from them, but Sawyer loops his arms around me and holds me tight.

"Didn't say you could move, Sunshine."

"Well, it's either I move or my phone keeps ringing," I counter, and he grumbles something under his breath I can't quite make out.

"Fine," he eventually grunts, rolling over slightly and grabbing my phone from the bedside table and handing it to me. "Tell them to fuck off."

"You're supposed to be the joyful one here," I tease, kissing the tip of his nose. "Not me, I haven't even had coffee yet."

"Who needs coffee when you have dick? Anyway, I am joyful, but someone is killing my joy by disturbing our time."

"Are you two going to keep talking or is someone going to answer the freaking phone," Asher complains from behind me. I giggle softly.

I check the screen and see Penn's name just before the line disconnects.

Seven missed calls.

Shit.

I sit upright and without me even saying anything, both of the guys are instantly alert.

"What's wrong?" Asher asks, scrubbing a hand down his face.

I frown at him and call Penn back. "Don't know yet."

She answers almost immediately, screeching down the phone. "What is the point in having a goddamn phone if you don't answer it? I swear on all that's holy, I nearly came to that house and beat down the goddamn door, Briar."

"Calm, Penn. What's wrong?"

She takes a deep breath and I hear someone crying in the room with her, followed by a low soothing voice.

"You need to get to the dorm building. Now."

My heart races in my chest. She sounds scared.

"Penn, what happened?" I ask again as I climb from the bed and start rooting around in Asher's stuff to get some sort of clothing that isn't undead cheerleader.

"It's Serena, B... she's, oh shit. She's dead."

LILY WILDHART

NINETEEN

"What the fuck do you mean she's dead?" Travis growls as I rush around the kitchen searching for my shoes.

"I'm not sure how else I can say it," I deadpan, shock still overwhelming me. Once I got off the phone with Penn, I told the twins what she'd said, then scrambled to get ready.

"I only have fucking stilts," I grumble to myself, wishing I'd planned ahead and brought an overnight bag.

Way to focus on the important things, Briar.

"You ready?" Asher asks as he rushes down the stairs, Sawyer and Cole right behind him.

I blink at him, realizing that everyone's coming with me, and nod. I don't have the energy to argue about having an entire fucking entourage of people with me right now. I just want to get to Penn and find out what the hell happened to our friend.

Everyone's watching me and it takes a second to realize that they're all watching me like I'm about to break.

Ha.

They have no idea.

"Yeah, I'm ready."

"I'm driving," Travis states, his tone brokering no room for argument. I don't really care who drives as long as I get to the dorm quickly.

I'm ushered outside by Sawyer and end up in the back seat of Travis's Range Rover squished between the twins. One thing I will give Travis, he doesn't fuck around in a crisis. He's calm, level headed, and drives like a bat out of hell.

Before I even get time to really think over the fact that Serena is dead, we're pulling up outside the dorm building. There are police everywhere, but we manage to get inside and up to my room after answering a dozen questions and proving that my room is my room.

Pretty sure we would've had more questions if Cole and Travis weren't with us. They really are like royalty in Serenity Falls.

"There you are!" Penn gushes when I enter our room. Connor is sitting on her bed, where I'm guessing she just jumped up from. I hug her back and the guys filter into the room around us. All of a sudden the space feels a little suffocating.

"What happened?" I ask her as I break the hug.

"I'm not entirely sure yet. I got home and saw all the police, and then I found Charli crying in the back of an ambulance. They've blocked off where they found her body behind the building, but that's all I know so far."

I squeeze her hand, watching as she swallows and blinks, obviously trying not to cry.

I look over at Travis who already has his phone in his hand. He and Cole seem to have a silent conversation and both stand. "We'll go see what we can find out."

"Thank you," I say sincerely, though I have no idea how they're going to find anything out. Then again, royalty.

"I need to go and see Charli," Penn mumbles as she starts putting clothes into a duffle. "I'm going to stay with Connor for a few nights."

"Okay," I respond, nodding.

I should probably feel something, especially since the shock has worn off, but I've always dealt with death a little weird.

Well, ever since Iris anyway.

Nope, not going there right now, Briar.

She hugs me before she leaves with Connor, who smiles sadly at me before the door closes behind them, leaving me with the twins.

"I should change," I say, heading into my closet and grabbing a pair of jeans, a t-shirt, some underwear, and a pair of Converse. I showered last night, so I don't worry about that and just get changed, not bothering with the screen since they've both seen me very much naked anyway.

"You're coming to stay with us," Asher says, matter-of-factly. "At least for a few days until Penn is back."

I nod, knowing that it's not worth the argument, and grab my suitcase from under the bed, throwing in an array of clothes. "You sure the other's aren't going to mind? I can just go back and stay with Mom and Chase."

"Don't be ridiculous," Sawyer scoffs, cracking his knuckles. "There's no way you're staying in that museum of a house. Not when you can stay with us, be close by for class, and where we can make sure you're safe."

Warm fuzzies fill my chest, but I refuse to trust them. Warm fuzzies usually just lead to a swift kick in the girl parts followed by a lot of tears.

Absolutely not.

Wow, my brain is fully trying to not think about Serena and what happened to her.

Asher's phone pings and he stands, leaving the room to take the call, and once we're alone, Sawyer corners me, stopping me from packing, wrapping his arms around me.

"Tell me what's going on in that beautiful mind of yours."

I shrug and rest my head on his chest. "Honestly, nothing really."

"She was your friend, Briar. I mean, you guys weren't exactly living in each other's pockets, but you were still friends."

"I know." I sigh. "I just… I don't know, maybe I'm still processing."

The lie slips from my mouth far too easily, but he won't understand. Most people don't. Everyone grieves in their own way, and I... well, death just doesn't really phase me anymore. But when you tell people that, they look at you like you need a shrink, and despite not wanting the warm fuzzies when I'm around him, I don't want him to look at me like that.

"Okay. Well, let's finish getting you packed, and then we can head home. I'm going to go and find the others. You okay up here on your own?"

I nod, smiling at him. "I'll be fine, there's police everywhere. Not like someone's going to gank me in here right now."

He laughs at me, shaking his head. "You really have watched too much Supernatural, you know."

I scoff in mock horror. "Blasphemy. That, right there. Just disgusting, no such thing was ever true."

He laughs again and kisses my forehead before heading out of the room. "You're crazy, but I kinda like crazy."

He winks before he disappears, and once the door is closed and I'm alone, I take a deep breath. Moving my suitcase over to Penn's bed, I lie down on mine and just take a minute to collect myself. Living with the guys for a few days will be fine.

I can totally manage that.

Especially if the alternative is potential death.

Though, for all we truly know, Serena wasn't murdered and that could just be the whispers of Saints U.

Anything is possible.

I get comfy, tucking my arm under my pillow, just to rest for a minute before the chaos I know is likely to come over the next few days, and feel something beneath my pillow.

Sitting up, I lift the pillow and find a piece of paper with my name scrawled on it. Yeah, that's not ominous at all.

I pick it up, my eyes darting around the room like I'm being watched, before unfolding the paper.

Roses are Red
Violets are Blue
Next time I won't miss
And it'll be you.

Three days turned into a week, which turned into three, and now it's almost December and Penn still isn't back in the dorm, which means I'm still not back in the dorm. Charli dropped out and went back home, which totally sucks, but I get it. She and Serena were friends long before they came here.

Add to that, Serena's death has been ruled a homicide and well… everyone's losing their damn minds.

I get it, bad shit happens. Lord knows I know that well.

Which is why I'm currently lying on my front on the floor of their living room, surrounded by puppies and trying to study for the upcoming test Professor Crawford told us we've got tomorrow in not just Intro to Psych, but also Abnormal Psych.

What a fun freaking day for me. So I came back here after class, let myself in with the spare key Travis begrudgingly handed over, and got to my study puppy pile like my life depended on it.

I pop another cherry Lifesaver in my mouth, the sugar the only sustenance I've had today besides coffee, which probably isn't the best brain food, but it makes me happy.

The door opens and Cole comes in, the corners of his lips tilting up when he sees me. "I figured you'd be back here. I brought coffee."

"Yes! Life saver. I've been too lazy to get up." I grin at him and do the whole grabby hands thing, which just makes him laugh and shake his head as he brings me the java awesomeness.

"I'm sure the fact that Shadow is asleep on your ass has nothing to do with you not moving…" He chuckles as he crouches to give me the drink.

These last few weeks he's warmed up a lot, and when it's just been the two of us, which it has been most Tuesday afternoons 'cause the others are all in class, we've had time to actually hang out and get to know each other a little.

I mean, he's not exactly talkative, so it's not like I know his life story, but I'm comfortable with him in his silence.

"It has nothing to do with that sweet little demon," I say, sticking my tongue out at him as he takes his bag off his back and sits down with us. Fi and Hellion come out of their beds and sit with him once he's comfortable and I narrow my eyes at the little traitors.

The puppies are totally all team me, but those two have been much harder to bring over to my side. They're loyal to the boys, I'll give them that.

"Have you told the others yet?" he asks, glancing up at me after we've both been quiet for about twenty minutes.

Dammit, he's never going to let it drop.

Cole was the one who came back to my room first the day Serena died, so he saw the note, but he agreed to let me tell the others in my own time. I still think it's a sick joke, but I also don't want to deal with it.

Because if I read too much into it, the guilt that Serena potentially died in my place is going to sink me.

I can't deal with another death on my conscience. I barely survived the first.

"You know I haven't. There's no point. It's been three weeks. Nothing else has happened, no one has come after me. No more notes. It was probably the same asshole from that night at the party just fucking with me."

He quirks a brow at me. "Or that guy at the party is the sicko that strangled Serena after raping her, and he was coming for you, except you've been here with us and the dogs since then."

"Don't be so freaking rational." I sigh, exasperated. "The odds of your version being correct are really small. I mean, I know my personality isn't exactly Little Miss Sunshine, but I don't think I've pissed anyone off enough for them to want to kill me."

"You should at least tell the twins. You're dating them. You shouldn't have secrets."

"Everyone has secrets," I counter, and he nods.

"You're right, but not all secrets could be deadly."

"I'll think about it. After tomorrow's day of hell with Crawford."

He frowns at the mention of my professor. "I thought he'd let up on you?"

"So did I," I grumble. "But his hatred of me seems to be back in full swing. I don't understand what I did to piss him off so bad."

"I have my own suspicions, but Sawyer's still sitting in on your classes with him, right?"

I nod. "He is, though I still don't know why. I also don't know what Sawyer said to him at the start of the year that made Crawford hate me so much."

"You're exactly Crawford's type," Cole smirks. "Travis didn't want you to be his next target, so he sent Sawyer to sit in since he's the only one of us with Wednesdays free."

"As if Travis cares that much." I snort a laugh.

"You have no idea," is all he says in response, leaving me speechless for the first time in a while. I try to push away the thoughts, especially when the conversation I overheard still plays in my head when I let it.

He packs away his stuff without saying anything and heads toward the stairs, but turns back to me before ascending them. "For someone who seems to know so much, you really have no idea do you?"

After Cole and his cryptic bullshit yesterday afternoon, saying I got no studying done is a bit of an understatement. Instead, I persuaded the twins that Chinese food was the best idea ever and we took the pack for a walk. Which was as much fun as I thought it would be.

Except now I'm staring at the test paper in front of me, wishing I'd have shut off my over-thinking, overly negative brain and just focused on studying, dammit.

I've already been through and answered all the questions I knew I had answers for, but this last one is killing me slowly, and I'm basically watching the clock run out.

Because Crawford needed another reason to rake me over the coals.

Yay freaking me.

Of course, this is the one time Crawford allows pen and paper in his classroom, because laptops mean cheating, apparently. My hand is so sore from writing so much, at one point I thought it was going to cramp out. But now I'm almost missing the pain, because at least the pain meant I had the answers I needed.

"Time's up!" Crawford announces, and a chorus of groans sound around the room. I glance over at Connor, who finished his test about twenty minutes ago. He looks cool as a cucumber. On the other side of me, Sawyer looks like he's going to fall asleep since he didn't actually take the test.

My misery officially has no close company.

I pack up my stuff as the TA collects the tests, groaning internally at just how bad I'm going to flunk this test and likely the one this afternoon too.

"Is Penn coming back to the dorm any time soon?" I ask Connor as we stand. Not that I don't like living with the guys, but I miss my friend.

He glances over my shoulder at Sawyer and shrugs. "Honestly, I don't know. She's all kinds of shaken about it all still. Doesn't think it's safe in that dorm."

"Is that why she's been avoiding me too?" I ask, trying not to be bummed out that I've barely seen her the last few weeks.

"She's not avoiding you," he responds, awkwardly rubbing the back of his neck. "She's just scared to let anyone get too close. She really liked Serena and it's hitting her hard. I think she's scared of losing anyone else."

I nod, understanding the sentiment even if I don't agree with it.

"Okay," I respond, giving him a sad smile. "Are you guys going to the memorial next week?"

"Yeah. Penn wasn't sure, but I figure she'll regret it if she doesn't. So I told her I wanted to go."

"I guess we'll see you guys there then."

He leaves while I wait for Sawyer to drag his ass up, and of course that's when Professor Crawford calls my name. "Miss Moore, do you have a moment?"

I roll my eyes and glance over at Sawyer, who is frowning at the professor.

"Alone," he tags onto the end, and Sawyer glares at him.

When we reach the front of the class I squeeze Sawyer's hand and smile. "It's cool, I'll only be a second."

He doesn't look happy, and I'm sure I'll hear all about it in a minute, but he gives me the space and exits the classroom, leaving me with the professor.

"Miss Moore, I'm sorry to say that with your grades thus far, and what I've seen of your answers so far today, you're not going to be passing this class."

Sorry my ass. The smile on his face tells me just how freaking sorry he is.

"So what can I do? I don't want to have to retake the class."

He laughs and shakes his head. "There isn't anything you can do."

"Then what was the point in even telling me?" I hiss.

His smile widens at my obvious frustration before he leans in way too close. "Because I wanted to see the look on your face when I told you."

I take a step back so he's not in my personal space, trying to shake off the major ick I'm getting from him right now. "What did I do to deserve you hating me like this?"

He quirks his brow and steps back into my space, and even though I try to back up, he mirrors my every step until he's got me cornered. "You know exactly what you did, you little whore. You thought you could run away and face no consequences? Maybe you got away with it before, but not this time. If I can make your life hell, like you made hers, then that's what I'll do."

His hand grasps my throat and he starts to squeeze as I claw at his wrist. Panic floods my system, but I'm saved by a knock at the door that distracts him. His grip falters and I manage to push away and run from the class.

Sawyer calls my name as I run past him, desperate to get away.

I have no idea what he was talking about, but this is more than Cole suggesting I'm Crawford's type. I need to find out what the fuck he's talking about before he makes good on his promise.

Which means I have to ask the one person I don't want to for help.

Travis.

Fuck my life.

LILY WILDHART

TWENTY

My reflection in the mirror is as solemn as I'd expect when dressing for a memorial. Obviously we couldn't attend the funeral, that happened back in Serena's home town, but the University thought the memorial would be a good way for those of us that knew her to say our goodbyes.

After having to explain the whole Crawford situation to Travis, he said he'd look into it. Considering I have no idea what the hell Crawford was going on about, I'm not sure he's going to have much luck, and he said about as much when we spoke.

But at the very least, he said he'd try.

Though after I told him and the others what happened, Sawyer hasn't left my side in class, and I'm pretty sure they did something to Crawford, because he hasn't so much as looked at me since I told them.

And he gave me passing marks on both of my tests from last week.

I'm just keeping my head down, doing my papers, and trying to do what I can. There's not much longer left in this semester, then I'll be free of him at least.

Well, so long as I don't actually fail his classes. If I do, then I have no idea what I'm going to do. I've already crammed so much into each semester that I can't afford to retake two freaking classes for the credits to graduate.

So I'm really hoping Travis finds something, otherwise I have no idea what I'm going to do.

We have a football game tonight, and obviously I'm going to support Cole. I haven't missed any home games since I've been at Saints U and I'm not about to start now.

But first we have the memorial for Serena.

I can't believe it's been four weeks since she was killed, and what's worse is the police still have no idea who did it.

Her parents are flying in today, and I'm pretty sure Charli is coming with them. My heart hurts for them all, but I still haven't really processed her death. Well, not like people would expect me to. I don't mean to seem callous, but while we were friends, she wasn't exactly my bestie, and sure I miss her, and I'm sad she's gone, horrified by how she was taken from her family, angry that it happened to her, but I'm not… overwhelmed by it like other people seem to be.

I haven't cried.

I haven't gotten mad.

I've just kept going, because that's what I do.

And I'm sure a therapist would have a field day with that little nugget, but that is why I don't do therapy.

However, I am hoping I can convince Penn to come back to the dorm today, because I can't keep living in the spare room here. I've basically taken it over at this point. The twins were great about helping me set it up when we realized Penn wasn't coming back after a few days, because there was no way I was going to keep living in their rooms.

But it doesn't feel like my place either.

Not that the dorm feels like home, but at least it was my space.

I know technically this is my space, the guys said as much, but Travis was *not* exactly sunshine and rainbows about me taking over the spare room.

I've stopped trying to figure him out. It makes my head hurt less.

I check my reflection again, knowing that I have so many other things to be worried about rather than the way I'm dressed, but it's all I've got to shut down the voices right this second.

I'm just glad Penn offered to speak when Charli asked us, because I wouldn't have had a clue what to say.

A knock on the door pulls me from my thoughts and I'm a little shocked to see Cole pop his head around the door. "You about ready?"

"I am. I didn't realize you were coming."

He enters the room fully and jams his giant hands in his suit pants pockets. I definitely shouldn't be drooling over how well he fills out his shirt.

No, absolutely not.

Especially when I'm dating the twins.

Bad Briar.

"Of course I'm going, we're all going. We weren't about to let you go alone." He leans back against the door, looking at me like I'm crazy.

"I'm pretty sure I'm safe from any would-be killers at the memorial, Cole."

He rolls his eyes and folds his arms across his chest. "Yeah, because people never get taken from public gatherings. Nope. It's unheard of."

His sarcasm makes me smile, and the corners of his lips tip up.

"But anyway, we're not coming to protect you, we're coming to support you. I thought you were a smart cookie," he teases.

Not going to lie, I've really enjoyed getting to know this side of Cole since I moved in. I might even miss him when I go back to the dorm.

"I *am* a smart cookie. Just apparently not when it comes to you four. You're a different breed," I tease right back, and his smile grows.

"Come on, Cookie," he winks. "Let's get going."

He opens the door and ushers me out. I smooth down my blouse and black skirt, feeling more like I'm going to a job interview than a memorial, but I didn't have a suitable dress, so this has to do.

"Stop freaking out," he murmurs in my ear as he places a hand on the small of my back to lead me down the stairs. I have no idea how he knew, but I've stopped questioning a lot of things when it comes to Cole Beckett.

He seems to just always know.

The others are waiting for us, all in a shirt and tie, and yet again I chastise myself for thinking how hot these boys look all done up.

Definitely wrong time, wrong place, Briar.

Travis drives us to campus—obviously—and the twins flank me as we walk across the quad to where the memorial is being held by the fountains. Charli said it was Serena's favorite place, so it made sense for us to hold it here.

We find Penn and Connor in the crowd, Penn's eyes already rimmed red from crying. I give her the biggest hug I can muster and she starts to cry again.

"Penn! Briar!" We turn to find Charli heading toward us with who I can only assume are Serena's parents. Penn wipes at her face as they approach.

"Sandra, Ben, these are the friends I was telling you about. Briar, Penn, this is Serena's mom and dad."

"It's so nice to meet some more of Serena's friends," her mom says, her voice shaking, and my stomach twists.

I feel guilt for not feeling more loss.

Penn and Connor go with Charli and Serena's parents while I hang back with the guys. More people arrive and I wander further and further to the back of the crowd. I spot Dante with some of the other guys from the football team and give him a small wave as I retreat. He looks like he wants to come over to say something, but he glances over my shoulder and seems to think better of it. I look back and see the four of them trailing me, never letting me go too far from them.

"Are you okay?" Asher asks when I've finally reached the back of the crowd of people gathered for the memorial.

I just shrug, because nothing I say won't sound callous and I don't want him to worry about me any more than he obviously already is.

He frowns at me and takes my hand, squeezing it before pulling me close. "You don't have to be scared," he murmurs, and I don't have the heart to tell him that's not my problem, especially when he's giving me the warm fuzzies again. "We won't let anything happen to you. Ever."

After the memorial, the twins brought me back to the house and Travis went with Cole for their pregame ritual. Penn still refuses to come back to the dorm, she even mentioned giving it up next semester, so I either need to find a new roommate, or figure something else out.

Exactly what I'll do is beyond me, but that is not my focus right now.

My focus is helping my friend, because she's obviously terrified, but I have no idea *how* to help her. Connor said she won't talk to a professional, so I'm clueless, but I need to figure something out, because she's retreating.

HARD.

It took everyone to convince her to come to the game tonight. It's the last game before Thanksgiving next week, so I guess it's a big one. The idea that Serena wouldn't want her to miss it is what I think got her to agree, but it's still worrisome.

After my shower, I put on a pair of jeans and a long-sleeved tee, pulling Cole's jersey over the top. November in the northeast is no joke, so I also pull on thick fluffy socks before putting on my Chucks.

I grab a knit hat and gloves too, because I'm going to freeze without them. I might *love* all things fall and being cold, but being cold *outside*, where I don't have a cozy fire and hot chocolate… yeah, that's not my favorite.

"You nearly ready, Sunshine?" Sawyer asks as he leans against my door frame, his arms above his head as he leans forward. His black t-shirt is skin tight, and the hem has risen up to showcase those freaking washboard abs of his. That lickable

V poking out the top of his jeans makes me lick my lips.

Yes he's a freaking Adonis, I'm aware, but jeez… do I *have* to be so aware of it all the time? And does he have to look so good in *everything?*

"You're drooling," he teases, flexing his arms on purpose.

"You're hot, so sue me," I shrug, and his grin widens. "But yes, I'm ready. Are we still getting food with everyone after?"

"Yeah, no party tonight, win or lose. Not after the memorial."

I grab my phone and wallet, pushing them into my pocket before grabbing my hoodie and zipping it up over my jersey.

"You know you're not going to get away with that right?" Sawyer asks, and I look at him sideways.

"Huh?"

"Put the hoodie under the jersey, Briar," he deadpans.

"Right," I say, nodding. "One day I'll get used to this football stuff."

"Yeah, maybe," he teases as I unzip the hoodie, strip off the jersey, then redress in a way I won't get crucified for.

"Better?" I ask once I'm redressed, and he moves toward me, wrapping his arms around my waist. I twine my fingers behind his neck as the fresh sea breeze scent that is entirely him overwhelms me. He kisses me softly, but with so much passion that all thoughts but him leave my head.

My fingers twist in his hair as he pulls me even tighter against him and my toes curl as shivers run down my spine.

"We're going to be late!" Asher calls up the stairs, and

Sawyer groans as he pulls back from the kiss and rests his forehead on mine.

"Such a freaking cock block," he moans, and I laugh softly.

"Oh, yeah, 'cause me living here the last few weeks, you've totally been suffering with the lack of orgasms."

"Sunshine, there is never enough time with you," he murmurs, tucking my hair behind my ear. "Also, you look fucking adorable in this hat."

"Thanks," I say, my cheeks heating.

"We should go before he starts sulking." He sighs and I can't help but smile. Considering how alike the twins are, they couldn't be more different.

He spanks me softly and I let out a little squeak. "Tease."

"Oh, Sunshine, you have no idea how much of a tease I can be yet." He winks at me before pulling back and leading me downstairs to where Asher is waiting for us. He's in a black henley with the sleeves rolled up, his ink very much on display, and my steps falter.

Yep, it's not fair.

I shouldn't be this affected by them, and yet… here we are.

Asher grins at me like he knows exactly what I'm thinking. "Later, Beautiful," he promises, and I'm going to hold him to it too. He holds out his hand for me and I move to him.

"I'll go warm up the car," Sawyer says before heading outside, leaving me alone with Asher.

"You look adorable," he says, and I grin wide.

"Yeah, I heard," I laugh, rolling my eyes.

"Hey, we're twins, of course we think alike. You got a sec before we head out?" he asks, and it occurs to me that Sawyer knew Asher wanted to talk to me, which is why he dipped outside.

Little sneak.

"Sure, what's up?"

He runs his hand through his dark blond locks. His hair has gotten longer now and it's almost falling in his eyes, but I definitely don't dislike it. "I just... this is going to sound nuts, I'm aware."

He pauses and I chew on my lip, staying quiet and letting him work through whatever it is he's going to say.

"Okay, I'm making this way more of a thing than it needs to be," he says, laughing softly. "You fucked the three of them before you met me, and I'm pretty sure Sawyer mentioned that they all agreed to share you... because they all wanted you. And then I met you, and I, very obviously, wanted in on that little deal they made."

I nod, pressing my lips together, wondering where the hell he's going with this.

"Sawyer and I are much less... withholding with how we feel about you—obviously—but you being in the house... I think the other two are weakening. Cole at the very least. So I just, *we* just, wanted to let you know that if either of them says anything, or does anything, and you're good with that, then we're good with it too."

He pauses again while I process exactly what he just said.

"I am not making a great moment of this," he groans, tugging at his hair again.

"Asher, I mean, it's a lot, but you didn't exactly mess it up. I doubt you're right about the others, but thank you for telling me, I guess?" I say, not really sure how to take the fact that Sawyer and he are okay with not just sharing me with each other, but with the other two as well. It's not exactly something that's done.

I don't think.

"It's not something we've ever done—outside of a one night thing—but you're way more than that. Obviously. God, I keep saying that a lot. I think I might actually be nervous," he rambles, wiping his hands on his jeans. "But Sawyer and I, we're all-in with you. If you hadn't been who you are, I'm pretty sure Travis wouldn't have ever put you at a distance, which means Cole wouldn't have either. If you'd have been okay with dating all four of us, I mean."

"Honestly, I can't say I ever really thought about it," I tell him, though Cole did kiss me that one time, and I didn't tell anyone… but that was before us three were a thing. "Though, to be fair, I can't say I ever considered dating twins either."

The front door swings open and Sawyer bursts in. "Are you guys done yet? I'm freezing my balls off out here."

I laugh, happy that Sawyer broke the tension, but I'm also kind of glad Asher said something so I'm not blindsided if Cole or Travis *do* say anything. Not that I think they would.

Now who's rambling, Briar?

"Yeah, we're good," I say with a smile. "Let's do this."

"We're good?" Asher asks, taking my hand and squeezing it.

"We are," I reassure him, and he kisses me.

"Good, let's go support our boy."

I let him lead me outside and prepare myself for two plus hours out in this frigid November night.

Please, God, let them have hot chocolate at the stadium!

The game is ridiculously close and it's halftime. I'm waiting in line for my fourth hot chocolate because it's too freaking cold tonight, even with the packed stands. I think it might snow soon.

My phone buzzes in my pocket and I check it in case it's one of the guys wanting a drink, even after they declined earlier.

Cole:

I need to see you. Meet me by the locker room door.

I groan, because there is definitely not enough time to see him *and* get hot chocolate, but I'm also fairly sure he wouldn't message me if it wasn't important.

Me:

Okay, coming.

I leave the line and head toward where the locker rooms are, which, thankfully, have directions on the signs, otherwise I'd be totally lost.

I spot him in the hall as I'm approaching. There's no one else around. I assume everyone is inside the locker room already.

As I approach, I open my mouth to speak, but he shakes his head. He grabs my arm when I reach him and pulls me further down the hall and round a corner.

He pushes me against the wall, tucked inside the alcove, my entire body covered by his. And despite the hundreds of people around the stadium right now, I'm pretty sure no one has a clue I'm here.

"What's wrong, Cole?" I ask, concerned.

"Nothing's wrong. I just wanted to thank you," he says coyly, a small smile on his lips.

"Thank me for what?" Confusion skits across my face, because I have no idea what he's talking about.

"For coming to every single game, despite everything. Plus, seeing you in my jersey… it's kind of distracting."

"You want me to take it off?" I ask, confused. Here I am doing what everyone told me to do, and I still got it wrong.

"Oh, absolutely not," he says, crowding against me so my back is flat against the wall, and all I can see or smell is him.

"But I still want to thank you."

He lifts the hem of my t-shirt and undoes the button on my jeans and my breath hitches as he pulls down the zipper. I press my hands against his chest and stutter his name.

"What are you—"

"Shhh, let me thank you. Let me look after you," he murmurs as he bites the lobe of my ear, pulling a breathy moan from me before pushing his hand beneath the lace of my panties.

What in the?

"The twins—" I start, but he laughs softly, cutting me off.

"Trust me, Baby Girl, the twins already know I've been restrained. We already agreed to share you."

"I know," I tell him, partially moaning as his fingers brush against my clit, still shocked about the sharing and what's happening right now, but I'm not exactly mad about it.

It's not like I didn't want him the first time I saw him, and it's not like that want ever really went away.

"Problem with that?" he asks, stroking against me again before biting down on my shoulder, and I swear any hint of a problem disappears from my mind like smoke. He looks into my eyes, an arrogant smile on his lips. "That's what I thought."

He kisses me, teasing my mouth with his tongue while painfully, gently stroking my clit, his kiss swallowing my whimpers.

This is insane, right? I mean, they did agree to share me without even consulting me. I'm trying really hard to make sense of this crazy situation, only, he's doing some voodoo magic with his finger flicking across my clit and making my stomach contract with each movement.

My mouth is prisoner to his kiss, his tongue controlling, his teeth a silent warning. The protective pads of his football pants pushing against my body are heavy and thick.

"Want me to stop, Baby Girl?" I'm pretty sure his question is rhetorical but, no, I absolutely do not want him to fucking stop. If anything, I want him harder.

"Harder it is, then." Fuck my life. I said that out loud, didn't I?

Cole's palm rubs against my clit as three fingers push inside of me and I gasp at the fullness of it. I'm breathless and lightheaded, the potential of getting caught is as exhilarating as the anticipation of coming on this man who seems bigger than life itself.

"When I have time, I'm going to fucking devour you. But right now, I need you to come for me or else you're gonna have a stadium full of people hating you for making me late to the second half of the game."

No pressure, asshole.

With his last word he pushes in deeper and, like some sort of wizard, he sets off some kind of magical button deep inside me that pulls the air right out of my lungs.

Immediately, his free hand covers my mouth, his lips at my ear. "Shh, Baby Girl. Don't want anyone knowing I'm making you come, do you?"

I don't respond. My brain is melting as every cell in my body explodes in ecstasy.

"That's my good girl. Get my fingers nice and wet and every time I bring it to my nose, it'll be like you're right there with me."

Oh, fuck. His words are making my climax last for an eternity and he fucking knows it.

"Cole, I—"

"I know, Baby Girl, I know. Now, turn around while I fuck you senseless."

Before I can register his move, he turns me and slams me against the wall, my face to the side as he slides the belt out of the double-D ring. Without even pushing his pants down, he reaches in and pulls out his long, thick cock.

Holy hell, it looks angry and instead of running, I lick my lips and spread my legs. I'd be lying if I said I hadn't thought about fucking him that night he was in my mouth, and since the twins already told me they were good with this, I'm going to go along for the ride.

What's the worst that could happen?

"Fuck, I can't wait to be inside you."

I yelp a little as he grabs my hair and pulls my face back from the wall, his mouth on mine and his tongue attacking mine as his cock slams inside me.

Every time he thrusts, I hit the wall hard enough I'm

convinced I'll have evidence of this on my body for days.

"Fuck yes, you're so fucking tight, Baby Girl. So fucking perfect." He slams inside of me as his tongue fucks my mouth. It's hard to concentrate on kissing him when his dick is making my brain melt.

I try to reach behind him, try to touch him somehow, but the way he has me positioned, I can only stand here and enjoy everything he's giving me as his balls slap against my flesh with every violent plunge inside of me.

Reaching around me, he places two fingers on my clit and my entire body convulses from the unexpected bolt of pleasure it provokes.

"That's it, baby, give me your cum and I'll give you mine." A long, drawn-out moan escapes from between my lips, and I nearly pass out as he pinches my clit right before he freezes with his dick buried fully inside me.

He fills me with his cum as I come around him. I'm about to cry out when his mouth drops onto mine and he swallows whatever sound was ready to escape.

The both of us breathing heavily, we take a second to get our bearings as the faint sound of the team song plays over the speakers. It's time for him to go and a small sense of victory fills my chest as I think of him needing me so badly he couldn't wait until after the game.

"Do not fucking clean up. I want you to walk around with my cum inside you, dripping out of you, while I go and win this game."

Pulling out, he tucks himself back into his pants and does his belt back up. When his dark eyes rise to mine through his long, thick eyelashes, he takes my breath away all over again.

"Every time you feel my cum drip, remember how good I felt deep inside of you." Then he brings his finger to his nose and inhales. "I know I will."

With a quick kiss to my lips and a smirk that's worth a million bucks, he's off to join his team while I try to put myself back together.

I dart to the bathroom and try to tame my wild hair and splash my flushed face with water before hurrying back to the others. The third quarter has already started by the time I reach them and I slide past Asher and Travis to my seat next to Sawyer, who knowingly winks at me.

"Have fun, Beautiful?" he asks, and my face heats again. "I wish I could have watched."

I bite the inside of my cheek. Deciding to play him at his own game, I lean in close and whisper, "Maybe next time."

BURN

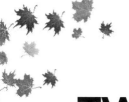

TWENTY ONE

Settling into my new version of normal this last week has been weird. The guys basically insisted I just move into the house officially. After I talked to Penn on Sunday, who agreed that she was just going to stay with Connor, we emptied the dorm of the rest of my things and officially moved me into the spare room.

Travis even helped without complaining… well, not *too* much, anyway.

Though, since Cole has been a lot more touchy-feely with me around the house, Travis has definitely been side-eyeing me like it's my fault that I'm fucking everyone but him.

It should probably weird me out that I fucked him, since our parents are married, but it just doesn't. The whole stepbrother thing isn't really a thing to me. We didn't grow up together.

Hell, we barely even know each other. Beyond knowing that his dad puts too much pressure on him, and he's pursuing a business degree, I have no idea what he does for fun. Or what he does in general.

Yet, I can't deny that there's a pull to him. Even when he was being a dick there was a magnetism about him that made me oh-so-aware of him whenever he was near me.

It's the same for all of them.

The difference is, I don't have to hide it with the others.

Not at home at least.

At the Kensington McMansion though... I definitely have to hide it. And considering today is Thanksgiving, and Chase and my mom decided to go all out and host the Becketts and St. Vincents—as well as two other families I've never met before—it is not a day to be thinking about all of my extracurriculars.

"Did you see Joan's nose job? Dr. Botch Job calling," Susie, one of the girls from one of the other families here, bitches to Jessica, the daughter of another. I can't even remember their last names.

"Oh, God, it was awful, but not as bad as Tiffany's boob job. She's lopsided, poor girl. That'll teach her to take the cheap route. I told her to go to Dr. Pearson. He never does a bad job," Jessica retorts, and it takes everything in me not to roll my eyes.

Somehow I got shoved in this room with my mom, these two vapid bitches, and their moms; who are currently gossiping on the opposite sofa.

Beam me up, Scotty. I am so *done here.*

The puppies came with us at least, and Shadow is lying beside me on the couch, keeping the gremlin-like women away from me.

If I'd have known the guys were going to just abandon me when we got here, I'd have refused to come at all. My only small mercy to this point is that my mom hasn't dropped news of her pregnancy yet, so everyone isn't cooing about the baby.

Just thinking about it makes me lose my appetite.

I can't lie and say that I don't have a lot to be thankful for this year. Hell, in the last three months my life has changed entirely. If you'd have told me at the start of summer that I'd be sitting here like this right now, I'd have laughed until I cried.

But there are still things in my past that haunt me, especially this time of year.

I already know Christmas is going to be dire. Usually, I hide away, and mom's always been too strung out, too drunk, or too focused on a man to really care what I did.

Christmas was Iris's favorite.

It was *our* favorite.

And now it's nothing but a reminder of the worst day of my life.

But I have a whole month to dread that and the rest of this day to get through first.

"—Briar?" I look up and realize my mom was talking to me and I hadn't heard a damn thing.

"Sorry, what?" I say, smiling apologetically.

She quirks a brow at me, but smiles anyway, though I can see the frustration in her eyes at me not being the darling little daughter like the other two. "I was just asking if you're looking forward to the Christmas break, sweetheart. Chase and I are going away with everyone to a ski lodge in the mountains, but I know the boys wanted to stay behind. I figured you'd be doing something with your friends."

She has got to be kidding me right?

Small mercies, I don't have to see her on Christmas Day.

"I haven't really thought about it," I tell her. "But yes, I'll probably make plans with my friends."

She doesn't have to know that I have all of about three friends, one of which is Emerson, who dropped off the face of the earth when I started at Saints U.

"That's lovely." Her saccharine smile makes my stomach twist and I'm thankful when the five of them start talking among themselves again about people from the club, and what happened at the latest charity gala.

God, I can't imagine that being my entire life.

I will never, ever, be the gala wife.

Not a chance.

"Ladies, dinner is served," Tobias says as he sweeps into the room like my saving grace. I let the others leave first, taking a deep breath in the silence to try and gather myself before this drama show of a dinner. "Are you okay, Briar?"

"Just fine," I respond with a tight smile. "But if you happen to slip some tequila into my drink with dinner, I'm not going to be disappointed."

He grins at me, shaking his head. "Wine is on the table already. Pretty sure putting tequila in that wouldn't go down so well, but I'll see what I can do."

"You, Tobias, are a freaking god!"

He chuckles as I walk past him into the hall. "Anything for you." He winks at me and heads in the opposite direction toward the kitchen.

I enter the dining room and take in the sight before me... including the smirk on the twins' mom's face when I notice that Jessica and Susie are seated by them both, with their parents cropping them in. Then I realize my seat is between Travis and Cole.

At least Cole won't make this insufferable. Except he's looking at me like he's about to apologize to me. I glance at Travis and he looks *pissed*.

Oh, fuck. What did I miss already?

I don't say a thing as I head to the empty space and Cole stands, pulling the chair out for me. I thank him as I sit, and wince when Travis chugs his drink in one breath and slams the glass down on the table.

I dare a look at the twins but neither of them will look at me, and a pit forms in my stomach.

What the hell is going on?

Before I get the chance to ask, most of the table is swept up into conversation about shit I don't care about as Tobias and the other staff bring out the mountain of food that's been prepared for today. I really wish I'd just spent the day volunteering at the shelter like I've done the last few years.

I have absolutely zero appetite, and just being here is setting me on edge.

Chase says grace and everyone goes around saying what they're thankful for. I mumble something about new beginnings before we start to eat. But I don't taste a thing as anxiety knots my stomach. I barely manage a few mouthfuls throughout the entire meal, and I don't touch the wine.

I get the feeling that whatever is coming, I don't want to be intoxicated for it.

Or maybe I'm wrong and I should be hella intoxicated. It's a little too late for that now though, as the staff reappear and start clearing away the dessert dishes. I didn't even touch my pie, which is basically unheard of, but anxiety has a way of stealing my appetite.

When most people are distracted, I finally manage to gain Cole's attention. "What the hell am I missing?" I hiss at him quietly, trying not to draw attention to us.

"I'm sorry," is all he says before Chase stands, clearing his throat.

"This year we have so much to be thankful for. For my new wife and stepdaughter. For my new venture. The support of my friends, but we also have another announcement."

Oh, fuck. Not this again.

I grip the edges of the table, trying to stop myself just leaving the room in front of all these people.

"Smile," Travis growls at me quietly.

"This year," Chase continues. "We get to be thankful for the joining of our families. So, to Cole and Briar, congratulations on your engagement."

What in the actual fuck?

I leave the house once dinner is over, get a set of keys from Tobias and just drive the hell away from whatever the hell that was.

ENGAGED!

This is not the early nineteen hundreds. They do not get to tell me who the fuck I'm going to marry. They can shove it all the way up their asses if they think I'm going to just go along with it.

Fuck all the way off.

Unwanted by Pale Waves blasts through the sound system in the sleek sports car I'm driving way too fast back toward Saints U.

I ignored everyone, including the four guys I'm supposed to fucking live with right now, and got the hell out of dodge.

My mother just smiled at me after Chase's announcement, and I would bet my entire life, and on Iris's grave, that she knew it was coming.

Selling her fucking daughter like some two bit whore to gain political capital for Chase.

Because that's what this is. That's *all* it is.

I don't imagine Cole got much of a say in it either, but he could have fucking warned me.

Cowardly little boys, all of them.

Well, newsflash: I am not from their world and I don't live by their rules.

By the time I get back to campus, I am still riled up and steam might as well be coming from my skin with the way rage radiates from my pores.

Driving or singing usually helps calm me down, and I already know that I can't draw right now because I'm way past the point of being able to numb myself and spill my pain onto paper.

Instead, I pull the car into an empty space by the library and get out. It might be fucking freezing outside, but maybe, just maybe, a brisk walk might shock out some of the blinding anger.

My phone rings for the umpteenth time, but I ignore it again. Though, I'm definitely glad I just wore jeans and a sweater to Thanksgiving dinner, my Chucks probably aren't the right footwear, considering the wet ground, but I'm too pissed to really care that much.

I walk around until the sun sets, and just keep going until I end up in the library. I'm pretty amazed it's even open right now, but the sanctuary of quiet is available and I take full advantage of it.

I wander through the stacks, aware that there's me and maybe one other person in the entire gigantic building, and take comfort in the fact that I could get lost in here for days and no one would find me.

I find a copy of *Pride and Prejudice* before finding a dark, quiet spot. It's almost perfect: a little lamp on a table next to a bean bag, a metal hour glass on the windowsill, and the giant window looking out into the darkness.

Moving the beanbag into the nook of the window, I curl up with the book and lose myself to my favorite book of all time, where even Lizzie got to decline marriage. But then, Lizzie's parents, fault ridden as they were, are still leaps and bounds ahead of my biological and now step parent.

If only life was as easy as it is the books I lose myself in.

Thunder rumbles through the sky outside, making me jump, but then I grin widely. I fucking love thunder storms.

Rain unleashes and cracks against the window as lightning illuminates the dark sky, the roll of thunder not far behind it again.

I abandon my book and run outside into the storm.

Running until I'm behind the library, in the middle of the quad, silence presses in around me except for the storm. It's so dark out here I can't really see anything until the lightning flashes.

I scream into the rain, trying to let out everything that's been building up inside of me. The thunder answers my screams with roars of its own and I scream back until I'm hoarse and soaked through.

But I don't care.

For the first time today, I don't feel like I'm going to suffocate, so I keep screaming and spinning in the rain with my arms spread wide.

The next time the lightning flashes, I scream again. But not in anger.

In fear.

I don't know how he saw me. Or how he got so close, but when I see him, he's so close I can practically feel him.

"Boo," he shouts between cracks of thunder, and I take off running as fast as I can. His laughter echoes behind me, mixing with the sounds of the storm as my heart races in my chest.

This can't be happening to me.

"You can't run from me. I told you, this is my world. Not yours." His shouts fill the space, and I keep running, trying to see where I'm going through the darkness and rain, but I don't see the rock until it's too late and I crash to the ground.

I scramble to my knees, but before I can get up I feel his weight on top of me and I slip in the slick mud.

I struggle and fight against him, but he's bigger than me.

Stronger than me.

And it's so fucking wet.

He laughs in my ear before manhandling me until I'm on my back beneath him, looking up into his dark, soulless eyes.

"I told you I would ruin you one day." His hands move from my wrists to my neck and he presses down on my throat, constricting all my air.

I claw at him; his face, his neck, his hands, but he just laughs and squeezes tighter, before leaning forward and licking my cheek. "Vengeance tastes so sweet."

Fight, Briar.

Iris's voice rings out in my head, but a part of me wonders if I have all that much worth fighting for.

Dammit, Briar. Fight!

Her voice is loud, as if she's here with me, and just for a second, I close my eyes and picture my little sister's face.

Fight.

I feel around, searching for the rock I tripped over, anything to help me fight against him. Beneath my nails fill with mud as I scrape at the wet ground, desperate for anything that can save me.

Darkness starts to take the edges of my vision as I feel the roughness of stone and I sag a little.

You can do this, Briar.

I grip the rock as hard as I can and swing for the side of his head, but he just laughs at me and squeezes my throat tighter.

Shit. I might actually die.

So I swing the rock again and he falters. I do it again, and again, and again until he's sagging against me and I can't tell if the wet on my face is rain or blood.

I try to push him off me, but he's too fucking heavy, and I'm so weak.

Instead, I reach beneath him to my pocket, and struggle for my phone, dialing the last number that called me.

It only rings once before I hear Travis's voice and I start to sob down the phone.

"Briar! What the fuck is going on? Where are you?"

I sob again, trying to move his weight off of me, but I feel like I can't breathe. "Travis, I think I killed him. I think he's dead."

To be continued

ACKNOWLEDGMENTS

Wow, yeah that happened. Honestly there were so many times I thought this book would never make it to completion. For those of you who follow me on social media, you know this year has been an absolute rollercoaster for me, and well… Briar became my release of every emotion I've been dealing with. So I hope you love her and relate to her as much as I do, because I love her strong but broken and vulnerable self.

I have a huge thank you to give to my sister, Kelly, for keeping my ass in line while I was writing this book, and to my wifey, Rose for keeping my mind on what was important. And to KC & Eva for dealing with my serious squirreling on sprints aha.

I have thank Kirsty-Anne Still for the most beautiful cover for Briar, along with David Michael & Rebecca Gibson for my copious rounds of edits.

David, you know you're my sparkly unicorn, you don't get to leave this boohoo emo unicorn ever. I will find you, ha!

Sarah Goodman & Sam Whitney, thank you so much for your final polishing of this one. I know it's been a rush, but you did epically as always.

To my alpha & beta team - Megan, Jeni, Lisa, Zoe, Keira, Jessi, Nicole & Nicole (yes there's two, I didn't screw up aha). Thank you for reading with such enthusiasm as always and loving Briar and her boys as much as I do.

Finally, thank you to you guys for taking a risk on a new series. It's only my second contemporary series, and I know that not everyone will pick up a new author, so there aren't words to truly express how thankful I am. But all I have is this, so thank you.

ABOUT THE AUTHOR

Lily is a writer, dreamer, fur mom and serial killer, crime documentary addict.

She loves to write dark, reverse harem romance and characters who will shatter your heart. Characters who enjoy stomping on the pieces and then laugh before putting you back together again. And she definitely doesn't enjoy readers tears. Nope. Not even a little.

If you want to keep up to date with all things Lily, including where her next book is out, please find join her newsletter at www.lilywildhart.com/subscribe.

ALSO BY LILY WILDHART

THE KNIGHTS OF ECHOES COVE
(Dark, Bully, High School Why Choose Romance)

Tormented Royal

Lost Royal

Caged Royal

Forever Royal

THE SAINTS OF SERENTIY FALLS
(Dark, Bully, Step Brother, College,Why Choose Romance)

Burn

Rebel

Avenge

Tame